CHRISTY

LYNKS AT TRYST FALLS
BOOK 2

BROOKLYN BAILEY

Copyright © 2023 Brooklyn Bailey
All rights reserved.

Lynks at Tryst Falls is a work of fiction. Names, characters, and incidents are all products of the authors imagination and are used fictitiously. Any resemblance to actual events or persons, living or dead, is entirely coincidental.

Any trademarks, service marks, product names, or named features are assumed to be the property of their respective owners and are used only for reference. There is no implied endorsement.

Cover by @Germancreativ on Fiverr

❀ Created with Vellum

Definition of "Sweet Romance"

As many readers already know there is no definition and levels within the category of sweet romance. Therefore, I would like to describe the definition as I use it to describe my stories before you commit to reading beyond this page.

My sweeter romances are **PG-13** versions of my steamy stories written as author Haley Rhoades. They are **a combination of Hallmark movies and Lifetime movies with a similar steam rating to shows that air on major networks during primetime hours**. While searching for their HEA, my characters face real-world situations, setbacks, hardships, personal faults, and must transform in order to find their happy ending.

While my characters might have relations prior to marriage, all of them occur off the page. Kissing and alluding to relations does occur in my books along with mature topics. My stories are not **"clean romance"** or **"Christian romance."**

DEDICATION

To all the ladies that put up with my novice skills on the golf course. Though my handicap is high, I feel I belong because of you. May the golf gods forever be in your favor and the birdie shots be plentiful.

To Enhance your Reading:

Check out the Trivia Page at the end of the book before reading Chapter #1.
No Spoilers—I promise.

Pull up my Pinterest Boards for my inspirations for recipes, characters, and settings. (QR Below or Link at the end of this book.)

PROLOGUE- CHRISTY
JANUARY

I return from the bathroom with seconds to spare in the commercial time out.

"Made it!" I cheer, assuming my seat between the girls on the sofa.

Looking up from her eReader, Brooks asks, "Is it over?"

"No!" my twins bark in unison, frustrated with her lack of football spirit and knowledge.

"Did they score?" Brooks asks.

"No!" the twins shout. "It's tied."

I barely notice as Brooks rolls her eyes in my direction, before I turn my attention to the TV screen. Fed up with the announcers' commentary, we turned the volume down at the beginning of the fourth quarter. We watch the screen with rapt attention.

The offense of our team, the Kansas City Cardinals, comes set. It is third and ten on our twenty-eight-yard line with five seconds left on the clock; the score is tied, 14 to 14.

The center snaps the ball, and our quarterback drops back for the pass. With only five seconds on the clock, this should be a long pass into the endzone.

The quarterback looks to the left side of the field and then to the right. He scrambles a bit, still looking downfield.

"87! 87! He's open!" Harper shrieks at the screen.

I pull my eyes from the wide receivers in the endzone; he is open. The QB throws a short-yardage pass to number 87, Ryan Harper.

He catches the ball on the 25-yard line, tucks it to his side, and runs. He shakes off one defender, finding a small opening in the center of the field.

"Run! Run!" the girls yell.

Please, please, please. Please let him score the touchdown to secure his team's spot in the postseason. I want this for him; he's worked so hard to get to the NFL.

A teammate makes a block. Ryan Harper leaps. He launches himself over two players, falling into the endzone for a touchdown.

"Touchdown!" Harper screams.

"We won!" Ry hollers.

"He scored!" I yell.

"Who scored?" Brooks asks, rising from her chair.

"Harper!" the twins exclaim.

Jumping up and down, the twins and I celebrate the Cardinals victory, extending our season by at least one more week.

Two minutes later, exhausted, I plop down on the sofa. Brooks looks at me, a smirk on her face. She knows next to nothing about football, but she knows my secret about Ryan Harper.

PROLOGUE- RYAN
JANUARY

"Playoff win, baby!" our quarterback, Nolan chants, slapping my back before squeezing my shoulder.

Behind us, the locker room still sounds like Mardi Gras in New Orleans. The game ended over two hours ago, and unlike the majority of my teammates, I am ready to escape that scene.

I listened to the coaches and owners give their speeches of congratulations. I gave interviews to the press, shook hands with the owner's family along with their special guests, and posed for too many pictures. Although I finally showered, I am once again covered in the spray of beer and champagne from the ongoing celebration.

"Moving the party to my place. You coming?" Nolan invites.

"Nah. I am beat." I shake my head.

"You do not have a wife to answer to," he argues. "C'mon, dude."

"I'm out," I state, turning to face him.

"Left it all on the field—I get you," he says, finally accepting my decline. "Will not be the same without you."

"I know, but I am sure you will party enough for the two of us," I smirk, sharing our signature handshake.

Back at home, my place feels like a mausoleum compared to our fans, Cardinals Nest stadium, and our locker room. The announcers on the 24-hour sports news station drone on about our advancing to the divisional championship game and do little to fill the large space that I call home.

Water bottle in hand, I walk to the bedroom, turning on the television as I strip to my boxers. Too keyed up for bed, I scan through the channels, trying to find something of interest. I should still be celebrating, but the only person I want to celebrate with disappeared years ago.

I open my cell phone, thumbing to my photo app. Buried in my favorites, I scroll through the photos I've saved for six long years—pictures in our golf carts, on my family's boat at the Lake of the Ozarks, at Worlds of Fun, and at concerts. The next is a video from my eighteenth birthday. With three quick taps, I stream the video to my TV screen on the wall.

I watch Mom and Christy carry my birthday cake with 18 flickering candles towards the table where I wait. A proud smile graces Christy's face as she presents the cake she made from scratch. Once the cake is sitting before me, she takes her favorite seat on my lap. I place a kiss on her cheek before I make my wish and blow out the candles.

The next video is Christy practicing her cheer routine in my backyard. This one I filmed myself. Wearing a tank top and practice shorts, I watch the muscles in her arms as she cheers, then the muscles in her legs as she jumps and tumbles.

The short video clips end too soon. Having saved these photos in their own special album, I set it on slideshow before tossing my phone on the nightstand. As photos appear, one after another on a loop, I prop myself on two pillows at the head of my bed.

I feel the weight of her eyes upon me as her smile warms me from the inside out. I imagine her delicate fingers upon my skin and her lips upon mine. As the cheer video begins, I close my eyes, and celebrate our playoff win with the memory of her.

PROLOGUE- BROOKS
NEXT SUMMER-THURSDAY, JUNE 8TH

"Hey, guys." I greet the gym rat and straight-laced man as they enter my tattoo parlor. "Looking to get inked today?" I ask as they scan the walls and approach me at the counter.

"I am bringing you a newbie," I-love-lifting-weights-and-chugging-protein-shakes guy announces proudly.

Called it. I knew the guy in the button-down shirt was uptight. *He probably wants a tattoo honoring his mom.*

"Any idea what and where you want it?" I inquire, dreading his answer.

"I am looking for something even a t-shirt will cover," he explains.

Under a t-shirt, so he plans to hide it 24/7.

"I am warring with two quotes by Nietzsche," he states.

Whoa! I did not see that coming. Maybe I judged these two guys too quickly.

"I am Brooks, by the way." I wave.

"I am Ryan, and he is Maddux," the taller and wider one says.

"So, Maddux, why a tattoo? And why today?" I sound nosey, but getting the inaugural tattoo is a major step, especially for a straight-laced guy like him. I need my customers to be happy when they leave my parlor and not spreading negative experiences.

"He's talked about finally getting a tattoo for two years now," Ryan states.

"Bro, I can answer for myself," Maddux chides.

My thoughts focus on the word "bro," wondering if these two are really brothers. They are tall, both over six feet and each has blonde hair, although styled differently. Ryan wears his blonde curls ear-length and tousled for that just crawled out of bed look. Maddux trims his short on the sides with about two inches of product-tamed, perfectly styled, wavy curls on top. Their matching blue eyes, sexy smiles, and dimples lead me to believe they are indeed brothers.

"I need an artist's help with the design. I do not only want a quote. I'd like it inside a tribal band or a tribal sun tattoo. I am open to a thigh tattoo if it is a larger design."

I like that. I love designing unique pieces. I get to show my creativity on paper as well as on the body. I tug my sketchpad from under the counter, opening to the first clean page. In the top corner, I write "M-a-d-d-o-x."

"It is u-x not o-x," he corrects.

I fight the urge to roll my eyes. *It is my sketch, not a government form. Chill, dude.*

"What are the two quotes?"

Maddux's tongue darts out to wet his overly-plump lower lip, his teeth dragging over it in contemplation.

I am momentarily distracted by his mouth. It's been too long since I allowed a man to kiss me.

"My first choice is, 'No artist tolerates reality.'"

My eyes fly to the purple bumper sticker hanging halfway up the wall to my right with the same quote in black lettering. I first read the line in high school and kept it near me ever since. I place the quote on the page under his name, along with the second, longer quote: "Without music, life would be a mistake."

Hmm... I love both of them.

"Do you have photos of the artwork you like without the quotes?" I ask.

Maddux shakes his head. "I like the sun because it is a symbol of strength and protection. Let's design a Polynesian thigh tattoo; include a sun and that quote."

I pull my arms from the counter when he points to the reality quote. Not quick enough, his fingers skim over my forearm. I freeze, awaiting a jolt that does not come. *Odd.* Even the slightest touch, especially with a stranger, brings on visions. I open my eyes, looking up at the tall, blonde hunk, looking down at me with concern. His sky-blue eyes ping pong between mine.

"I am sorry if I scared you," he murmurs, tucking his hands into his pockets.

Biting my lips, I nod then return my gloved hands to the sketchpad. As I sketch a thigh, I attempt to decipher what happened a moment ago. I always see the future when a stranger touches me. I did not imagine his fingertips grazing my arm. I can still feel the heat where he made contact. Fingers hold the longest, most vivid visions. Sometimes, I block them out, but only when I focus and only with family and my close, close friend. I spare a glance up at the two men before I place a sunburst on the thigh then design repeating patterns around it.

"Usually, a band tattoo symbolizes rebirth or that life continues," I explain. "The arm bands often commemorate a death. Is there anything or anyone in your life you would like to include in the design?" I pause my pencil, looking only at Maddux.

He looks at Ryan for a long moment before his blue eyes return to me. "I had cancer when I was four." He shrugs nervously. "I do not want a long band of ribbons; I do not want pity."

"Oh, I would not do that," I vow. "Are you still…"

He shakes his head, answering my unspoken question. "I am in remission and have been for over 20 years now."

He smiles, and I am lost in the faint lines at the sides of his mouth, the parenthesis at the edge of his cheeks, and the crinkles at the corners of his eyes. He really is a marvelous specimen of a man. I long to sketch his face. Instead, I attempt to burn it into my memory to draw later when I am alone.

"Let me play around with this," I say, my pencil once again

sketching. "I will hide a cancer ribbon within the design. Discreet but a celebration of the life you live."

"Thank you," he says, his voice further hypnotizing me.

He places his palm on top of my wrist on the counter. I fight my instinct to pull away, welcoming visions of his future. I need to figure out how his first touch produced no images. I stare at his hand touching me. Still no visions. *Maybe I am sick. This has never happened before.* I look up at this neat-as-a-pin, perfectly-put-together man, marveling that he's blocking my gift. *Perhaps he has a gift like mine.*

"I will spend a day or two on the design. You can call the shop after that, and we will set up a time for you to come and approve it."

Maddux nods.

In a final attempt to figure this all out, I remove my glove, extending my hand to shake his. *Nothing. Even if he had no future, I'd see his death.* Instead, I receive no visions. Next, I shake Ryan's hand.

Mistake. Big mistake. Vision after vision swarms my head. Not just one event. Many. I see tomorrow, next week, next month, next year, and beyond. There are so many visions, I nearly faint before I withdraw my hand, waving them away.

1

THURSDAY, JUNE 8TH

Christy

> ME
>
> we're home

I text my best friend and roommate, Brooks. She's covering until the closer shows up at her parlor downstairs. On nights like these, I am in charge of dinner.

"Hey, you two," I call to my twins. "Go find pajamas."

My five-year-old daughters promptly obey. The days they accompany me to work at the pool wear them out. They enjoy an hour of swim lessons with my lifeguard staff in the mornings then play on the pool deck until the pool officially opens. During the day, they play on the playground when I am not able to watch them swim.

While I rarely work a full, eight-hour shift, it is a lot for their little bodies. They go hard all day long. I talk to them on the 15-minute drive home to keep them awake. I learned if they nap that late, it makes for a rough night.

I hurry through prep then place the chicken and rice in a casserole dish inside the oven, setting the timer for 30-minutes. When I announce bath time, Harper and Ry strip while I run the bath water. Harper climbs in first, then Ry. They play with their favorite water toys as I lather then rinse their hair and soap their sun-tanned bodies. I think their swimsuit tan lines are adorable. I keep them slathered in sunscreen, but we are outside nearly every day in the summer.

When their hair and bodies are clean, I sit back to watch.

"Two-minute warning," I announce from my perch on the toilet seat.

I take a moment to text Brooks.

> ME
> dinner 15 min

> BROOKS
> (thumbs up emoji)

I am blessed to have her in my life. She allows me to swap the hours I work at her tattoo shop downstairs for my part of the rent. As she owns the building, she's really letting the girls and me live with her. I work for her out of guilt. I can't afford a two-bedroom apartment and daycare on my salary from the club alone. I am grateful, and that is why I try to cook and clean as much as I can. I dread the day she finds a man, and I will need to make other arrangements. But for now, this is the perfect arrangement for the girls and me.

When my cell alarm signals bath time is over, I wrap Ry in a towel on the rug, then do the same to Harper. I towel dry their curly, long blonde hair. I am jealous, my dark hair does not lighten in the sun like theirs does.

Tub drained, I leave them to dress while I check on dinner. I am placing utensils on the table when they emerge in their *Nightmare*

Before Christmas pajamas. Brooks bought them, and my girls love that I complain that they look scary.

"Bones! Yuck!" I play along, faking a shudder.

Giggling, my twins climb into their seats at the table.

"Where is Miss Brooks?" Harper asks.

"I am right here," Brooks announces, entering the kitchen, as I pull the baking dish from the oven.

"Go sit," Brooks instructs. "I will carry this to the table."

I note she is not smiling. Brooks's normal, energetic personality is not emanating from her every pore.

"Bad day?" I dare to ask as she takes her seat.

She bites her lips tightly between her teeth as she nods.

"Wanna talk about it?" I offer as I scoop rice onto each plate.

"I can't," she bites.

Bites? Calm, fun-loving Brooks is not sitting beside me. Hmm... What happened today that my best friend would not share? She always shares; she overshares. Usually, I hear many stories from her in the evening. Apparently, as she jabs a needle repeatedly into people, they love to spill their guts. I keep telling her we should write a book with the confessions on her tattoo tables.

"I want to tell you, but I can't," she states flatly between bites.

I focus on the girls, cutting chicken into bite-sized pieces for them. I have known Brooks for six years now, and I have never seen her this…quiet. This might be my most uncomfortable meal since I left home in high school. My exhausted girls slowly eat as their eyes grow heavier, and Brooks does not want to talk. Rather than fill the void, I opt to chance an occasional glance at my friend.

"I guess I can share part of it," she offers. "A new guy and his brother…" She glances up at me then back to her food.

Weird.

"Well, he wants his first tattoo. While I was sketching, he touched me."

I gasp. *This is what's upset my friend.* She saw a vision that scared her.

"Actually, he touched me three times," she states.

I choke on my food, coughing and sputtering for a minute. She is careful, uber careful, to avoid touching everyone, even my girls. It is on very rare occasions, a stranger will catch her off guard and touch her. She wears her gloves at all times in her shop. It is a protective barrier for her. *One touch is an accident, but three times? Three times means she let her guard down, and she never does that.*

"Tell me," I urge. "Tell me about the visions, so I can help you work through them."

She shakes her head. *Hmm...* She's shared some pretty screwed up and freaky visions with me. *It must be bad if she will not tell me in front of the twins.*

"Girls, go brush your teeth and get ready for bed," I instruct, anxious to hear this story.

Brooks and I watch two sleepy kids slide from their chairs and trudge to the hallway. Little ears now gone, I look to Brooks for an explanation. Again, she shakes her head. I prepare to demand to hear about the visions but am silenced by her hand between us.

"He touched me three times, and I had no visions. None." Eyebrows raised, she looks for my reaction.

"No visions?" I murmur, scared what this means. "Were you blocking him?"

She shakes her head. "The first touch, his fingers accidentally grazed my forearm as he pointed at my sketch."

"No visions?" I ask.

Again, she shakes her head. "He perplexed me," she admits. "A million thoughts flooded to mind as I continued to sketch, so I was not focused when he placed his hand on mine."

My eyes grow wide. *It was not an accidental touch. She allowed him to make contact.*

"Part of his hand met my wrist and nothing. I began to worry I was sick. So, I removed my glove to shake his hand goodbye, and still no visions. To be sure I was not broken, I shook hands with his brother, and..."

I can't help but finish her silence. "You had a vision."

"I had the most vivid, fast playing flashes I've ever experienced. Like, ten visions all in a minute's time. It made me light-headed," she informs.

Christy

"So, your gift is still intact. What does this mean?"

She stares at me as if I missed a punch line or the real reason for her story, then she seems to shake off the cobwebs.

"I am not sure why I did not have visions when Mad—he touched me," she states. "Maybe he was blocking me."

My friend shrugs. *Hmm... He was blocking her.*

"You should ask him; maybe he could teach you to do it," I encourage.

"And how would that go?" she scoffs. "So, I have visions with everyone but you. Do you have a gift, and if so, can you teach me to block visions like you do?"

I pick up the sarcasm she lays down.

"I can't tell strangers I have a gift. Word will get around, and I will lose clients."

I purse my lips. It is a dilemma for sure.

"Tell me about the visions his brother gave you." I attempt to change the topic.

She shakes her head, leaving no doubt this is not up for discussion. *Crud.* That bothers me more than her not having visions with the other guy. There are only two types of visions she will not share. Visions involving me and the girls—I requested she keep those to herself—and the others are heinous. As a mom, I can't hear them, or I will never leave the house with my daughters.

It sucks that she has those on her mind now. It can't be easy to move on and unsee those.

"You should read to the girls tonight," I suggest, hoping their innocence will help push out the visions.

Together, we make quick work of clearing the table. I load the dishwasher while she joins the twins. It only takes me a minute, and I peek my head into the bedroom I share with my girls.

Brooks is not reading; instead, she is staring at the football posters on the girls' wall.

"He runs fast." Ry runs around the room as a demonstration.

"And he always catches the football," Harper brags, tossing her little Cardinals football and catching it.

"What's going on in here?" I ask, leaning against the door frame.

Both girls point to Brooks. "She asked," they defend in unison.

"To bed, both of you," I order, and they assume their spots on their pillows.

Brooks, however, does not move. She stares at the poster as if studying every feature of the NFL player.

"Brooks, is everything alright?" I ask, wishing I might wrap my arm around my friend's shoulder.

"Everything is perfect," she says with conviction.

I watch her; she is not herself tonight. Most of the night, she acted as if she saw a ghost, and now everything is right as rain. When she bends down, kissing each girl's hand and placing it on each twins' cheek, I gasp. *Touching.* She physically touches the girls. Her eyes are closed; that means she is having a vision. *Maybe she needed sweet visions to erase those she saw today.* She smiles at the girls and turns off the light. We exchange a look at the door.

"Let's talk," I urge.

Back in the kitchen, I pour two glasses of our favorite rosé, sliding one stemless wine glass across the butcher block countertop to her.

"Explain," I instruct.

She shakes her head, lips tight between her teeth.

"Brooks, it is clear the visions today upset you." My eyes beg her to open up. "You kissed the girls; you were seeing their futures. What is up?"

Again, she shakes her head.

"Who were these guys?"

More head shaking.

"Brooks, help me understand," I plead.

"They were good visions," she states, leaving me curious.

"The girls?"

She shakes her head. "The guy at the shop. So many happy times, events, and a long, happy life."

"So, why are you so sullen?" I probe.

"I am not sullen. I am restrained," she smirks. "You ordered me not to share any visions I see for you and the girls."

With no more detail, she mimes zipping her lips and locking

Christy

them, then tossing the key over her shoulder. This is not the first time this has come back to bite me on the butt. Part of me wants to know everything she experienced today, even with the twins. Although I believe her visions and have witnessed them come true, I do not like knowing what lies ahead. I detest waiting around for the scene she saw to unveil itself. I become anxious, looking everywhere for it to happen. I am much too busy for that. I will stand firm and not give her permission to tell me what she saw for Harper and Ry's future.

"I love our lives," Brooks ensures, smiling before sipping her wine.

"No hints. You know the rules," I warn, shaking my finger at her.

"I am calling it a night," she states. "It is a big day tomorrow," she smirks, taking her wine with her.

I shake my head. She dropped another little hint there. *Damn her.*

2
FRIDAY, JUNE 9TH

Ryan

"Thanks for doing this," I greet my brother, Maddux, in my driveway.

He smiles, replying, "You live next door; it is not a hardship."

It is not quite next door. I built my new house in the Breakstone Cliffs neighborhood two doors down from his, but it is a quarter of a mile at least. His house overlooks the tee boxes on number three, and mine sits between holes number four and five. At least it is close enough I am only a golf cart ride away.

For the time while he was at Northwestern, followed by my time at Georgia, we lived in different states. Despite our four-year age difference, we were close growing up in Overland Park. Through our frequent family vacations and family dinners, our parents instilled in us the importance of family.

"The contractor is already inside," I inform, motioning toward the open garage doors; he follows me inside.

I am handed a clipboard checklist and a pen to make notes as we tour the house during my final walk through. After months of waiting, it is done. On Monday, appliances arrive, and on

Friday, my new furniture. By this time next week, I will be moved in.

Together, we listen as the contractor describes each room, and he makes notes of an exposed nail head, chipped paint, and a drippy faucet. My open floor plan kitchen, dining, and family room area looks amazing. With only a double-sided fireplace in a six-foot wall in the center of the space between the family room and formal dining space, combined with the light walls and blonde wood floors, it is huge. It is exactly what I hoped for.

Next, we walk down the long, wide hallway toward the study, two guest rooms, and the primary suite across the hall. Despite my designer's protests, I continued the blonde wood throughout the main level. My custom-made desk will look perfect in front of the long, wooden, backlit shelves in the study, and the matching cabinets below offer me plenty of storage options. My favorite room is the oversized master which gives me room for my Alaskan King bed. I am a big guy at six-foot-six; I enjoy my space when I sleep.

Opposite the wall for my bed, the built-in shelves frame a space for my over-sized television. With built-in speakers throughout the house, I ensured—from TV to music—I will enjoy sound inside and out. We tour the ensuite next. Crossing my fingers that someday the woman of my dreams will live here with me, I opted for his-and-hers bathrooms, vanities, and jumbo walk-in closets with a two-person whirlpool tub between them.

I spared no expense; I look forward to using the heated tile floors and towel warmer this winter. Maddux's career in the real estate field proved helpful in suggesting upgrades and a layout for my home. I am happy we made this journey together. While the house is all mine, I will always remember his help.

In the walkout basement, we examine the theater, the game room, the bar, and the kitchenette. Totaling five bedrooms, six bathrooms, and a four-car garage, it takes quite a bit of time to tour the entire house. Next, we explore the deck, patio, pool, 50-yard turf field, and the landscaping.

All in all, there are only a handful of necessary touch-ups. I sign the form, and I pass the clipboard back to the contractor.

"Not bad," Maddux says, making the gesture of dusting his hands. "Ready to play 18?"

I nod, leading the way back to his golf cart in the driveway. I have not played much golf in the past six years. I know I will suck during this celebrity charity tournament. Living here at the Lynks at Tryst Falls Country Club, now I will play tons of golf in the off-season.

Christy

I turn my head to the left then to the right, releasing some stress from my tight neck and shoulder muscles. Over six hours at the pool were put in today, and now another five to six hours will be spent waiting on members and celebrities at the charity event. I offered to tend bar outside tonight; with one person calling in, I will be both in front and behind the bar for hours.

I tug at the tiny black uniform dress for the fifteenth time this hour, wishing it were three inches longer. The waitresses urge me not to fight it, claiming it leads to great tips from the men. *That is why I signed up to work this event—the money. I need the money; I always need money.*

Choosing to make the best of it, I focus on the music playing and filling drink orders. Swaying to the beat behind the bar helps my mood. The hours fly as do the drinks. Now the only pitfall is I need to kindly brush off the comments and advances of all levels of inebriated men.

Ryan

Christy

After our round of golf, I remind myself I am a member of this country club and resist the urge to leave the charity dinner and auction that follows. I will need to make friends here as these are the members I live next door to and golf with.

As a popular NFL player for the local team, I pose for photos, shake hands, and listen to strangers' favorite memories and games. Many ask which house I bought and about my predictions for next season.

I would rather they welcome me to the club and ask if I am married. I am looking for friendship here. I hope I am not always the celebrity on display like a zoo exhibit.

I observe Maddux mingle with members and friends. When I hover, he introduces me as his little brother, sharing details of my house and golf game. Perhaps his friends will become mine. I can't keep hanging around with the NFL couples and their kids. I need to create my own family; I want to find someone to share my life with.

As the hours pass, we take custody of a table on the patio. I watch my brother consume glasses of scotch, one after another. He is not slurring his words, but his always-put-together personality slips. He flirts with the wait staff and teases some of his friends.

"I will get the next round," he offers, pointing to the bar.

I shake my head. I hold myself to a strict two-drink policy, which I adopted the summer after high school graduation. It serves me well, especially now that I am in the public eye. I can't afford any scandals. My agent, my team, and my sponsorships expect me to honor my clean image.

I glance at Maddux at the end of the bar, temporarily distracted by the female bartender swaying with the music as she fills orders. I need to pull my brother back to the table before he embarrasses himself by hitting on her.

It looks like her; it can't be. As I approach, I know my eyes are playing tricks on me, and it's not due to alcohol. After all these years and all my attempts to find her, the love of my life is tending bar at the country club I recently joined. I can't believe the one that got away is right here in my life once again. *I will not waste this lucky break.*

After dinner, a local band performs outside, and Christy works the bar as she sings along to the band as they sing covers.

She looks the same as six years ago, maybe more mature. She seems happy, dancing and conversing with the members and other guests. *She still enjoys music and dancing—I love that.*

Too many nights, her memory has haunted me. I've tried to move on, but no one compares to the memory of her and our time together.

I cringe, remembering our fight after I drunkenly hooked up with another girl. Admittedly, I made out with a girl or two before that. In high school, alcohol and I did not make the wisest decisions. I can't believe I "accidentally" slept with the other girl. Christy was so mad, she cut all ties with me immediately. I did not even see her at school. I graduated two weeks later, and although I tried, I never saw her again. When I finally worked up the nerve to knock on her door, her father stated she had run away. I did not believe him, so I camped outside the house, down the block, but she never showed. I asked her friends, and they also thought she ran away.

I went off to college but attempted to find her on social media. When I visited home each summer, I asked, but none of our friends ever heard from her again.

Let's see… If I am 24, she is 21. Wow! It has only been six years. It seems longer. I've beat myself up for six years. I can't believe she fell back into my life.

I spend the remainder of the night enjoying my view.

I feel like a stalker, lying in wait. The distant lights of the parking lot, cast shadows around me.

"Christy," I call, approaching her from behind as she walks out the staff door at the back of the clubhouse.

Startled, she jumps, fists raised between us.

"Easy. It is only me." I can't help but chuckle at her defense moves.

"Ry..." My name lodges in her throat. Her hand to her mouth, tears reflect the distant lights.

Without a word, without any thought, I pull her tightly to my chest, arms cocooning her. Like no time passed, she snakes her arms around my waist and rests her cheek on my chest.

"Why are you here?" she murmurs.

"I am a new member," I inform her.

She looks up at me, tears clinging to her dark lashes. "Here?" she asks in disbelief.

I nod, smiling. She pulls away. Although I attempt to hold her, she takes two steps backward, shaking her head.

"I can't." She scans the area nervously. "I need to go."

"Wait!" I call, taking a step toward her.

She holds a hand up between us, palm toward me. "I need to get home," her voice firm, I halt. "It was nice seeing you again." Her tone urges me to let her go, to leave her alone.

"Can I..."

She cuts me off. Walking backwards, she shakes her head.

"I could lose my job by talking to you." She bumps into a beat-up, old, blue Honda Civic. "It is a staff/member thing," she says, as if that explains everything.

I stand frozen in place as she climbs into the car and drives away. For long moments, I am alone in the staff parking lot. I hang around, hoping she might come back. Only two other cars remain.

"Can I help you find your car?" A male voice jars me from my thoughts.

I shake my head. "Do you know Christy Wainwright?"

He shakes his head.

"She just left," I explain, pointing my thumb over my shoulder.

"Oh." He chuckles nervously. "That was our pool manager. Her name is Christy, but that is not her last name. I think she's trying to give you a fake name to brush you off, dude." As he speaks, he shakes his head, crossing his arms over his chest. "I bet she does not know that you are famous."

Ah… So, he recognizes me. Hopefully, I can use that to my advantage.

"We went to high school together," I begin, then lie. "I thought her last name was Wainwright, but after six years, I probably got it wrong."

He smiles widely, answering, "Yeah. Her last name is Carlton."

Carlton. That means she is married. Crap. That explains her hurrying to leave. But…I did not clock a wedding ring on her hand when I looked for it. *Could she be divorced? I hope so. Wait. That's a horrible thing to think. I hope she's single, but I also want her to be happy. Maybe she is happily divorced.* I realize this guy is watching me mull this over and say good-bye.

I turn on the headlights before aiming the golf cart toward Maddux's house. High on the feel of Christy in my arms once again, I can only think of her. *I need to win her back. I need a plan.*

3

SATURDAY, JUNE 10TH

Christy

I find myself constantly looking over my shoulder, as I scurry to prepare the pool for the day. Now that Ryan is a member, he could be anywhere at any time. I hear a startled scream. My thoughts elsewhere, I sprayed a little girl perched on the pool's edge.

"Oops. Sorry," I beg her pardon.

Harper takes the hose from my hand. "I will do it, Mommy," she states.

Even my five-and-a-half-year-old sees I am struggling with simple tasks this morning. I return to my office, reading through the evening note I make a mental list of the tasks to complete before opening at 11. Swim lessons will be over soon. My lifeguards will have over an hour to set up the pool deck, so I hop on a cart, heading to the clubhouse for supplies.

Even as I drive along the path, I watch nervously for Ryan. I quickly load toilet paper and napkins on the cart, looking over my shoulder. *Hmm... There was something else.* I try to recall the note on my desk. *What was it?*

"Christy!" A waitress named Rose calls my name as she hangs up the phone behind the snack bar. I ascertain from her wide eyes and tight lips that something is wrong. "One of your guards called." She points to the phone. "One of your girls is hurt."

I wave my thanks as I dart out to the cart. I press the pedal tightly to the floor, but electric carts can only drive so fast. *"One of your girls."* I wonder *if she meant my lifeguards or my twins.* I look at my cell phone, wondering why they called the club house instead of my cell. My number is posted at every phone around the pool. I will the cart to speed up as a pit settles hard in my stomach.

Crud!

Approaching the pool, Ryan extracts his large frame from a red golf cart near the pool entrance. I jump from my cart, not taking the time to set the brake. The area is flat; it will stop on its own.

"Hey," Ryan greets.

"I can't," I state, brushing past him.

"Mommy, she's hurt." Harper points as soon as she sees me.

I note Harper's arm wraps around her sister's back.

"She broke her arm," Harper claims.

I bend to one knee. "Let me see," I urge, my fingers already gently moving from Ry's elbow toward her wrist.

"It snapped," my little girl states, as if talking about a twig and not her arm. "Right here." She points with her left hand.

Ry hisses when I gently press that area.

"I think she needs an X-ray," a swim lesson parent informs me. "It is swelling fast."

"I will take care of the pool," a lifeguard offers, and I nod.

"Let's go," I urge the twins toward the cart.

"I will drive," Ryan offers. "Before you argue, you need to focus on your daughter."

My girls climb onto the backward facing seats on his golf cart. Reluctantly, I slowly take a seat beside him, keeping my right hand on the "oh crap" handle above me as I turn toward the twins behind us.

Christy

Ryan

A zillion questions come to mind, but I focus on following Christy's directions to her car in the staff parking lot and then to the nearest Urgent Care clinic. As I drive, I feel panic grow in my chest. *It can't be. I can't be right. She...She would...Christy would tell me. I would know, wouldn't I?* I glance in the rearview mirror.

The mirror images wear their long blonde curls in a ponytail. They share my big blue eyes and curly blonde hair. *I wonder what other traits they inherited from me—perhaps athleticism. What reason would Christy have to keep them from me—to keep them a secret? Pregnant and scared at age 16, why didn't she come to me? I would never have left her side. She did not need to raise them alone; I should have been by her side through it all. I thought we were careful. I thought I kept her safe. Would have, could have, should have no longer matter. I am a father. What matters is from this point forward.*

In the waiting room, two patients in line before us, I can't take the tension. My mind still focuses on questions and possible reasons. I need to start a conversation with them.

I can't help but ask, "How did it happen?" I jut my chin at the injured arm.

"We were playing football," the outspoken twin answers and looks at her mom. "Two-hand touch. I promise."

"I fell, and it snapped," the injured twin explains.

"How many times have I told you not to play football?" Christy chides. Looking at me, she explains, "Some of the older kids stick around and play touch football while waiting on their siblings to finish swimming lessons before the pool opens at 11. They play on a tiny patch of grass near the playground area. I keep telling them someone will get hurt."

"I caught the pass," the girl with the broken arm brags, looking in my direction. "We always win."

Both girls smile wide. They really are identical; I can only tell a difference because of the injured arm.

"You win?" I ask.

They proudly nod.

"Harper is quarterback, and I am a tight end like you, Mr. Harper," she brags, holding her arm and smiling.

Ah-ha! So, the girls do know who I am.

"I want to be the tight end, but I am better at quarterback than Ry is," Harper shares.

"And I am a better tight end than Harper is," Ry states.

Interesting… Christy named them Harper and Ry.

I imagine these little girls playing touch football on the grass with a group of boys. *If the girls often win, I'd love to see them play. They must have skills.* A warmth fills my chest, and a smile slides upon my face. *I think it is pride.*

"Not everyone can be a tight end," Christy reminds her girls.

"But…" they say in unison and break into a fit of giggles.

"But the best position on the offense is the tight end," I state smugly.

"Yep!" Again, they speak at the same time.

"Do they…" I point at the girls.

Christy nods, "You get used to it. I think it is a twin thing."

I hope I get the chance to get used to it. A glimpse is all it took. I am a dad. I missed six years—I will not miss any more. I will find a time to talk to Christy alone. They look like me; I know they are mine. We will be a family. I will be sure of it.

I wait with Harper while Christy escorts Ry to see a physician.

"Football, huh?" I pry before the door closes behind Christy.

"Yep," Harper grins. "Mommy is a big Cardinals fan, but she does not like us playing. She thinks the older kids might…" she pauses as it clicks that her mom was right; the older kids did hurt Ry.

"Your mom likes the Cardinals?" I interrogate further.

"Ry and I do, too," she shares smiling proudly. "We watch every game. Sometimes, she lets us stay up late on a school night for your games."

"Every game?" I ask, and she nods.

"Mommy yells loud at the TV," Harper informs. "But she gets mad when Ry and I yell at the game. You are her favorite player."

Bam! I knew it. I still mean something to her.

"Who is your favorite…"

Harper interrupts me before I finish my question. "You are," she giggles. "You are Ry's favorite, too."

"Ry is a weird name," I blurt before I think better of it.

"Her name is Ryan, silly," she laughs. "We call her Ry."

Identical twins. Harper and Ryan. Ryan Harper. Christy gave her daughters my names. Our daughters. My daughters. If I was not sure before, I am now.

Butterflies flutter in my abdomen at the knowledge I am a father. My mind whirls with everything I want to teach them. When I thought I was finally getting myself together, building a house, God threw me another curveball. Well, two curveballs—two absolutely perfect curveballs.

An hour passes before Christy returns, a royal blue cast on little Ry's forearm.

"Mr. Harper, will you be the first to sign my cast?" Ry asks once we are in Christy's car.

"Of course," I answer. "But you can call me Ryan."

This causes the twins to giggle. Christy rolls her eyes at me.

"Mommy, we need a black marker," Harper announces.

"I have some in my office," Christy informs.

"Mr. Harper—" Again, the two giggle. "—will you come to Mommy's office for us to get a marker?"

"Of course," I answer to continued giggles and then gibberish.

"Girls, I told you that's like whispering, and that is…"

"Rude," they say in unison.

"Somewhere, my parents are enjoying my pain," Christy mumbles.

I cringe at the mention of her parents. Her father verbally abused both her and her mother. I also suspected he hit his wife, but I never saw definitive proof. I make a mental note to ask Christy about her parents and her running away.

"Mr. Harper... I mean Ryan," Ry giggles. "My cast is waterproof so I can still swim."

"That is cool," I reply.

"Mommy," the girls sing-song.

"You got a text from Miss Brooks," Ry informs.

"I really need to log out of the iPad," Christy mutters, pulling her cell phone from her purse on the floorboard.

"Yes, I will sit the twins..." Harper reads, stopping at a word she does not know.

"Tonight," Ry helps her read.

"Too smart for their own good," Christy mumbles.

"What is with all of the mumbling?" I ask.

Her wide, startled eyes notify me she was unaware she spoke out loud.

"They seem to keep you on your toes," I chuckle.

She nods.

"Are you going out tonight?" I inquire.

"No. Why?"

"Miss Brooks offered to babysit," I remind her.

She blows out a loud breath. "My friend thinks she can predict the future," she replies.

I pull my eyes from the road for a quick glance in her direction.

"So, you are going out," I state, fearing she's trying to hide from me.

"I do not have plans," she assures me.

"Yes, you do. I think we should talk tonight," I urge, careful to keep my tone firm but not overbearing.

Fear upon her face, she nods.

"Miss Brooks can tell the future," Ry states, her eyes never leaving the iPad in her lap.

"She does it all the time," Harper adds. "Miss Brooks says Mommy is in the Nile."

"Let Miss Brooks keep the girls so we can talk," I urge. "We can go to my place."

I only get a nod from Christy while I hear more gibberish from the backseat.

Christy

The girls talk about my team, football plays, and ask me questions the rest of the drive, then on the golf cart ride back to the pool.

"Why a blue cast?" I ask, printing then signing my name.

"The nurse said pink or purple is popular," Ry says and makes a gagging gesture.

Christy rolls her eyes in my direction, causing me to laugh.

"Would they ask you if you want a pink or purple cast?" Ry asks me.

I shake my head and make a gagging gesture.

Christy swats me and admonishes, "Do not encourage them."

The girls laugh loudly.

Looking at the clock, I remember I am not able to spend the entire day with these ladies.

"I'd better head over to the driving range. Our tee time is at one. I'll see you tonight."

I can see in her eyes she wants to argue. Our conversation later will not be an easy one. I long to pull her into my arms and hold her. It takes all my strength to leave my three girls to go golf.

While they are not quite my girls now, soon they will be.

4

SATURDAY, JUNE 10TH

Christy

I lean against the door to my car, mentally preparing myself. I wish I'd suggested we meet in a quiet restaurant, but as a public figure, someone might overhear us. I should have asked Brooks to keep the girls at the tattoo parlor, so we could talk at our apartment. *Anywhere but here, now, at his place would have been better. Who am I kidding? I am dreading this conversation; it is not the location that bothers me.*

With hesitant steps, I approach the double glass doors of his high rise and enter the lobby.

"I am here to see Mr. Harper," I inform the woman behind the front desk, positioned directly in front of the elevators.

"Is Mr. Harper expecting you?" she questions, her tone leading me to believe she thinks I am a random fangirl.

When I nod, she asks for my name before she picks up the phone. "Mr. Harper, I have a Miss Christy Carlton here to see you." Her stern gaze remains on me as she listens. "Yes, sir."

A smile now upon her face, she informs me, "Mr. Harper asked me to add you to his approved visitors list. If you will follow me, the elevator is right this way."

Apparently now, I am worthy of a friendly face and her undivided attention. She presses the button on the farthest elevator, and the door opens. Before signaling for me to enter, she scans her keycard and presses the button for the eleventh floor.

"Enjoy your visit," she says as the doors close.

I wish I had a minute to prepare myself as the elevator slowly ascends, but it is an express elevator. It seems like the doors barely close before they swish open again. Ryan stands ready, greeting me with his crooked smile.

"You made it," he announces, swinging his arm for me to enter. "I mean, of course, you made it. I worried you might have trouble finding the place or change your mind and text that you were not coming," he rambles nervously.

I do not confess I wanted to chicken out; I do not tell him I would choose a gynecologist visit over our time together tonight.

"Soooo…" he drawls. "This is my place for one more week. Pardon the boxes."

I scan the large, open loft with stacks upon stacks of boxes, pondering what Ryan might collect to fill them all. I imagine there are trophies, jerseys, and helmets.

"I am drinking water," he says, making his way toward the kitchen. "I also have beer, wine, and ginger ale." He looks expectantly at me, one hand on the refrigerator door.

"Water is fine," I respond.

Ryan efficiently pulls a reusable glass bottle from the door and pours water into a red-tinted glass on the counter. He adds three ice cubes before sliding the glass across to me.

"Thank you," I murmur anxiously.

"Let's make our way through the towers of boxes to the sofa," he suggests, rounding the island towards me.

His large hand presses into my lower back, and he walks beside me. Electric currents flow from his warm fingertips, spreading quickly throughout my body. It should be weird, allowing him to touch me familiarly, but it feels second nature.

I place my glass on a coaster on the table in front of me as I assume the spot near the arm of the sofa. Instead of the leather bachelor furniture I expected, the tan sofa is soft with several large pillows. I pull a red corduroy pillow into my lap, hugging it tightly to my chest. Ryan sits on the center cushion beside me instead of at the opposite end, and his water joins mine on the table. I fiddle with the corner of the pillow, my eyes on my fingers and not the man beside me, as several long moments pass between us.

I decide to put us out of our misery.

"We need to…I do not know how to…" I stammer. "What are we going to do? How do we…?"

He shrugs and moves closer to me on the sofa, pulling me into his arms, my back to his chest. "We will figure it out," he whispers near my ear.

"We can't mess it up. The girls need us to get this right," I murmur, loving his warm body holding me.

I've missed this for six years. I dedicated myself to the twins. I left no time for the possibility of dating. I've missed this feeling of not being alone, of having someone to hold me. Brooks is the best friend I could ever ask for, but her inability to hug or hold my hand-- her words, and actions do not feel like this.

Ryan

I am holding Christy again. I must find a way to have more moments like this.

"Let's talk," I suggest, ready to plan.

Christy turns, positioning her knee between us.

"It could not have been easy parenting on your own," I state the obvious.

"They are very smart and keep me on my toes; that is for sure," she chuckles nervously.

Christy

"I do not want to move too fast or overstep my bounds," I explain. "I need to be their father in all ways I am supposed to be and can be. I want to be with the three of you; I want to support all of you in every way I can."

She makes a move to argue.

"I am not talking about financial support. Well, I am, but I also mean keeping them while you work, spending time with the three of you, helping when they are sick or hurt... All of it. I *am* going to be here for all of it."

Tears stream down Christy's face. "I am sorry. So, so sorry," she cries. "I did this. I did this to you; I did this to them. I am the reason we are in this mess."

"Shh..." I soothe. I hold her to me; I hug her tightly. "Shh... No, you did not."

"If I had partied less... if I did not sleep with someone else, you would have told me," I argue. "If I had not messed up at the party, I would have been by your side through it all."

I scrub my hands over my face, mentally kicking myself yet again for my straying libido.

"Hell, if I had been more careful, you would not have been pregnant. You did not get pregnant on your own. I had a hand in that," I pause, my mind running through that scenario. "But then we would not have Ry and Harper."

Christy places her hand upon mine.

"I never regretted having the twins," she whispers.

I am so glad to hear that. In less than a day, I already love them. I do not want to imagine a world where they do not exist.

"They are the best parts of both of us," I murmur, my throat tight.

She nods her head against my chest, and I feel her wet tears through my shirt.

"I kept you apart. I kept them a secret for too long. How can you ever forgive me?" She looks up at me through tear-filled eyes.

"How about you start at the beginning and tell me everything?" I prompt.

I do not interrupt while Christy reminds me, she did not feel well, so she stayed home that night. While I partied with my classmates, she took a pregnancy test, and her life changed forever. She planned to tell me the next afternoon, but two of her friends told her I cheated on her at the party. Hurt and afraid, she did not know what to do.

My chest aches, remembering the pain I caused after partying without her that night. I hurt her and broke us for a quick roll in the sheets. It was meaningless sex that I did not even remember the next morning. The hickey on my chest corroborated the story the guys shared about my behavior the previous night. When I showed up at her door, she pushed me away with red, puffy eyes and a broken heart.

Unable to confide in me, she desperately told her parents Monday before school. My insides turn to concrete when she tells me how her father's rage fell on her. She remembers the hateful words he spit at her and the hurt she felt as her own mother would not intervene when he kicked her out.

That explains the disdain he directed at me the next week.

"He told me you ran away," I murmur, my voice breaking at the painful memory.

Confused, Christy's tear-filled eyes search my face.

"When you missed two days of school, I knocked on your door," I explain. "Your mom answered when I skipped school the following Monday to find you. She told me you'd run away and to stop coming by. I looked everywhere for you. I wanted to…"

She interrupts, continuing to share the horrors I initiated with my selfish behavior. "I was visibly upset in homeroom," she confides. "Mrs. Greenberg pulled me into the hall. When I claimed nothing was wrong, she escorted me to the counselor's office. They requested my assignments and allowed me to remain in the office for the day."

I watch in silence as Christy's shaking hand reaches for her water. I listen to her gulps as she swallows hard. *I wish I had tissues.* I hop from my seat, returning with a roll of toilet paper.

"That is all I can find right now." I shrug.

She wipes her eyes and blows her nose. Then, repositions herself on the sofa cushion, a pillow clutched tightly to her chest.

"When Mrs. Greenberg returned at the final bell, I realized I had

Christy

no home to return to. I was not ready to tell my friends, so I told them the truth."

Christy's eyes avoid mine.

"I am not sure if you remember, but she attended our church." She glances up through wet lashes then continues, "Mrs. Greenberg had a pamphlet for a church-run home for unwed mothers. What happened next is kind of a blur. I remember crying myself to sleep on a cheap twin bed in a room with two empty beds."

Christy literally shakes away the memory, gathering herself. "Anyway, that is where I met Brooks. Her mom forced her to volunteer every Sunday in hopes it would prevent Brooks from having sex."

A tiny smile perks up her face, and her eyes flicker a bit.

"Brooks told me she detested her visits before I showed up. We hit it off. She started coming on Wednesdays, too. In my fifth month of pregnancy, the women that ran the center began discussing the adoption process with me, and I freaked. I think as the twins started to kick, it became real to me. I realized they expected me to sign documents and give my babies away."

"I had to find another option. I confided in Brooks, and together, we devised our plan. It is like the stars aligned for me. Brooks was an apprentice at the tattoo shop while her family thought she worked as a barista. Her mother blew a gasket when, on Brooks's twenty-first birthday, she used her trust fund to buy the tattoo shop and moved into the apartment above it. She made a large donation to the unwed-mothers center as she plucked me from them in the nick of time. She has been my boss, roommate, and best friend ever since."

I clear my throat as I search for words. "You overcame so much. Alone. I am humbled by your fortitude…"

"Do not," Christy argues firmly. "I do not deserve your praise. I essentially lied to you and the girls for…"

I interrupt by grasping her face in my hands at her eye level, and I speak, "You gave me those two miracles. You kept them safe from your father; you kept them safe for six long years, and you raised them to be the intelligent, resilient girls they are today. I mean, Ry broke her arm today and reacted like it was nothing."

I break eye contact to place a long kiss on her forehead. I close my eyes, fighting the urge to move my lips to hers. All the old feelings rise to the surface, and I long to pick up where we left off. *We need to talk.* A thought pops into my head. *Lying to the girls.*

"Did Harper or Ry ever ask about me? I mean, about their dad?" I hate that the quiver of my voice broadcasts my emotion.

Christy's tiny smile grows.

"From the time they could talk, I told them 'Daddy is at work and very busy, and someday, he will be home.'"

Christy

I watch Ryan's eyes grow wide at my words.

"My intention was never to keep the girls from you," I explain. "I planned to contact you after you graduated from Georgia."

I cringe, waiting for him to mention that was two years ago. I search his face, anticipating his anger towards me.

"So, they do not think I abandoned them?" he asks, disbelieving.

I shake my head. "I never spoke ill of you. I did not want them to harbor negative thoughts where you were concerned."

"So, how do we tell them?" he asks with a sense of urgency. "I want to tell them as soon as possible. I would like to spend as much time with them as I can before the season starts."

My rapid heartbeats feel as though they might break through the walls of my chest. *It is happening so fast. I bumped into him last night, and tonight we are talking about telling the girls. We must think this through; we can't get this wrong.*

5

SUNDAY, JUNE 11TH

Ryan

Two nights after bumping into Christy, we prepare to talk to the girls.

"Ladies, I am taking you out to eat anywhere you want," I announce at the door to their tiny bedroom.

Harper and Ry squeal with excitement.

The far wall of the tiny space is covered in two Kansas City Cardinals football posters and several pennants. One poster is mine, dancing in the endzone after scoring a touchdown, and in the other, I stand beside our QB, Nolan. *When Harper claimed they were huge fans, I did not imagine this.*

"You will regret allowing them to choose," Christy warns behind me.

"Sonic! Sonic! Sonic!" the twins chant, hopping up and down.

"Really?" I ask in disbelief.

"I warned you," Christy taunts. "It is their absolute favorite."

"Sonic it is," I agree, and they award me with raucous cheers.

"Let's go. You know the drill," their mom prompts.

The girls use the restroom, grab a backpack, and wait by the door.

I answer more rapid-fire questions from the backseat about my teammates and playing football. It helps to calm my nerves.

In our slot at the drive-in, I ask, "What does everyone want?"

"Wacky Packs," the twins reply.

My head spins toward the back seat in confusion. "What?"

"We like grilled cheese Wacky Packs," Harper assures me.

"A Wacky Pack?" I seek further confirmation.

"Look." Ry points to the menu. "The kids' menu."

I scan the large sign, which lists meals, sides, slushes, shakes, and ice cream until I finally see the kids' section. Sure enough, the kids' meals are called Wacky Packs.

"You order," I instruct Christy, who shakes her head with a giant smile.

"I remember all the times we used to go to Sonic in high school, and I never once saw the kids'…"

"Wacky Pack! Wacky Pack!" the girls chant.

"I am not saying that," I protest. "I will ask for a kids' grilled cheese meal."

"Wacky Pack! Wacky Pack!" they cheer even louder.

Through laughter, I press the red button, ready to order.

"Welcome to Sonic. Order when you're ready," a male voice crackles through the intercom.

"Say it! Say it!" the girls chant from my backseat.

"I would like two Wacky Packs," I order over the twins' cheers.

Whoever named these were not thinking about dads having to order them; that's for sure.

When meals are delivered to our vehicle, Christy directs me to the nearest park for us to eat. I follow her directions over the gibberish conversation in the back seat.

"Ry and Harper…" Christy chides their use of twin speak.

I fight a smile, hearing their names sounding so much like mine.

"Mr. Harper," Harper calls for my attention. "What's your middle name?"

I glance in my rearview mirror. The girls giggle, hands to their

Christy

mouths. When I answer it is Carlton, I watch them look at each other with wide blue eyes. Looking at the road again, I hear more gibberish. When silence fills the vehicle, I wonder how to start this conversation.

"Mommy," the twins sing-song.

"*Cruuuud*," Christy draws out in a low growl. "They know," she whispers.

My head snaps to her at my right side. Wide-eyed, she nods, mouth quirked to one side.

"Are you our daddy?" Harper blurts.

I guess this is how our conversation will start. From the mouths of babes. I continue to drive, unsure how to respond as Christy seems stunned beside me.

"Mommy said our daddy was busy with his job." Ry works it out aloud. "And now *you* are here." She pauses for a second. "Ryan Carlton Harper is your name, and it is our names," she states.

"Mommy said she went to school with you," Harper adds.

Five. They're only five-and-a-half, I remind myself. Although they often act much older, I need to remember they are not quite six yet.

"Let's take our food and talk about this sitting at a picnic table at the park," Christy suggests, giving me more time to attempt to figure this out.

Who am I kidding? If I have not found the words in the last 24 hours, I am not about to in the next 10 minutes.

⁂

"May I have one cheese tot?" Christy asks from across the picnic table.

I slide my long container of tater tots covered in melted cheese towards her. I extend my plastic fork with one tot skewered upon it. Her eyes squint as she assesses the meaning behind the gesture.

"It is a tot, nothing more." I fear my eyes betray me as I watch her lips upon the black utensil in my hand.

"Thank you," she mumbles as she chews, her eyes alight.

"They are still your favorite," I state the obvious, and she nods. "I only ordered them because you did not."

"I watch what I eat," she claims, eyes looking away.

I place my hand on top of hers on the tabletop. "You are gorgeous. You have nothing to worry about," I state, hoping she takes it to heart.

She keeps her eyes on the twins, who are eating near us. "I work harder to keep my swimsuit body these days," she murmurs.

I shake my head, my hand still on hers. "You have always been hard on yourself. I saw you in the bartending dress—you can eat cheese tots and still stay hot."

"Girls, please toss your trash," Christy directs, changing the subject.

As the twins return from the nearby trash can, I invite them both to sit on my side of the table. I maneuver myself with one leg on each side of the bench, facing both girls as I straddle the board.

"So, your mom and I need to share some stuff with you," I stammer. I take a deep breath to center myself. *They are five-and-a-half-year olds, not the defensive line of the Seattle Seagulls.*

"You are my daddy," Harper blurts, unable to wait for me to pull myself together.

"And my daddy," Ry chimes in.

I smile in Christy's direction. She mentioned they are intelligent. I grossly misjudged the magnitude of that.

Turning back to the girls, my smile grows, and a warmth fills my chest. "Yes. I am your dad. I have been very busy, but now I am here, and I will never leave again."

I cringe at my choice of words. *I will travel for work; they might consider that as me leaving them.* I look at Christy across the table. She smiles, tears in her eyes, and nods. *I guess I did not screw this up.*

Focusing back on the twins, I find they're carrying on a full conversation in their unique language.

"Girls..." Christy interrupts.

"Can we...um..." Ry stumbles.

"Hug?" Harper finishes for her sister, looking from her mom to me for permission.

I do not hesitate; I spread my arms wide. Harper and Ry, with excited smiles, cling tightly to my neck and shoulders, and I wrap my arms snuggly around their waists.

Christy

Ryan looks at me over the twins' shoulders. His blue eyes swim with unshed tears. My two tiny girls brought this strong man to tears. My heart hurts, and tears burn my eyes. *I did this. I kept them apart for over five years. I deprived my twins of a dad in their lives. I denied Ryan a chance to be their father.*

I stand, struggling to catch my breath. I need air; I need to walk. Ryan's large hand grasps my wrist, halting my escape.

"Stay," he pleads.

My feet are concrete; I am stuck in place. Slowly, the girls release their grip on Ryan, taking a seat on the picnic tabletop, feet on the bench. He pulls me around to stand beside him, facing our girls.

Harper looks at her sister beside her then back at us. "Can Daddy come home with us?" she asks me.

It is a punch in the gut.

"Daddy has his own house," I tell them. "It is not football season, so he has lots of time for us to play," I offer instead.

In a perfect world, I would have forgiven him for hurting me all those years ago. In a perfect world, we would be a true family under one roof.

"Mommy," Ry whimpers, "I want Daddy to read me my bedtime story."

Harper jumps in, "I want Daddy to play football with me."

I am unsure what to do; I denied them for too long.

"How about we play catch right now?" Ryan suggests.

Like me, he wants to make the girls happy. The twins clap.

"I will go grab the ball," Ryan says, walking backwards toward the SUV.

For a moment, I am surprised he is prepared; then I remember his job. *He probably keeps several with him at all times.* I help the girls hop down, holding their little hands in mine to prevent them following him to the parking lot.

My stomach does a flip-flop when Ryan approaches, a proud smile on his face. It flips again when I realize we gave in to Harper's wish, and now Ry will expect her daddy to go home with us.

Ryan

Time flies by. We play football for half an hour. I love every minute, every giggle, and every tackle with tickles I make on the girls. Even Christy joins in our game.

When little yawns slow our tosses and catches, we load the twins into their booster seats and set our course for Christy's apartment in downtown Liberty. With each block I drive, I dread saying goodbye more and more.

I wish my house were furnished; I would drive them to my place instead. I can't force Christy to let me come in. I can't make her allow me to read a bedtime story, and I can't fall asleep on her sofa, so I am here when the girls climb out of bed. I find I am always at her mercy. After parking, I draw a long breath as I turn off the ignition.

"Shh…" Christy signals, index finger over her lips.

Glancing over my shoulder, I find both girls asleep; their little heads have fallen to their shoulders. A glimmer of hope blossoms.

Christy

She will need my help to carry them upstairs. Simultaneously, we open the backseat doors and unbuckle their seatbelts. I pull Ry from her seat, holding her with one arm flat to my chest. I mouth, "Wait," to Christy before I hurry around to help her.

"Help me lift her. I will carry her," I whisper.

She does not argue and helps place Harper in my other arm. I pause, enjoying the feel of them in my arms and against my chest. I can feel their breaths on my neck. I hold two little miracles in my arms. Christy closes the doors, backpacks in hand.

"Want me to help?" she asks.

I roll my eyes at her silliness. She bites her lips, a wide smile bursting onto her face. "I forgot I was talking to an NFL player," she murmurs, unlocking the door.

I follow Christy up the narrow stairs toward the apartment over the tattoo shop. This might be part of my new workout; the girls grow heavy as we near the door at the top of the stairway. While Christy holds the door open, I step inside the small space. I still marvel that four people live in this tiny, two-bedroom walkup I stand in.

I am in awe as Christy helps the two partially asleep girls go potty and slip on their pajamas. They are the most adorable critters in their black pajamas with white bones all over them. I know I have seen the cartoon drawing on their bellies, but I can't think of the name of it.

When they climb into the tiny twin bed, I realize Christy must sleep on the other twin in this room. While I sleep in a massive Alaskan King, they occupy this little room and these tiny beds. I tuck that away to try to fix someday soon.

"Story," Harper whines.

"Daddy, story please." Ry lifts her head, tired eyes piercing through me.

I look from my stance in the doorway to Christy for guidance.

"One story," Christy tells the girls. "One story, a short one, then to sleep. It is already an hour past your bedtime."

I hesitantly step toward their bed, unsure how to pick a book for a bedtime story. I am sure there are rules.

Christy pats my shoulder as I pass by. "Make up a story, a short one," she instructs.

I nod and plop myself down at the end of the bed. *Hmm... Make up a story.*

"Once upon a time, there was a handsome guy in high school." I smirk at Christy, and she rolls her eyes. "He played football and was the smartest guy in class. One day, a new girl joined his class. She was so smart, her teachers wanted her in class with the smart, handsome guy. The girl loved football, so she went to all of his football games." I pause to take a breath.

"They are asleep," Christy says.

When I look up from the tiny hands I hold, I find they are asleep for the second time tonight.

"C'mon," Christy encourages, shutting off the bedroom light. "Can you stay for a bit?" she asks, one hand on the wall, head tilting toward the living room and kitchen.

Hmm... It is my lucky day. Wide smile on my face, I nod and follow her into the tiny galley kitchen. She sets two stemless wine glasses on the counter.

"Join me for a glass?" she asks, pulling a partially drunk red wine bottle from the refrigerator.

"Let me," I state.

My fingers graze hers on the bottle before she relinquishes it. I fill her glass halfway and only pour a sip in mine. Following her lead, I join her on the sofa. She sips her wine for a moment as we sit in near silence. The only sounds are music from the parlor below.

Uncomfortable in her silence, I say the first thing that comes to mind, "I have been here before."

Her eyes widen.

"I mean, not up here. I have been in the tattoo parlor downstairs."

She tilts her head now, curious.

"Last week, I was down in the shop. My brother wants a tattoo."

"Maddux?" she asks.

"You remember him? You met him a few times when he was back from college at Mom and Dad's."

Christy

She contemplates this for a bit before nodding.

"Are the two of you still close?" she inquires.

"We were apart for college; it was a long eight years. Drafted by KC, we are back in the same state, and believe it or not, I built my house down the road from his." I chuckle, still amazed we will be neighbors at the course.

6

SUNDAY, JUNE 11TH

Christy

It all makes sense now—the two men in Brooks's shop and the mysterious visions she was not able to share. They were not bad visions; they were visions that included me, and therefore, she could not share. She saw Ryan coming back into my life. She saw the twins with their father. That is why she stared at the football posters for so long that night.

"What?" he asks.

I shake my head, unwilling to share my thoughts.

"My house is done, and my furniture arrives on Friday," Ryan shares. "Maybe you and the girls could spend the day with me on Friday." He searches my eyes for a reaction. "I think I need to spend more time with all three of you before the girls stay alone with me while you work."

I nod. "They will want to spend every day with you." I cringe as my voice shakes. "We will not be able to give them everything they want."

"I understand that, but I am on a countdown to my season starting. I would like to spend as much time with them as I can while my days are free," he confesses.

Christy

"Maybe you could come hang out with them at the pool this week while I work," I suggest. "I will be busy, and you will see them interact with their friends."

He likes that idea.

"Mommy?" one of the girls calls from the other room. "Is Daddy still here?"

Our eyes meet. While he smiles, I frown. Before I hop up, two little heads peek from the bedroom doorway. Sly smiles grace their faces.

"Bed," I order, pointing in their direction.

Giggles erupt with the sound of their feet racing across the wooden floor to their bed.

"Want me to help?" Ryan hedges, not knowing if his presence would further hinder their sleep.

I signal for him to join me. Every experience is a new one for him. He is out of his depth here.

"We want Daddy to sleep with us tonight," Harper declares, smiling proudly.

"Honey," I respond. "Daddy has his own house and his own things to do. He works out, he sees his friends, and he plays golf with his brother."

"Brother?" Ry asks warily.

"My brother's name is Maddux," Ryan answers. "He is older than me and ugly."

The girls laugh. *This is not good. They will never go to sleep now.*

"Can we see Maddux?" Harper asks. "Do you have a mom and dad?"

Her questions fly rapid fire as her little brain tries to learn all she can.

"Mommy does not have a mom and dad," Ry states, rubbing her fist into her left eye.

"Climb back into bed," I urge.

"I will tell you about my family, but only if you keep your eyes closed." He smiles proudly in my direction.

Tucked in, kisses given, Ryan sits on their bed, and begins.

"My brother Maddux…"

He is interrupted by the sound of the front door closing and the alarm keypad beeping.

"Brooks!" the twins scream with glee, climbing out of bed once again.

I close my eyes, attempting to take a calming breath. They will never fall asleep at this rate.

"Brooks, Daddy is here!" Ry cheers. "Come see Daddy."

The girls run to Ryan's side, each taking a hand.

"See?" Ry points. "He's our daddy."

Ryan nods his chin in that purely masculine guy way, his panty-melting smile greeting my friend.

"Hi again," Brooks waves.

"Hello. I am Ryan Harper."

"She knows," I bite. "She could have given me a heads up," I say through gritted teeth.

"But someone has a pesky rule about me sharing those things."

I remember Ryan is in the room. Looking in his direction, I find his brow furrows at our talking in code.

"Sounds like the two of you share your own language like the twins do," he chuckles.

"Back to bed," I order again. "For the third time." I look at Brooks, hoping she gets my meaning.

"Daddy has a brother," Ry tells Brooks.

"And a mom and dad," Harper adds.

Brooks smiles. "I will leave you to this," she says, swirling her finger toward the twins in bed near Ryan.

She is in the doghouse. She really could have hinted without sharing all the details.

"Eyes closed," Ryan says, kissing their little hands.

This time, I shut off the light as he speaks.

"My brother Maddux is four years older than me. His house is by my house. He is your uncle, so you can call him Uncle Maddux. My mom and dad live an hour away. They will be coming up next weekend to see my new house. You can call them Grandma and Grandpa."

Christy

"I wanna see them," Harper says, keeping her eyes closed tightly. "When can we meet your brother, your mom, and your dad?"

Ryan shrugs my way. "When you fall asleep, your mom and I will make a plan. We will tell you tomorrow." Again, he looks at me to see if he is doing okay, and I nod. "Keep your eyes closed and roll over," he directs. "I will rub your backs like my mom used to rub mine at bedtime."

I slip from the room as memories of Ryan's hands on me come to mind. Luckily, they fall asleep within five minutes. I find Brooks enjoying wine in the kitchen, a glass poured for me beside hers on the counter.

"This was too big for you not to tell me, and you know it. You knew he would bump into me; you knew he would be here tonight, and you know…" I trail off as Brooks raises an eyebrow.

"Want me to tell you about tomorrow? Or Thursday? Or Friday?"

I shake my head. *I do, but I do not.*

"I need to know…" I begin before Ryan joins us.

"Sorry to interrupt," he says.

"I will let the two of you chat," she says, smiling like the cat that ate the canary.

Leaning near my ear, without touching me, she whispers, "Spoiler alert! Happy ending."

Does she mean tonight, this week, or forever? I hate her hints more than knowing what her visions contain.

When he hears the sound of Brooks's bedroom door latching, Ryan shares an idea he had while rubbing the twins' backs. He invites the three of us to camp—well, sort of camp—at this empty house on Thursday night. He proposes we could watch movies on an iPad, play games, order pizza, and use sleeping bags. Then we could hang around for furniture delivery on Friday and meet his family.

I hedge, "I am not sure the girls will be ready to meet…"

"Christy," he soothes. "You know my family. They are laid back, easy-going; it will be a smooth meeting. And they will love everything about the girls."

I cringe, and he notices.

"They will love you, too." He places his hand on my knee between us. "My parents love you."

I open my mouth to argue, but he stops me.

"They only worried about our age difference when I turned 18. And given what they knew of your dad, they were warranted that he might have me arrested for statutory rape. They loved you; they were worried."

I nod. *He is right; they were nothing but nice to me.* It is all moving so fast. It has only been two days since I bumped into Ryan. Now, he has met the girls, is proposing the three of us "camp" at his place, and wants us to meet his family. He wants to make up for lost time before he reports to camp, but I need to think about how it will all affect the girls. They are young and eager.

"So..." Ryan prompts. "Can we plan a campout?"

He looks like a little boy asking for permission to hold a sleep-over. Well, an over six-feet tall, muscle-bound boy, but eager all the same. I nod. Instantly, he hops up from the sofa, overwhelmed with excitement.

"What kind of snacks and drinks should I ask Josh to buy for the girls?"

My brow furrows. "Who is Josh?"

Ryan chuckles, "He is my house manager."

I quirk one eyebrow.

"Uh-uh." He shakes his head. "Do not judge me. I do not clean house, and I don't find time during the season to shop and run errands. I have appearances here and across the U.S. You will see; Josh is a must for me."

"I don't doubt it," I remark. "It seems weird, hearing it come from you. That is all."

I can't believe I agreed to any of this.

Ryan

After planning with Christy, I hurry to my new place to talk to my family.

"Sit down," I instruct my parents, motioning to the two folding chairs in the wide-open space that will soon be my open floorplan living area. My parents begin to argue, but my look conveys I am serious. Maddux hands a water bottle to Mom before sitting on the wood floor beside them. Pacing back and forth, my nerves threaten to mess me up. I remind myself my parents are level-headed and supportive; they will be shocked but excited.

"Bro, you asked me to get the entire family at your empty house late on a Sunday night, so we know you have something major to share. Spit it out," Maddux urges.

"I have children," I blurt, my eyes locked on my father's, waiting for his disappointment.

"Children as in more than one?" My brother, ever the analytical one, seeks clarification.

I nod. "Twins," I inform them. "Identical twin daughters." Now, I look to my mother. "You are a grandma."

Tears form in her eyes, her hand over her mouth, as my father sits stoically shocked beside her.

"How?" Maddux interrogates.

"Christy," I answer. "The girl I dated my senior year in high school."

"You mean the girl you cheated on and then spent years pining over?" he scoffs.

"Did you just use the word 'pining'?" I laugh.

"Son," Dad's serious tone cuts in.

"I had no idea. I promise. If I did, I would not have left her side," I vow. "It is a long, sad story that she shared with me today."

"When did..."

I interrupt my brother, "Friday night at the club. She was the bartender you hit on."

He chortles.

"That was Christy. That was the first time I've laid eyes on her since before high school graduation. I looked for her everywhere, and she was under your nose for over three years as a lifeguard and waitress at the club. Now, she is the pool manager."

I explain how I went back to talk to her, I describe the girls, and I share how Christy named them after me. My family listens without interrupting, although they have questions.

"Want to see a photo?" I ask, dying to share the picture I took with them tonight, and I extend my cell phone.

"They look like you," Dad states, a little choked up as his shock fades.

"They must be..." Mom does the math out loud.

"They are five-and-a-half," I state.

"Wow," Mom gasps. "They are tall."

I nod proudly. *Odd how fast my paternal instincts took over.*

"Christy says they are in the ninety-eighth percentile for height, and they are intelligent."

"Clearly, they inherited their brains from their mother," Maddux jabs.

"Can we meet them?" Dad asks, sitting on the edge of his seat. "If she works at the club, she must live nearby."

Nodding, I tell my family they live in Liberty. While they will be at the club all week as Christy works, I encourage my family to let me set up a meeting after my furniture arrives on Friday. That bursts their bubbles, but they agree. Mom informs me I need to meet with my designer to plan bedrooms and a playroom for the girls.

"Plan on Friday," Maddux instructs. "I will take the day off to be here with you for furniture and everything else."

Of the three of them, my brother's reaction surprises me the most.

7

TUESDAY, JUNE 13TH

Christy

I sit on the closed toilet lid, my head in my hands, recounting the morning's events.

> *I stared at the text while I drove a cart toward the clubhouse. "My office, please." While my boss often texts, it's never to call me into his office. My senses were on high alert; I knew something was up but had no idea. When I walked in, the hair on the back of my neck stood up at the sight of the Human Resources Director on the sofa of my boss's office.*

Finally ready to exit the safety of the bathroom stall, I approach the sinks; my abysmal reflection haunts me. Red, puffy eyes, tear-streaked cheeks, and a runny nose are billboards to my crying jag. As I wash my hands, a member enters to wash her hands beside me.

"Honey, are you okay?" Paige, a mom I recognize from the pool asks, hands frozen beneath the water from her faucet.

I am afraid if I speak, I will cry again, so I simply nod and flee. I climb into the golf cart, driving towards my office. I can't believe she had printed a copy of a photo of Ryan with us on our way from the pool to my car for Urgent Care on Saturday. Adrenaline coursing through my body with Ry's broken arm, I did not consider the no fraternization rule when Ryan offered to drive us on his golf cart.

Ryan

Why is my publicist calling? I tap my cell phone to accept the call.

"Hello," I greet, mentally preparing myself for the next appearance she plans to volunteer me for.

"Where are you?" Mel barks without a hello.

"Umm…I am home," I answer.

"There are pictures of you popping up all over social media," she informs. "My research shows three people posted the original photos, then others reposted and tagged you on Instagram, Facebook, and Twitter. They began popping up last night. Who is this woman with the two little girls?"

Crap!

"I need to go. I need to find Christy before my fans find her," my voice is frantic.

Mel asks, "Who are they? Do I need to…"

I interrupt, already on my way out the door. "I will explain later, and no, I am not dating her. Gotta go."

I attempt to text and call Christy but get no response. I figure she works this morning, so instead of her place, I drive to Maddux's house at the club. Of course, Kansas City traffic does not cooperate between my downtown loft and the country club. Fifty minutes later, I am finally parked in Maddux's driveway and on his cart, headed toward the club house.

Christy

While looking for Christy, I glance at the screenshots my publicist sends me of Facebook and Instagram posts I am tagged in. None are negative; they speculate who the three females are in my SUV and why I would take them to a Sonic Drive-in. Fortunately, no one seemed to follow us to the park.

"Excuse me," I say, approaching a female member exiting the club house. "Have you seen the pool manager, Christy, this morning?"

The slender blonde in golf attire and Birkenstocks smiles widely; she must recognize me. "She was crying when she left," the blonde informs, pointing. "I think she was returning to the pool."

"Why was she crying?" I stupidly ask.

She shakes her head. "She did not speak when I asked if she was okay in the locker room."

"Thanks," I say as I return to the golf cart.

Not wanting to find myself delayed by other golfers, I take the cart path only used by employees. I park Maddux's cart where Christy parked when I saw her here last and enter through the employee gate. I do not see Christy around the pool or in the guard shack. I hope to find her in her office but fear she might be in the women's locker room. The twins sit quietly outside the open office door.

"Hey, guys." I smile at my daughters.

"Mommy's crying," Harper says, barely above a whisper.

I nod before peeking my head into the office.

"Christy?" I call, not wanting to interrupt if she is working.

My hand pushes the door open wider; she is not alone. An older woman in a silk blouse and pencil skirt stands at the edge of the desk, shaking her head as she glares at me. *What the hell?*

"It is not a good time," Christy's voice shakes.

My stomach plummets when I realize she places items from her desk into a box.

"They fired you?" I scoff, returning the death stare to the stranger.

"Um, Christy?" a pimple-faced teen male interrupts nervously. "There is a new rumor post, and it is about you."

A rumor post? She was fired? What is he blathering about?

"Excuse me." An assertive female guard presses past the boy and me, not stopping until she is by Christy's side. "Look." She extends her cell phone to Christy, who wipes tears from her eyes in order to read.

"Can I see?" I ask the boy.

He hands me his phone. I stare in disbelief at a photo on Facebook—taken Saturday morning—of me driving the four of us on a golf cart to take Ry to Urgent Care. Above the photo, I read:

The Back 9 Talk
By now, we all know "Superman" and tight end for the KC Cardinals is our club's newest member and resident of Breakstone Cliffs.
But did you know "Aqua Woman" hooked up with "Superman," and our very own "Wonder Twins" are actually his?
It is a story over five years old, and I don't know about you, but I want ALL the details.

"Who wrote this?" I ask, looking at the boy, the girl, and then the cranky lady.

All three shake their heads.

"It is anonymous," Christy sniffles.

"Well, it is not true," I declare. "It is not true." I look at the strange lady. "She has not broken any policies. You can't fire her over a rumor."

I am angry; I feel rage growing within me.

"Sir, we fired Ms. Carlton prior to the rumor post and photo on the Facebook blog. The club has a strict no fraternization policy, and clearly, Ms. Carlton crossed the line."

I open my mouth to defend her, but Christy stops me.

"Let's go. Can you drive the girls and me?"

The woman from the club house approaches me near the cart.

Christy

"Excuse me, Ryan. I am Paige. I live next door to your brother Maddux. Anyway, my nanny texted that a ton of cameras are at the gates. I saw the rumor post and thought I would come over to warn you." She looks to Christy and the girls at my right before continuing, "Christy, I am sorry. I will be voicing that I strongly disagree with club management, and I know many of my friends will protest on your behalf, too."

"What gate?" Ry asks, her small voice no longer vibrant.

"We have a gate to enter our part of the neighborhood." I explain, looking from the girls to Christy. "Someone leaked it to the press."

"Christy, I know you do not know me very well, but you know my children, and they love your girls. If the two of you need some time, Ry and Harper can play at our house or swim in our pool. I am close to Ryan's house and safely inside the privacy gates."

"Thank you," Christy murmurs.

"Here is my number. Text or call anytime." Paige shakes her head then, eyes locked on mine, states, "I still can't believe the club did this to you."

"It might be good for the girls…" I begin to suggest.

Christy interrupts, "I need them with me."

"The kids and I could grab some toys and meet you at Ryan's," Paige offers. "You need some time to process all of this. I could watch the kids play close by."

I shake my head as I respond, "Nah. My house has no furniture. Let's meet at Maddux's house. He gave me the garage code."

Paige nods, turns on her Birkenstocks, and bounces toward her cart, her ponytail swaying from side to side.

"I should go home," Christy argues.

"The press is probably there, too," I inform her.

"I need to escort her off the property," the grouchy office lady informs.

I urge all three girls onto my cart.

"There," I spit. "Now, they are on my property. I know my membership is only a week old, but you upset the wrong family. My brother, Maddux, has belonged here for over 10 years and sits on the board. He will be contacting you soon."

"Your cart is on club property," she states.

"So, you are standing there, telling me—a paying member—that I can't drive my cart on the club's cart path? Are you revoking my membership?"

Eyes like saucers, she backpedals. Shaking her head, she apologizes.

"You messed up big time. Do me a favor and tell your boss Ryan Harper said so, and he will be hearing from me soon."

With that, I steer the cart toward hole number two on The Breakstone Course for my brother's house. I need to find whoever writes for the *Back 9 Talk* page and put an end to this rumor mill.

"They think I am sleeping with a member," Christy states when the children take off to explore Maddux's home.

"I will make a call; you will have your job back in the blink of an eye."

I pull her tightly to my chest, unable to endure another second without touching her. When she does not protest, I know she is emotionally spent. I look at Paige across the room.

"We are not...I mean... Christy did not break that rule," I inform her.

Paige shakes her head and shares, "I called my husband on my way home from the club. He is in entertainment law... Wait. You know him. You are at the same agency."

I do not know her last name. I scramble to recall if Maddux ever shared their last name with me.

"Anyway," she continues, "he said the way the policy is worded, by riding on your cart and spending time away from the pool with you, Christy did violate the rule." Paige's eyes share that she is sorry to be the bearer of this news.

"You will not lose your job because of me," I vow, taking Christy's face in my hands.

"It's too late. I can't go back now; the damage is done. They did it in front of my twins. There is no way I will go back," she protests.

Christy's stubbornness failed to fade in the years since high school.

"I can work full time for Brooks," she tells me, studying art on Maddux's wall, not looking at me. "We will be okay."

Apparently, she forgot our discussion about me helping with finances. I am not going to argue in front of Paige; instead, I table the issue.

Turning her gaze toward our guest, Christy continues, "Paige, if the offer still stands, the kids should probably play at your place for the afternoon."

"Kids, let's go!" Paige yells up the stairs.

The twins follow her excited children to play next door, waving over their shoulders on their way out the door.

"I wish my furniture was here." I think out loud.

"When did you say it will be delivered?" Christy asks, glancing at me.

"Friday. I can take you over to see my place now if you want," I offer, hoping to distract.

"Let's wait a bit," she urges. "Right now, I need to sit a minute and process everything. I think I will call Brooks."

I offer to leave the room, but she assures me she does not want privacy. I sit on the overstuffed blue sofa, tugging her beside me. She looks ready to cry again, and I can't take it. I pat my thigh.

"This used to be your favorite seat," I remind her.

She shocks me when, after she presses to connect her call with Brooks, she climbs onto my lap.

"What in the world?" Brooks asks in greeting, loud enough I can hear her.

"There is more," Christy tells her friend, switching over to speakerphone.

"I saw the *Back 9 Talk* post," Brooks states. "That did not help your case."

"She did nothing wrong." I butt into the conversation, unable to stop myself.

"Well, hello. Is this Ryan?" she queries.

"Yep," I reply.

"There are better things coming this week. Well, from today on the future looks good for you," Brooks says, causing me to search Christy's face for her meaning.

"Let's wait until you meet in person to scare him with your freakiness." Christy chuckles hollowly.

The girls mentioned something about Brooks predicting the future. *They were not serious about that, were they? Is Brooks telling Christy about her future?*

"I am here to stay," I declare.

Brooks laughs on the other end of the phone.

She can laugh all she wants; I will prove it to her. Had I known, I would have never left Christy's side.

"I'm glad you are on the phone Brooks. Maybe together we can convince Christy to let me help her out financially," I plot, enlisting her best friend, knowing Christy will fight me tooth and nail.

Christy climbs off my lap, standing across the room hands on her hips and scowl on her face.

Brooks chuckles, "Go ahead and try. Act like I am not here."

I am not sure if that means she is on my team or not, but I plead my case.

"I mean, legally, I owe Christy over five years of child support. Please do not fight me. Christy, they are my daughters—my flesh and blood."

I pace to the windows, looking across the yard and golf course beyond.

"It kills me to think of you struggling to raise Harper and Ry on your own. You know me; you know the kind of man I am. They are my family. You are my family. I need to take care of the three of you. I need to help with finances, childcare, education, healthcare, and everything else."

I run my hand through my hair. My eyes remain on Christy as I speak.

"I missed too much. I do not plan to miss any more. I take the role of being a father seriously—just like you do being their mom."

Christy sucks on her lower lip, her eyes contemplating my words. I love this woman, and I plan to spend the next 90 years showing her how much. I tuck a dark brown lock of hair behind her left ear.

"I understand it is hard for you to allow me to help. You were a single parent, making every decision on your own." I pause, wetting my lips. "I am in the picture now and expect to make important decisions with you. I will not be a jerk about it, but I will remind you and I will contribute financially."

I press two fingers to her lips, halting her protests.

"You made your opinions known on Saturday. I listened and thought about it. I need you to hear me. I am the twins' father, and as their father, I have a responsibility."

Later in bed, I replay my conversation today with Christy. Losing her full-time job, she seemed at her wits end with the financial ramifications.

She was not happy that I brought the topic up in front of Brooks. In this case, I believe it was better to ask for forgiveness than for permission. I wanted Brooks to hear straight from me rather than from Christy retelling it in a rant. I feel I defended my point of view and as two rational women they will discuss it.

I hope tonight, once the girls are in bed, she thinks about this conversation and understands that, while I will not force myself on her, I will be a father to my daughters in all ways. She need not worry about finding another job; financially, they will be cared for.

8

WEDNESDAY, JUNE 14TH

Ryan

"Remember, you do not have to answer every question," Mel, my publicist, states. "If you do not know what to say or do not want to answer, look at me, and I will move to another question." She straightens the waistband of Harper's shorts as she speaks to my daughters and Christy.

My daughters—Will I ever grow used to the sound of that? I am a dad.

"Ready?" my agent asks.

I look at Christy, who—in turn—looks to the girls.

"Yes!" they say in unison.

I love it. I take Ry's left hand then extend my other hand to Harper, and I lead my girls into the press room. While they enjoyed a tour of the stadium today, I doubt they will enjoy the next hour. As we enter, following my agent and publicist, camera clicks fire like a swarm of locusts. Harper waves with her free hand, eliciting laughter from the journalists.

"Hi, guys," she says, now standing beside her mom to my right.

"Well, I guess she gets that from me," I announce, winning over the crowd as I always do with my humor. When the laughter calms down, I turn halfway towards my girls.

"It is my turn, okay?" I tease.

My two little ones nod, big smiles upon their faces, sweet puffy cheeks and all.

"So, as you can see, my life has been anything but boring this off-season," I begin. "I hope, with the statement we released and this press conference, that I will be able to focus my attention on these three beautiful women without worrying about interference from the press."

I pause, murmured promises are made, and others nod in agreement.

"We volunteered to stand before you in person today to clear up some rumors and answer a few questions. If you behave."

"I behave," Ry says, looking up at her mommy for affirmation, and Christy nods.

"I have a lot to catch up on and learn, and I am excited to do so. Oops! Where are my manners? Let me introduce everyone." I squat and place my hand on each girl's shoulder as I speak. "This is Ryan. She likes to be called Ry, and this is Harper. Last but not least…" Rising, I place my hands at her hips while I stand behind her. "This is their mommy, Christy."

Returning to the podium, I glance at the outline I created with my publicist for today. "The girls are five."

"This many," Ry states, holding out five fingers.

"We are five-and-a-half," Harper corrects. "I am almost six."

Laughter fills the press room.

"You have competition for the spotlight," a reporter raises her voice, and I nod.

"Christy and I dated in high school. We lost touch until last week. By now, you've read the statement we released, so I will not waste time repeating that information. We called this press conference to answer questions that remain. In a moment, I will open the floor for questions." I point to each of my daughters. "Please remember the tiny ears in the room."

I nod, and the room fills with everyone calling my name, hoping I call on them.

"Bobby." I point to the bald, heavy-set man from the KC Crescent.

"Are your daughters football fans?"

I breathe a sigh of relief that I chose the right person to demonstrate the type of questions to ask today.

"I mean, they are wearing your jersey, but..."

"They already owned the jerseys and two posters on their bedroom wall. But do not believe me. I will let them tell you in their own way."

I pull out the football we tucked under the podium, holding it in their direction. Their fingers signal, "Gimme, gimme." As they reach up for the ball, I hold it over their heads. Laughter and camera clicks break out.

My publicist scrambles to find a second ball when I hand the one I hold to Ry. One-armed, my daughter struggles a bit, but finally, she tucks the large ball under her arm proudly. Harper holds her ball in front of her with two little hands.

"Yep. They like football," I chuckle, back at the mic.

I scan the crowd, selecting my next journalist.

"What do you think of the Lynks at Tryst Falls firing Christy for being seen with you?"

I take a breath before I answer. "We are not together," I reply. "Yet."

The room fills with oohs, hmms, and laughter.

"So, you want to be a couple?" a random female reporter asks over the crowd.

Without pause, I answer honestly. "She is the love of my life. Of course, I long to be more than co-parents."

All eyes look to Christy, putting her on the hot seat for a response to my declaration. She wets her lips.

"While our focus will remain on our twins, I will not deny that old feelings have..." She glances up at me. "...surfaced."

Holy crap! Did that just happen? Christy announced she wants to be with me to the entire world. My chest heats and throat grows tight. A

Christy

tear perches on the edge of my left eye. *Nope. It can't fall. I can't cry in front of the cameras. I am a freaking NFL player. I can't break down at her words.*

"You all heard that, right?" I chuckle, still fighting the precarious tear.

"I have it on audio," one helpful journalist states.

"Funny thing, I talked about Christy with two of my teammates last year. As a rookie, they wanted to know everything about me. So, you know me. Give me the floor, and I talk forever."

While we laugh, I covertly swipe my tears, hoping the motion goes unnoticed. Before the room silences, Christy lifts Ry onto her hip. I am not sure if it is nerves or if Ry signaled. Not wanting to be left out, Harper motions that she also wants Mommy to pick her up. I grab her at her waist from behind and spin her in my arms. Harper smiles widely.

"See, I already mastered that Daddy move," I joke, motioning to a nearby reporter.

"I noticed the twins' last name differs from yours. Is there a reason for this, and will they be taking their father's surname?"

I look at Christy, hoping she will take this one. I am relieved when she maneuvers in front of the mic.

"I wanted the girls to share their father's name, but it felt wrong for me to give them his last name without his permission. Since he was not aware of the pregnancy, he was unavailable at the hospital."

Silence weighs heavily in the pressroom. After Christy's explanation, they still want more.

"I can't believe you did not know this one," I say, leaning toward Christy and the mic. "The twins' last name is Carlton, and Carlton is my middle name."

While a few reporters claim they knew this fact, the rest now nod in understanding.

Christy shakes her head and laughs. "I knew he could not relinquish the mic to me."

Now, my woman is working the room like a pro. Well, she is not my woman, but she will be.

"Christy, what are your thoughts about the club firing you for talking to Ryan?"

Dang. I thought we avoided that question from earlier.

"While I was very upset at the time, they acted well within their rights as my meeting with Ryan outside of work violated their policy. I will miss working at the pool every day, but I harbor no hard feelings."

"Ryan?" the reporter calls. "Same question."

I grit my teeth as I take a moment to scan the room. "Ours is not the usual relationship. What angers me most is they did not speak to us. Our relationship began before she took a job at the course. I know for a fact that a golf pro is married to a member. That situation is similar to ours. I hate that they took a job she loved from Christy, a job that many members felt she excelled at."

I pause when two of my teammates pop their heads into the room.

"Y'all giving my boy Ryan grief?" our running back asks the crowd, walking up the aisle towards us.

A constant in the press for his raucous partying and children outside of marriage with more than two women, the press takes notice of his presence.

"He was young, dumb, and in love," he continues, defending us. "It is not like he was in his twenties…"

I clear my throat, pointing at Harper, reminding him to choose his words appropriately.

"See what I mean? He knows he is a father for less than a week, and he is already a better dad than I am. And I have been practicing for two years."

"For three years. Your oldest is three now," a reporter corrects him.

"C'mon. Don't hate on me. I came in here to defend my man," he continues. "Unlike me, he has children with one woman and plans to be a present father. Cut the man a little slack."

He extends his hand for a high five, and Harper beats me to it.

"I think you've hogged enough of their time. What do you say we take these pretty ladies to the snack bar? Are you hungry?"

Christy

Ry speaks up. "I am."

As the press chuckles, we make our escape, leaving my publicist to handle the rest of the press conference.

9

THURSDAY, JUNE 15TH

Ryan

CHRISTY
here

Glad she remembered the code at the gate, I press the button mounted on the wall, and the garage door opens. As she pulls her car inside, I see the girls wave excitedly through the back window. I stand nearby as Christy exits the driver's side, looking at me over the roof of the car.

"Are you ready for this?"

With a wide smile, I state the obvious, "Of course, I am."

She shakes her head. "You should be warned, Brooks fed them copious amounts of sugar all afternoon. They will be wound up for hours."

"I have got this," I promise, not believing sugar highs in children exist.

When I open the back car door, I am greeted by my twins yelling, "Daddy!"

Christy

I unbuckle Ry while Christy tends to Harper.

How will I tell them apart when she gets her cast removed? I'd better focus on finding differences between them. I notice Harper is a bit more outspoken, but that's not enough, especially when they are quiet.

Free from their seats, the girls wrap their arms around my legs, speaking a mile a minute.

"Let's go inside," I tell them. "I have lots to show you."

The girls fly up the two stairs into the mudroom. I glance briefly at Christy before I chase after them, Christy laughing behind me. I catch up with the twins in my kitchen, standing open-mouthed, their wide eyes staring at Josh.

"Girls, this is Josh," I introduce. "Josh, this is Christy, Harper, and Ry." As I point to the girls, they wave.

"They are even cuter than you described," Josh gushes. "Call me Josh. I help Ryan…" Shaking his head, he corrects himself, "Your dad run this house. If you need anything just let me know."

"I stocked the fridge. Girls, the lower drawer is full of your juice boxes and water bottles." He smiles at each of them. "In this drawer are small containers of carrots, grapes, and yogurt. You can reach it, too. I stocked adult-friendly beverages and snacks, too. I put them up here so you can't reach them." He glances at Christy flashing her a sweet smile.

Next, he opens the pantry. "In here, the bottom shelf holds dried fruit pouches, baked crackers, and nuts." Josh again looks to Christy for her approval.

She smiles, nodding, and he lights up with pride.

Josh winks at me. "Toodles!" He waves over his shoulder as he heads for the door.

"I love him," Christy states, peeking at the upper section of the refrigerator.

"He is handy," I admit. "He helped me find games, books, and sleeping bags, too."

Patting me on the shoulder as she walks by, Christy comments, "I have no doubt you could figure it all out on your own with internet searches."

I shake my head. *That would be too much work. Someday, I will know what the girls eat, but not yet.*

"Mommy, look!" the girls shout, pointing to my once empty living room.

"This I did on my own. We can watch movies using the projector on the wall, and I made this big circus tent with sheets and boxes for us to sleep under."

The girls run to investigate.

"Wanna give me a tour?" Christy asks, bumping my shoulder.

I motion for her to follow me.

"Me, too! Me, too!" the girls cheer, following us.

Friday, June 16th
Ryan

I stretch my body this way and that. It hurts more than after any football workout I endure. I am much too young for my body to hurt like this from head to toe. While I wait for the coffee to brew, I stretch my thighs, arms, and back, but it does little to suppress the stiffness.

"Daddy," a little voice calls from behind me. I turn to find little Ry at the end of the kitchen island. "I'm hungry," she mumbles, rubbing her eyes.

I begin opening cabinets, as if Josh magically filled them overnight.

"Umm… What do you like for breakfast?" I ask, hoping to find something Josh placed higher up in the pantry.

"I've got this," Christy states, pulling milk from my refrigerator.

I watch in silence as she emerges from my pantry with two boxes of cereal. Coffee ready, I place a mug by Christy as I start a second cup for me. She pours a small amount of cereal into one paper bowl then a small amount of the second cereal into another bowl. She places a plastic spoon in each bowl then pours milk in one and hands it to Ry.

Maybe Josh deserves a raise for knowing which two cereals the twins would like. Or am I an idiot for having no clue?

As if reading my mind, after a sip of coffee, Christy says, "I have not found a cereal they don't eat yet. Thanks for the coffee."

I nod, stuck in a weird limbo world. I am not sure how to act; it feels uncomfortable, like the morning after a one-night stand. I am surrounded by my daughters with Christy, and I would not want to be anywhere else.

"What time did your family say they would be here?" she asks.

"The furniture arrives between nine and ten. My brother said he'd be here at noon, and my parents said they'd arrive in the afternoon." I smirk.

"What?" she chuckles.

"We should get dressed. They will probably all be here at nine," I admit, knowing my family will not be able to help themselves.

It has been a miracle they waited until today to meet the girls.

Christy

"Camping" at Ryan's has its moments. The sleeping bag on the hardwood floor sucked, but the shower in the master bathroom is heavenly. I have to force myself to shut the water off and exit. *Who knew a shower with so many knobs and shower heads even existed?*

Ryan and I currently lean against the railing on his deck, watching the girls run up and down his faux football field. With every passing minute, my nerves ratchet up another notch. While I've met his family before, now I am the woman that got knocked up and kept his daughters from him, only to pop up in his third year in the NFL.

Although I did not get pregnant on purpose, it is true. Ryan assures me his family is not angry with me, but my worries still grow.

"Bro," Maddux calls from the open doorway, scaring me. "I rang your bell for over five minutes. You need a butler for this monstrosity."

I stand nervously at the rail as Ryan gives his brother a one-armed guy hug, patting his back.

"Christy," Ryan motions for me to join them, "you remember my much older and uglier brother, Maddux."

While he chuckles, I note they look alike. There is no doubt they are brothers, even with the slight difference in their height and hairstyle.

"Hey." Maddux lifts his chin in my direction as he approaches the railing.

I smile and wave. "Thank you for allowing us to use your house the other day."

Maddux is silent, looking down at the girls. I hope his silence is not because he is mad at me.

"Do they go by Ryan and Harper?" he asks.

Ryan smiles at me, tugging me to his side. As we walk back to the railing, he informs his brother, "Ryan prefers Ry."

"Harper and Ry," Maddux hollers. "You'd better get up here and see what I brought for you."

My girls freeze for a minute to process who yelled and sprint towards us. It hurts a bit when they find safety behind Ryan's legs instead of mine.

"Girls, this is—" Ryan attempts to introduce.

"Uncle Maddux," they interrupt in unison.

They slowly step out, smiling and waving at him.

"Let me guess." Maddux scratches his brow. "You are Ry, and you are Harper."

The girls giggle, shaking their heads.

"I am Harper, and she is Ry," Harper corrects.

"Good. Now, that is cleared up." He pulls an envelope from his back pocket. He extends it, but the girls only stare.

"Open it," Ryan encourages, bending beside them.

Christy

Harper takes it, and she slowly lifts the flap and pulls a card from inside. Harper passes it to Ry, the better reader of the two. Her eyes study the letters on the front.

"Let's party," she reads, pointing to each word.

When she opens it, nothing falls out, causing me to worry about how my five-year-olds might react to only a card as a gift.

"Hap-py Birth-day." Ry continues to read the card. She puzzles over the interior for a minute, before passing it to Ryan. "You read."

"I owe you five birthday gifts. Please make a list of places you want to go and things you want to do. We will choose five of them, one for each birthday I missed."

I study Maddux, disbelieving he came up with such a perfect gift. With this card, with his gesture, he accepts his nieces with open arms.

"Daddy, we need paper and pencil," Harper states.

"Harper," I chide.

"Please?" the twins say in unison.

Ryan looks over his shoulder toward the nearly empty house.

"Girls, we will work on your lists tonight," I state. "Today, we are here to play with Daddy and Uncle Maddux and meet your grandparents."

"And get Daddy's furniture," Ry adds, causing me to chuckle.

10

FRIDAY, JUNE 16TH

Ryan

"Hellooo," Josh calls from the deck.

"Hey," I yell back. "I will be right up."

I leave the girls playing football with my brother. As I make my way back into the house, wondering where Christy disappeared to. Last I noticed, she was leaning against the railing, watching us. Josh hollering means he did not pass her when he arrived.

"Furniture truck is backing into the driveway now," Josh informs when I enter the kitchen area. "I figured you would like to know. I will handle the furniture; you focus on your family." He pats me on the shoulder as he walks by me to the garage.

"Where is Christy?" I ask his back.

Over his shoulder, he informs me, "I have not seen her."

Hmm... I make my way down the hall in search of her. With no furniture or art, the house is quiet enough I hear rustling in the master suite. I follow the sound and movement into the bathroom.

"Christy?" I call as I approach, not wanting to startle her.

"I am in here," she answers.

I lean against the door frame and ask, "What are you doing?"

"The wind messed with my hair," she offers. "I wanted to straighten it up before your parents arrive."

I move behind her at the vanity mirror. My hands settle on her hips, and my cheek presses against her head. The scent of her vanilla shampoo and body wash floods my senses with memories of our youth. I bought her vanilla lotion for her birthday and told her often how good she smelled. All these years later, she still smothers herself in vanilla. As if she were not yummy enough to eat before, now she is downright delicious.

"They already love you," I murmur, my eyes on hers in the mirror.

"A lot has changed since they saw me last," she argues.

"You are still gorgeous. You fought tooth and nail for six years to raise two beautiful daughters. That is all that matters," I explain.

"I kept the twins from them, from you; they will hate me for that," she quibbles.

"Christy, one look at Harper and Ry and my parents will melt," I enlighten her. "One look at how happy I am with you back in my life, and they will welcome you with open arms. They thought the world of you back in high school."

When her mouth quirks, I spin her to face me.

"You are an excellent mom, and they will love you like I do." I implore her to believe what I know to be true.

"The furniture is here," I inform her. "Let's go see what my designer chose for me."

Exiting the bedroom, she chuckles. "I can't believe you allowed someone else to make all the decisions for you."

"She showed me a few items and built the rest of the room around them," I defend.

Her words do worry me a bit; I put a lot of trust in my publicist and designer to fill this house. It seems like a wrong decision now. With Christy and the girls in my life, every piece of furniture now has importance. I pull out my cell phone to text my decorator.

> ME
>
> may need to change my furniture
>
> call me

"Ryan, darling." My decorator's voice greets me when we return to the kitchen. "They have not carried in a single piece of furniture yet, and you already doubt my vision? Who is this lovely woman?" she asks, motioning to my side.

I open my mouth to introduce Christy when my mother walks through the front door.

"Yoohoo!" she greets loudly. "We are here!"

Too excited. I knew my family would be. I excuse myself to head off my parents. I hear Christy introduce herself to the decorator then offer a drink with Josh's help.

"Mom, Dad, you're early," I growl, ushering them into the room I plan to transform into my office. "Take it down a notch. You do not want to scare the girls, do you?"

"Of course not." Mom acts offended.

"I told you not to make a scene when you walked through the door," Dad tells her. "She is under control now. There will be no scaring the girls by either of us." He gives my mother a pointed stare.

"We could not wait until afternoon; imagine if you knew the twins were at our house, and we asked you to wait until after lunch to come meet them for the first time," Mom challenges. "There is no way you would wait. It was asinine to expect us to."

I nod; there is no arguing with her statement. I can't imagine if I heard from Christy I had daughters but had to wait days until I was allowed to meet them. I thank my lucky stars I ran into all of them at once.

"Are you ready?" I jest.

"Ryan Carlton Harper, do not tease us," Dad chides. "Lead the way."

Christy

My mother beams, bright-eyed; her excitement is palpable. My father offers her his hand, and I lead them toward the deck.

"Will they…" Mom's thought gets lost in her throat.

At the threshold, I pause, turning to face her.

"They are lively, smart, caring, and look like me," I inform my parents. "Harper tends to be the outspoken one while Ry seems more in tune to emotions."

"Ry?" Dad asks, brow furrowed.

"Ryan goes by Ry," I explain. "They will cling to you immediately. They are going to love you, so be ready."

The fear in my mother's eyes slides away, and her excitement returns.

"Yo, Maddux," I yell from the railing into the backyard. "Time to take a break."

My brother and the twins look up in my direction. Maddux nods, and the girls sprint towards me.

"Daddy! Daddy!" they chant on their way up the stairs. "Uncle Maddux taught us how to…"

They freeze midstep at the sight of my parents. Their blue eyes grow wide and mouths hang agape.

"Harper and Ry," I begin, "let me introduce my mom, Jackie, and dad, Warren. These are your grandparents."

When we discussed meeting their grandparents last night, the girls seemed excited. I thought they would be balls of energy at this moment.

"So, do we call you Grandma and Grandpa?" Harper asks, placing her hands upon her hips.

"Well," Mom looks at me, and I smile to urge her on, "I would love for you to call me Grandma or Grandma Jackie or even Gigi."

Harper's face pinches as she considers this.

"We never had a grandma and grandpa before," Ry states, her voice barely above a whisper.

Christy approaches her daughters, crouching in front of them. She places a hand on each of the girls' hands.

"They have always been your grandparents," Christy shares. "Like Daddy, you get to meet them now."

Harper nods once in affirmation; Ry scratches her cheek. Then, Harper takes Ry by the hand and leads her toward my parents, who remain frozen in place.

"I like the name Gigi," Ry announces, smile upon her face as she looks up at Mom.

Harper asks, "If you are Daddy's mom, are you Uncle Maddux's mom?"

Mom smiles, bending down to eye level. "Yes, I am."

Harper's hands fly to her hips, and her tone turns haughty, "Well, your son said a naughty word while we played football."

Christy bites her lips while I lose my battle and laugh out loud.

"Did you tattle on me?" Maddux acts affronted.

"Mommy does not allow naughty words," Harper says over her shoulder at my brother.

"I will talk to him about his language," Dad tells the girls.

"Thank you, Grandpa," Harper says.

My father smiles wide, and his chest puffs out. My mother's hand flies to her chest over her heart, and she looks as if she might cry.

"Grandpa, did you teach Daddy to play football?" Harper asks, looking over her shoulder in my direction.

Maddux answers instead. "I taught him how to play football."

Harper looks to Mom. "Gigi, is Uncle Maddux lying?"

Dad, Maddux, and I break out in laughter. At five years old, Harper is already calling him on his antics.

11

FRIDAY, JUNE 16TH

Christy

As the girls color with Ryan's parents at the kitchen island and swim in the backyard pool, I watch in utter amazement as the movers carry in furniture. Room by room, Ryan's designer—with her team—stages the areas. I figured once the furniture arrived, he would spend months decorating, filling shelves, and buying rugs. Not in Ryan Harper's world; in one day, his house goes from empty to finished. Ryan lives a life which is polar opposite of mine.

I guess it is not 100 percent complete. I did overhear Jackie and the designer discuss setting up the girls' room and play area, but Ryan suggested we let the twins help decorate those. I worry they may never want to return to the room they share with me at Brooks's apartment once they create their space here on Ryan's budget.

"Penny for your thoughts," Josh says, nudging my shoulder as I stand near the refrigerator.

I shake off my worry, smiling up at Josh.

"Put me to work," I plead. "Tell me what to do to help you with dinner. Finding out at the last minute that you are fixing a meal for eight will not be easy."

Josh grins. "While I stocked the bar and kitchen today, I assumed Ryan's family would hang around. I thought we would prepare good, old-fashioned barbecue. I plan to make burgers, hotdogs, potato salad, baked beans, and apple pie with ice cream for dessert."

Wow! Ryan is right; Josh is phenomenal at running things.

"I already made the patties and potato salad," he informs. "You could peel the apples for the pie if you really want to."

As I begin peeling, I share, "I am not used to watching others do the work. I've felt useless all day. I need to clean and cook, not watch."

Josh stands close so only I can hear him when he speaks. "Ryan shares a lot with me; it may not be everything, but I understand. You spent the last six years working two jobs and raising the twins on your own. He feels guilty that you struggled without his support, he feels he has a lot to make up for, and he longs to prove he is worthy of being their father. He does not treat me like his employee. He treats me like a close friend, like you treat Brooks. I help him keep the house running, and he pays me, but we are friends. Please let me do my job. Let me give you time to relax. You will enjoy more time with the girls; you've earned it. Besides, I love my job."

I bump his shoulder with mine. "It will not be easy, but I will try. Please know that, from time to time, I will need to help to keep my sanity," I chuckle.

"I will do my best to encourage you to enjoy your free time. When you do feel the unrelenting urge, I will accept your help for a little while," he promises, smiling widely. "You have this under control, so I think I will start the grill."

"Did someone say grill?" Maddux's baritone voice startles me.

"Grill?" Ryan asks, walking from the deck towards us in the kitchen. "What are we grilling?"

"Josh planned burgers and hotdogs for us," I share.

Maddux wraps his arm around his brother's shoulders. "We will man the grill," he states, looking at Ryan for approval. "We men. We make fire. We grill." Maddux grunts like a neanderthal.

"I knew you were a barbarian," Brooks barbs, walking into Ryan's house without knocking.

Christy

I give her a pointed stare, hoping she will refrain from causing a scene. I love my best friend, but she tends to speak her mind and stir things up. I do not want this to happen around Ryan's family.

As Maddux and Ryan return to the deck and the grill area, I ask them to encourage the girls to climb out of the pool. They have been at it for hours; I am sure Jackie and Warren are ready to return for adult interaction.

I continue peeling apples and sipping beer while Brooks watches. I hear the girls bound up the stairs.

"Mommy! Mommy!" they holler.

"Stop," I order, and they freeze in place, towels wrapped around their shoulders. "Inside voices, please."

"Guess what," Harper says, approaching the counter opposite me.

I do not miss Jackie and Warren pausing behind my daughters, eyes locked on Brooks. Coming here straight from work today, Brooks's green, blue, and gold plaid, pleated mini skirt with thin black lines, paired with her skin-tight, black sweater vest—while normal for her—shocks Jackie and Warren. The spiked black collars at her neck and wrists, along with her black biker boots, are not commonly seen in their Overland Park Country Club and social circles. My best friend might look scary with her tattoos and what some refer to as gothic attire, but beneath her armor, she has a heart of pure gold.

"What?" I ask, faking excitement.

"Gigi said we could spend the night at her house," Harper announces, a big smile upon her face.

My heart clogs my throat. *It is happening. It is really happening. I am sharing my girls with their father's family; I am going to be alone.*

"Breathe," Brooks instructs, hand upon mine on the countertop. She speaks low, for only me to hear. "Make an excuse, take a minute, and step outside."

I nod to my friend.

"Wow! That is exciting." I pretend for my daughters' sake. "Do me a favor, girls. Go out and ask Daddy if the grill is ready for Mr. Josh."

Excited to tell their father their news, they jog onto the deck.

Ryan

"Daddy! Daddy!" Harper cheers, running towards me. "Gigi asked us to spend the night with her!"

"Cool," Maddux responds while my mind floods with worry.

"Let's talk about the sleepover at dinner," I tell my girls.

"Mommy wants to know if the grill is ready for Mr. Josh," Ry relays.

"Will you two stay out here to help Uncle Maddux watch the grill while I go help Mr. Josh and Mommy?" I ask, looking between the girls.

Both of them nod and move to my brother's side. Concerned, I make my way back into the kitchen. Without a word, I stride toward Christy. I place my hands at her hips and lower my mouth close to her ear.

"If it is too soon, say the word, and I will talk to my parents," I murmur.

I catch Brooks's expression at Christy's side, and it confirms that Christy is not thrilled with the girls having a sleepover with my parents.

"I am okay," Christy whispers. "It...I...It caught me off guard; that's all."

"I will make an excuse that I want them to spend the first night in my house with my new furniture," I offer.

"No," Christy says a little louder than a whisper. "They are excited and want to spend time with your parents. I... I need to... I should let them go have fun."

"Then we will have fun, too," Brooks proclaims.

Christy

"Yeah," I join in, spinning Christy to face me. "Let's celebrate my new place. You, Brooks, and Maddux should stay over. We will party; we can break in the pool table. I have plenty of bedrooms when we all decide to crash."

Christy's tear-filled eyes pierce my heart. She hates the idea of my parents keeping the girls. It is too soon; I see it written all over her face.

"I need to let them go," she whispers shakily.

"I will keep you company," I vow, and she nods.

"We will not leave you alone," Brooks promises. "We will keep you busy until they come back tomorrow. We can make it a girls' night."

Christy nods, wiping her unshed tears from her eyes. She turns to face her friend.

"The apartment will only make me think of them," she confesses. "Will you stay here with me?"

Brooks glances at me before agreeing.

"I need to talk to your folks," Christy states. "And I need to pack their bags."

"Let's eat," Brooks suggests. "Then you can talk while the girls pack their bags from last night."

I am liking Brooks more and more. She takes great care of Christy.

"Brother?" Maddux shouts from the deck through the open French doors. "Where are the burgers?"

"And the hotdogs?" Harper yells.

Christy laughs. "You'd better get to work, Dad."

She pushes me away, returning to the apples. Brooks smiles and shoos me out; I take that to mean my work here is done for the moment. I carry a tray full of meat and grilling utensils with me as I return to the deck. Sending the twins to change from their swimsuits, I enlist Maddux's assistance in distracting Christy for the night.

12

FRIDAY, JUNE 16TH

Christy

Ryan catches me looking at the time on my cell phone. "They are already asleep." He says what I already know. "I could call Mom and see how the night went."

As hope floods my face, he is already connecting a video call.

"Hello, dear," Jackie greets.

I wave from his side, noticing it is too quiet for the twins to still be up.

"Are the girls asleep?" he asks.

"Yes. See for yourself." She swivels the phone camera toward the twins, who are asleep in the guest room. Her husband sleeps between them, a children's book on his chest. She waits until she exits to the hall to speak again. "The girls were angels. You must let them stay over again soon." Her hopeful eyes meet mine.

"Of course. They will want to visit you often," I say, while all I want is to keep them all to myself for months to come. I know it is not healthy, but I am never away from them overnight. Even though they are asleep, I feel the need to be there with them.

"They are fine; they are asleep," Ryan whispers into my ear, snapping me from my thoughts. I did not even hear him say goodbye to his mother. "Let's have fun while they sleep, and tomorrow morning, we will find the twins here bright and early," he promises.

No longer feeling up to having fun, I only nod.

"Drink up," Brooks prompts, slipping a shot glass into each of our hands. "The girls are safe, we are awake and not at work, so let's drink," she urges, on the brink of a demand.

"Is that what you consider a toast?" Maddux asks, chuckling.

"Can you do better?" she challenges.

"Whoa," Ryan orders. "One toast per shot."

He holds his little shot glass higher. We follow his lead then down the shot. My body sputters as I gasp for breath, my tongue and throat on fire. Ryan and Maddux chortle loudly at my discomfort. The desert heat relents slightly, and I roll my eyes at them.

"What shall we play first?" Brooks asks, scanning the game room.

"Darts," Ryan says at the same time Maddux says, "Air hockey."

Brooks and I exchange a look and giggle. We do not want to play either option.

"I would prefer we play darts before you drink much more," Ryan tells his brother.

"That only happened one time," Maddux laughs. "And it was at my house."

Brooks turns towards me, rolling her eyes. I laugh; she does this a lot. She sneaks looks at me, and I can't help but crack up. Not sure how to really play darts, we attempt to mess the guys up on each throw. *Throw? Do you throw darts? Shoot darts?* Whatever it is, we attempt to screw them up. While all I can do is laugh, Brooks easily gets under Maddux's skin, and his game suffers. Or so Ryan says it does.

"I need a shot," Maddux says, pretending to mope from his dart game loss.

I enjoy a glass of wine a time or two each week, but it is clear Maddux enjoys alcohol as much as Brooks does.

"Ryan, break the rules. C'mon," he encourages, shot glass extended.

"What does he mean by 'break the rules'?" I ask, nudging his shoulder.

Ryan's blue eyes melt into mine. "I only have two drinks," he shares.

"Why?" Brooks asks.

"A long time ago, I had too many, and I hurt someone I cared about. So, I only allow myself two drinks."

He holds up two fingers between us. My breath hitches. *Holy crap! He means me.*

"Really?" I croak.

"Yes," Maddux answers, disgusted. "So, since you are here tonight, can you forgive him so he will enjoy another drink with us?"

In my periphery, I catch Brooks's hand fly to her heart. Tears well in my eyes at his gesture.

"C'mon, man." Maddux wiggles the shot glass as he begs.

"Only for tonight. Because you are here and no one plans to leave, I will have more than two drinks." Ryan's eyes lock on mine. "If you are okay with it."

I nod. I never asked him to only drink two drinks for the past six years; he did that as penance after he hurt me. A bitter taste rises up my throat at the painful memory of hearing he slept with someone else.

"Hey, hey," he coos.

"Crud! I did not mean to kill the party mood," Maddux modulates louder than necessary.

"Shots," Brooks says. "Shots will help."

I look wearily at my friend.

"No twins, no work, and no driving. We are drinking," she cheers.

She will make it her mission to see that I enjoy the night off from being a mom. I have only been away from the girls while they were at school, and I was at work or had fallen sick with the flu. *This is my first mom's night out. Or should I say mom's night in?*

All four of us throw back our shots of whiskey.

"High five," Maddux prompts, palm in the air. "A much better toast."

Christy

I watch my friend hesitate for a moment, then give him a high-five. Her eyes smile at me. She has finally found someone she may touch and not worry about seeing visions. With Ryan in the girls' and my life, Maddux and Brooks will be seeing each other often. I hope they will become friends, too.

"We should play pool, girls against boys," Brooks announces, causing me to quirk a brow.

"Uh," Ryan hedges.

"We have a table in the back room of the tattoo parlor. We can hold our own," Brooks assures, patting her palm against Maddux's chest.

Hmm. She touched him again.

"Game on," Maddux states, clapping his hands loudly one time.

Brooks hands me a fresh beer as we approach the pool table. She leans into my side and whispers, "Take it easy the first game. We will run the table for the second one."

I nod, unsure if, after two shots and now two beers, I will still have any game. Ryan breaks; no balls fall into a pocket. Brooks plays with the pool cue in her hand, getting comfy with the feel of it. She addresses the white ball, lines up her shot, and sinks the nine-ball in the center pocket.

"Yay! We are stripes," she cheers, shifting her hips from side to side playfully.

I bite my lips to keep from laughing hysterically at her. She does not act like this. Ever. She must be playing this up for the guys because she has not reached her drink limit.

She sinks one more ball before scratching. Maddux expertly removes three solid balls from the table before missing his fourth shot. I glance at Brooks and then Ryan, who smiles supportively. I sink two balls before purposefully flubbing up my third shot.

"Losers do shots," Maddux states confidently before Ryan's turn.

"Nooo," I answer, shaking my head. "This is just a practice game."

The guys stare at me, trying to ascertain if I am serious.

"Practice is over," Brooks announces. "Maddux, rack 'em up. Let's start the real game."

Ryan fetches four beers while Maddux racks the balls on the pool table.

"Let's make it interesting," Brooks says, winking in my direction. "But first, let's fix this."

She approaches Maddux, extending her arms and messing up his perfectly styled hair. His eyes bug out, and shock sweeps upon his face. When he lifts his hands to attempt to restyle his hair, Brooks swats his hands away.

"Trust me, it looks better," Brooks declares. "But you are so uptight, I bet you can't leave it like this for the rest of the night."

Tight lips and squinted eyes display his anger.

Unbothered by his reaction, Brooks turns to Ryan and me.

"How about we play strip pool?" Brooks suggests, causing me to nearly sputter beer onto the felt cover of the table.

Ryan's head snaps in my direction. I am not sure if his eyes flash with fear or hope.

"What are the rules?" Maddux inquires, as if it has been decided.

Ryan leans into me, whispering, "I am game if you are."

I am not sure if it is the alcohol in my system or the glimmer in his eye that spurs me on.

"We remove one article of clothing at the end of our turn," I suggest.

Ryan's blue eyes liquify, and his pupils dilate. "Really?" he asks.

"Really," I state, surveying the group as I count clothes.

Both guys wear t-shirts and shorts. So, with our bras, we wear one more piece of clothing than they do.

"Guys break," I instruct, faking my bravado.

Not wanting us to back out, Maddux points his pool cue, breaks, and balls scatter in all directions. Two solid balls and one stripe now rest in pockets.

"We will take solids," Maddux announces, lining up his next shot.

His cue nearly misses the white ball entirely, causing us to laugh as he removes his shirt, folds it neatly, and places it on a barstool. Brooks looks at me; her eyes bug out. Clearly, she did not expect him to be muscular with a trim waist.

Christy

Ryan

"You're up," Maddux challenges Brooks.

She shakes her head. "Christy will go next," she suggests, looking at her friend.

I watch as Christy wastes no time lining up a shot. When the white ball clanks against a striped ball, dropping it into the pocket, both women cheer. It does not escape me that she's perfectly placed the white ball in line for her next shot. Christy taps two more balls in before missing.

My stomach flutters at the thought of her removing her clothes. *I am loving strip pool. For the first time since high school, I am going to see Christy's bra or panties.* I lick my lips in anticipation.

Christy's fingers grasp the hem of her shirt, hesitating instead of lifting it over her head. Her fingers move to the button then the zipper of her shorts before sliding them slowly down her thighs.

I did not think this through. There is no way I will be able to make a shot with Christy's bare skin nearby. When she turns to toss her shorts toward the bar, I catch my first glimpse of her cheeks peeking out of her heather gray boy shorts. *Who knew boy shorts could be as sexy as panties?*

"Earth to Ryan," Maddux calls, interrupting my fantasies. "You are up."

I move around the pool table, appraising each angle, looking for the shot I know I can make. I find it hard to think; my eyes keep darting to Christy's thighs. *Focus. Focus. Focus.*

I stand to the left of Christy, line up and tap our ball into the corner pocket. *Shew.* Even if I can't keep my mind on the game, at least I made it look like I am focusing. Of course, I miss my next attempt, and I remove my shirt.

"Yummy, yummy." Brooks licks her lips playfully. "How will I ever concentrate with so much man meat on display?"

Christy rolls her eyes at her friend. Brooks adds a little extra sway to her hips as she moves to the other side of the table and takes her shot. Their purple striped ball falls into the center pocket on her first shot, and she misses her second.

She promptly lifts her black shirt over her head, tossing it to the pile of discarded clothes. Apparently comfortable in her body, Brooks places her hands upon her hips, not hiding her exposed, tattooed skin or her lacy black bra.

Maddux chews on his lower lip, his eyes stuck on Brooks's bare skin and the intricate designs of her many tattoos. I smirk, watching my brother's reaction.

"Bro," I call. "Earth to Maddux."

"Huh?" My brother shakes away the lust-filled haze, suddenly aware we are watching him.

He closes his eyes as he draws in a long breath through his nose. When he opens his eyes, it is easy to see he is fighting the urge to ogle Brooks some more. Focusing, he knocks in two solid balls before missing horribly on his third shot. The four of us laugh for several minutes at his huge mistake.

It hits me that, unless Christy runs the table to finish the game, I will soon see her remove her shirt, because I assume she will not remove her underwear before her shirt.

I covertly draw in a long breath and release it, hoping no one senses my excitement. I clinch my jaw, studying the table. I focus on the balls remaining and not on Christy bending at the waist, her bottom sticking out. I fight a groan when she pumps her cue through her fingers before knocking the white ball into a striped ball on the table. Moving in slow motion, it rolls to the edge of the pocket, seems to hover for a moment, then tumbles out of sight.

The girls leave only one striped ball and the eight-ball on the table. Two expert shots from Christy and they win. I couldn't care less if we win or lose. I do, however, hope she misses so she must remove her shirt. My imagination runs wild, but I prefer to see the real skin beneath her t-shirt.

Christy

She lines up her shot, closes her eyes for a moment as if in prayer, then takes it. Although perfectly planned, she neglects to hit it hard enough. The striped ball stops rolling an inch from the center pocket.

Yes!

Christy points her index finger across the table at her friend. "This is all your fault," she reminds Brooks before turning her back to us and removing her t-shirt.

After tossing it on the pile, she turns back toward the pool table. Unlike Brooks, she's uncomfortable with so much on display. Her hands on opposite shoulders, her elbows and forearms cover most of her chest.

When she attempts to move to the end of the table, I snake my arm around her abdomen, pulling her back towards me. The warmth of her soft skin pressed to my forearm sends sparks through my veins. Even though I caught her off guard, she does not fight me.

"So. Damn. Hot," I growl into her ear.

I feel her tense. Not wanting to upset her, I release my hold. She spins. Nearly nose to nose with me, she smirks.

"So, you like what you see?" she teases. "This is all you get. Brooks will finish the game, we will win, and all of this..." she motions her hand up and down her body, "...will disappear."

I try to listen, but this gorgeous woman in her matching gray bra and undies pushes all of my buttons. For six long years, I relived the memories of her in my arms. Now that she stands in front of me, I am unsure how to react.

She turns around, snags her beer, and takes a sip, no longer attempting to cover her body. She moves in the way of my next shot. I grip her waist, guiding her from my left side to my right. Trying to remain in control, I quickly release her, taking my pool cue in hand.

I address my ball, fantasies of all the things I long to do with my hands upon her hips occupy my mind. My hands on her bare skin seem natural, meant to be.

"Concentrate," Maddux urges from across the table, pulling me back to the game.

"Do not miss," Christy murmurs huskily while leaning into my side.

She breaks the connection immediately, leaving me longing to hold her. My head is not on the game; no matter what I try, I can't think of anything but her. Before me is an easy shot, but I mess it up like I knew I would.

I turn toward Christy as I unbutton my shorts and lower my zipper. She watches; her mouth forms an "O." I can feel the heat of her gaze on my hands as I slide my shorts down my thighs and step out of them.

13

FRIDAY, JUNE 16TH

Christy

Ryan stands between me and the pool table in only his snug gray boxer briefs. I stare as he cups and adjusts himself. There is no place to hide in briefs. A squeal escapes when, in the blink of an eye, he grabs my wrist and pulls me flush against him.

"Like what you see?" he whispers, his lips brushing my ear, his hot breath tickling my sensitive skin.

I gulp. He was mine; for over a year, he was my boyfriend. We spent so much time together, clothed and disrobed. He is wearing underwear, but I can only imagine him naked.

Through my heavy eyelids, I look up into Ryan's soft blue eyes. Longing to taste him, I lick my lips. His eyes clock the movement, and a guttural growl rumbles in his chest, signaling he struggles like me.

I lift my right palm to his chest and press firmly against his hard muscles, urging him to turn back to the game. Caught up in our own interactions, we missed Maddux's turn. We find him standing proudly in his boxers, sipping from his beer.

"My turn," Brooks announces, cue already in hand.

She winks at me, sinking the last striped ball. Like she planned, the white ball sets her up for the next shot.

"Eight-ball in the center pocket," Brooks calls, pointing to the other side of the table.

The balls smack together, and the black eight-ball drops into the correct pocket. Brooks takes two steps towards me, while clapping and cheering.

When we settle down, she leans in, whispering, "I am commando."

Crud! That means she is only in her bra and skirt. Had she missed on her last shot, she would stand only in her plaid skirt.

Reading my mind, she murmurs, "I knew we would win." She taps her temple, letting me know she saw the outcome in a vision.

Ryan

They won. The girls beat us at pool. Mesmerized, I watch as Christy and Brooks cheer in only bras.

"Beat ya," Brooks taunts when their celebration ends.

I've never felt so lucky to lose.

"Time for more shots," Maddux announces, eyes glued to Brooks.

"Clothes first. Shots second," Christy commands.

Standing at the pile of clothes, I pass Brooks her shirt, then Christy her shirt and shorts. A big part of me wants to suggest we remain in our underwear for the rest of the night, but the adult in me thinks better of it.

The women make quick work of dressing. I, on the other hand, move in ultra-slow motion, distracted by Christy's body. She works out, more than swimming alone. I long to run my tongue along the curves of the long muscles of her arms and legs. Thoughts like this will torture me all night. I force my eyes from her body to her face as I step into my shorts. Her eyes follow the movement. She sucks on

Christy

her lip while watching me button and zip my shorts. Toying with her, I pretend to lightly scratch my abs. My effect on her is visible; I smirk.

Brooks whispers something into Christy's ear. This causes her to pull her eyes from me and adamantly shake her head no.

"Two shots are better than one," Maddux declares, proudly displaying eight shot glasses atop the bar.

"Told you!" Brooks yells. "Why do you ever doubt me?"

"I do not doubt you," Christy grumbles under her breath. "I do not want to take two more shots."

"My house, my rules," Maddux proclaims.

"Um, it is my house," I clarify.

Maddux thinks about it for a minute then chuckles. The alcohol slows his brain as he processes that this is the first time I've hosted anything at any of my places.

"Line up, ladies and gents," Maddux invites, sliding one shot glass closer to each of us.

"Whose turn to toast?" I ask, scanning the group.

Christy and Brooks hold empty shot glasses inches from their lips, having already downed theirs.

"You did not see that one coming?" Christy asks her friend.

"What's with all the talking in code about predictions?" I ask, looking at the two women beside me.

They share a conspiratorial look.

"Bottoms up," Brooks goads, her second shot glass in hand.

Maddux and I shoot two shots in record time, slamming the empty glasses on the bar between us. I do not let Brooks's changing the subject distract me.

"Glasses are empty, so now you must answer," I urge. "The predictions."

"I need to sit down," Christy groans, trudging toward the large leather sofa.

I tilt my head in her direction, and the others follow me to join her. I plop down on the opposite end, leaning against the arm of the sofa. Maddux claims the recliner, and Brooks does me a giant favor by forcing herself into the tiny space to the left of Christy, causing her to move about a foot away from me; it seems like a mile.

"Should I tell them?" Brooks whispers, loud enough everyone can hear.

"Tell us what?" Maddux inquires.

All eyes move to Brooks.

"Brooks has a gift," Christy announces, eyes ping-ponging between Maddux and me.

"You brought us a gift?" Maddux asks.

"No, stupid," I correct, frustrated.

"I have the gift of sight," Brooks declares.

"I hate to burst your bubble, but all four of us can see," Maddux deadpans.

"Will you shut up?" I growl.

"She's not making sense," he complains in return.

"She has visions that predict the future," Christy states with a huff.

Maddux must be annoying her, too.

"When I touch someone, I experience flashes," Brooks shares. "I see events for that person."

"So, when we high-five, you can see my future?" Maddux asks, disbelieving.

"If I hug Christy or high-five Ryan, I will see a vision," she explains. "I can't control it."

"How does that work during tattoos?" I ask.

"At work, I keep my gloves on at all times." Brooks repositions herself, tucking her legs beside her on the sofa cushion. "Though I try, I can't avoid all contact and visions."

"How so?" I wonder out loud.

"It is impossible to keep the twins from hugging or holding her hand," Christy states. "Sometimes, strangers bump into her in public. That kind of thing."

"What's in the visions?" Maddux inquires.

"I see dates, parties, holidays, illnesses, visitors, vacations…"

"Death?" Maddux interrupts.

Brooks nods. "I can't choose to only see happy visions. What plays in my mind is random."

"So, you know everything that will happen to Christy and you," Maddux continues, very interested in this topic of conversation.

Brooks shakes her head at the same time Christy answers, "I asked that she not share visions she has for the girls and me."

Huh... I wonder why she does not want to know what is coming. I make to ask her, but Brooks speaks first.

"Occasionally, I am in a vision with the person I am touching, but I can't see my own future. I only see their future, and I might be present when it happens." Brooks's shoulders rise and fall with a deep breath.

"You have no control over it?" I ask.

"Nope," Brooks responds. "Well, maybe I can. Something weird happened last week."

When no one speaks, she continues. "The other day, two guys came in. I had my gloves on, standing behind the counter," Brooks recalls. "While I sketched a design, one of the men reached to point at the paper. His fingers grazed my forearm for just a second."

She shares a look with Christy.

"That's the only time a stranger touched me, and I did not experience a vision," Brooks confesses.

"And you did not know the guy?" Maddux asks.

"It was you, dummy," Christy laughs.

Through my alcohol fog, I attempt to recall the day we visited the parlor. She sketched a quick design for Maddux and told him to come back to see it. I think I remember her shaking both our hands as we left. That can't be right; she said she always wears gloves and avoids contact. I shake my head, shooing away the thoughts.

"Prove it," Maddux challenges, extending his hand.

"I touched you twice at the shop and gave you high-fives tonight, and I get no visions from you," Brooks tells him.

"So, touch Ryan or touch Christy," he urges.

"I do not need to," Brooks announces. "I shook Ryan's hand at the tattoo parlor. I saw plenty."

She saw "plenty" of visions of me. Did she know I would bump into Christy? Meet my daughters?

"So, tell me something that has not happened yet so I can believe you when it happens," Maddux commands.

"Come with me," Brooks orders, waving her hand for Maddux to hurry up.

The two disappear down the hall for less than a minute. I attempt to read into the smirk on my brother's face. *What could she possibly tell him that has yet to happen involving me?*

"Let's watch a movie," Maddux suggests.

Is that what I was doing in the vision Brooks revealed to him? Is he gonna set the scene up to see if I do what Brooks predicts?

My thoughts are too much for me; I need to move.

"Beer run," I announce. "Who wants one?"

Christy raises her hand while Brooks and Maddux say, "Me."

I make my way to the bar, wondering how I am supposed to watch a movie now, knowing Brooks has seen my future. *Should I ask her to share everything in her visions? Or is Christy right in not wanting to know about them?*

"Hey. You okay?" Christy asks, startling me when her hand touches the small of my back.

Turning, I find concern in her eyes.

"It is not an easy thing for her to share, but it is also not easy for us to know she has knowledge about us." Christy's tone further expresses her concern for me.

My head is fuzzy with the alcohol shots. I am sure it further muddles my opinions.

"It is heavy," I reply. "Have you seen proof?"

She nods. "It is freaky, but she sees the future."

"So, the other day, she saw my future. She probably knew we would bump into each other... Wait." I swallow quickly as awareness slams into me. "She offered to babysit for you before I suggested we talk."

Christy pulls her lips between her teeth and nods. I lose myself in her brown eyes. Her life is very different now, but she is still the girl I knew in high school—the girl I always loved.

Christy

When my eyes move from hers to her mouth, primal attraction takes over. My hands find her hips, pulling her to me at the same time as I crush my lips to hers. Christy's body and mouth mold to mine. Her hands fist in my shirt, and her lips part. I take it as an invitation to deepen our kiss. I swipe my tongue over her lower lip before seeking her tongue. My fingers tighten at her hips.

"Told you!" Brooks yells, intruding upon our moment.

Christy slowly pulls away, her hand wiping her lower lip, eyes looking downward. I am not sure what Brooks is up to, but I can't allow Christy to regret our kiss. I lift her chin, encouraging her eyes to meet mine. Smiling softly, I silently will her to do the same. For a moment, she bites her lip, then a wide smile graces her face. I feel my heart swell.

"Dude," Maddux excitedly calls at the bar, only a couple feet away, "she said you would kiss Christy."

"There was a 50 percent chance we would kiss tonight," I scoff.

Christy swats my chest.

"Well, probably more like an 80 or 90 percent chance," I tease.

Maddux shakes his head. "Brooks said the two of you would kiss behind the bar tonight before we turned on the movie. She even knew we would be watching *Die Hard*. Dude, that is my favorite movie!"

I squint my eyes at Christy's friend. *With alcohol involved, it is no surprise I kissed Christy, but who could predict when and where it would occur? Well, I guess Brooks could predict it.* This leaves me anxious to know everything she saw in her visions.

"I am so jealous," Maddux announces, causing all of us to furrow our brows at him.

"Jealous that she does not have visions of me," he clarifies. "Unlike Christy, I would want to know all about them."

I thought I wanted to know everything; now, I am not sure I would. The excitement and spontaneity of our kiss would be diminished if I knew when and where it would happen. *Nope. When it comes to Christy, I prefer for it to happen organically. If her kiss is a sign of what is to come, I need to prepare for my world to be rocked.*

14

FRIDAY, JUNE 16TH

Ryan

Halfway through the movie, Christy sleeps curled up on the sofa, her head in my lap. I catch myself absentmindedly running my fingers through her dark brown hair. She never partied much or stayed up late in high school, so I am not surprised she sleeps now.

Brooks yawns loudly from the other end of the sofa. "I am calling it a night," she declares before another yawn. "I will walk her to bed."

I shake my head. "Let her sleep," I instruct. "I am going to finish the movie."

I have no intention of waking her at the end of the movie. I plan to remain motionless for as long as possible while I enjoy touching her.

"I am gonna crash in a spare room," my brother states, stretching. "I am too tired to ride my golf cart home."

I nod; I intended for him to spend the night.

Quietly, they each wish me good night before disappearing down the hallway.

I tentatively press the button on the side of the sofa, and it slowly reclines. I pause, ensuring it did not cause Christy to stir, then press again until I am fully reclined. *Why did I not think of this earlier?* If I had, I would be asleep, and Brooks would take Christy off to bed with her. I am better off. Remote in hand, I set the sleep timer for one hour, then settle in to finish *Die Hard*.

Saturday, June 17th
Ryan

"Noooo," Christy groans, her arm moving from my chest to cover her eyes.

"Wake up, sleepyhead," I sing-song.

"My head hurts," she grumbles. "Why did I ever think I could keep up with you guys drinking those shots?"

I chuckle, causing her to slap my chest.

"Stop moving," she mumbles, her cheek pressed hard against my pec.

"Mom will be here with the twins in 30 minutes," I inform.

Now, she pops her head up, aware of our position.

I woke 15 minutes ago. I could have woken her then, but I enjoyed watching her sleep while I held her. Somewhere in the middle of the night, she moved from lying perpendicular to me, with her head in my lap, to parallel to me, cuddled to my side. Not that I have any complaints.

"How did you sleep?" I ask, fighting a smirk.

She claims she does not remember falling asleep or how she came to cuddle with me. I want to tell her we are drawn to each other and not to fight it but think better of it. Her body reacts like mine when we are close, when we touch, and when we kiss. She might fight it now, but soon, she will give in to our attraction.

Christy

"What the hell?" I nudge a sleeping Brooks on my way to my duffle bag.

"I did not wake you up," she gripes defensively.

"No, but you did leave me sleeping on the couch with Ryan all night," I growl, toothbrush in hand.

Walking behind me, I track her movements in the mirror. She shrugs before lowering her sleep shorts to pee.

"His mom and the girls will be here in 20 minutes," I inform. "There is no way she will not think I got drunk and slept with her baby boy again last night."

"First, he's no baby boy," she says, flushing the stool. "Second, he is an adult, and who he chooses to sleep with is none of her G-D business." With her hip, she pushes me from the sink to wash her hands. "And third…"

"Please do not let there be a third. I am too hung over for it," I whine.

"And third," she drawls out, "I will make you bright-eyed and bushy-tailed before she arrives."

"There is not enough fairy dust to rid me of this headache," I warn.

"Swallow," she instructs, hand extended with two pain relievers in her palm.

If I were not hungover, I would give her grief for her choice of words. I take the proffered pills and the bottle of water from her other hand to wash them down with.

"Shower," she orders, index finger pointed.

I am too tired to argue. I choose a setting a bit cooler than my preferred temperature, in hopes it will spark me to life. I make quick work of washing my hair and lathering my body. My mood lifts, knowing my girls will be here soon.

Wait. Vanilla? Ryan had Josh buy my favorite scent of body wash.

Christy

"Breakfast is served," Brooks calls from the vanity.

Stepping from the shower stall, I find two pieces of toast and a small glass of juice waiting on me. I award a smile to my best friend, grateful she has my back this morning. I allow her to apply a quick swipe of eye liner and a coat of mascara on my eyes, then I secure my long hair in a high ponytail. I do not wear makeup, but she insists it will help me appear well-rested.

"Maddux is cleaning the game room and bar. I think Ryan is showering upstairs," she informs casually. She loses her battle, a large smile climbing onto her face. She waggles her eyes at me.

"Stop it," I chide. "There was alcohol involved."

It is not totally a lie; we did drink too much last night. Considering Ryan has practiced a two-drink limit and I barely sip on wine, last night's shots were too much for us. Now that being said, alcohol is not the reason for our kiss or my laying my head on his thigh during the movie. I can't fight his pull; it is as strong as the sun's gravitation.

"Happy ending," she states, hinting not for the first time to the visions she experienced after shaking Ryan's hand.

"Cut that out," I warn, pointing my finger at her. "I do not share your gift, but I'd be blind not to see what is developing between Maddux and you."

Fire lights in her green irises, and her lip snarls. I touched a nerve. She can deny it all she wants; their bickering is foreplay. My friend will fight. She is stubborn. I hope she does not fight her feelings for Maddux too long. She's finally found someone she can touch, and she should grab a hold of him and hang on for the ride.

"Ready?" she snips.

I nod, following her from our guest room. I wave at Maddux, who is loading a dishwasher behind the bar, unable to fight my grin. I barely clear the top step when the front door bursts wide open and my girls run inside. I open my arms, preparing for the force of them colliding with me, but they run into the kitchen to the waiting arms of their father. Owning 100 percent of their attention for over five years, it will take more than a week for me to grow used to sharing their affection with Ryan.

They talk a mile a minute, sharing everything they did at their grandparents' house, while he crouches, and they hug his neck. Standing in the open doorway, his mother clutches her hand to her heart, tears filling her eyes.

Crud! I did that, too. I kept the girls from Ryan's parents; she must hate me for that. I had the best of intentions when I kept the pregnancy from Ryan and his family. I thought I was protecting him, allowing him to follow his dream and talent for football. I told myself I sacrificed to allow him to be happy. *I...*

"Christy?" Ryan's mother calls my name, pulling me from my thoughts.

"Hmm?" I mumble.

"They were angels, but now we realize why we parent children when we are young," Jackie chuckles. "We are exhausted."

I smile. "So, you had a good night?"

"Of course," she croons. "You raised perfect little angels. They even helped with the dishes."

"Perfect angels"? I want to argue and shake my head. No one is perfect, including my girls. I raised them to be respectful and helpful. As for the dishes, with no dishwasher at Brooks's place, we recruited them to help us.

I find myself wrapped in her arms as she whispers in my ear, "Thank you for keeping them safe and healthy. Thank you for loving Ryan enough to give them his name. You allowed him to play the game he loves while you gave up so much. Thank you."

When I am released, tears in my eyes, my girls smile up at me, and Ryan looks on with wide, worried eyes. I force a small smile upon my mouth. Her words struck me at my core.

15

SATURDAY, JUNE 17TH

Christy

Later in the afternoon, after hours in the pool, my girls are beat.

"Ryan, I should take the girls home," I announce, rising from my lounger. "They had a big night with your folks last night and a long day today."

He swims to the edge of the pool, looking up at me through his wet lashes.

"Stay."

He is not serious; he can't mean what I think he means. His one word pierces my heart.

"Stay here; let them sleep here," he encourages. "My house is humongous. There is plenty of room for all of us."

Tilting my head, I try to gauge what he wants. *Is he asking the girls and me to spend one night in a guest bedroom? Or is he asking me to share his bed?*

"The clock is ticking," he reminds me. "If you stay, the girls will feel comfortable; they will feel more at home. We can play games, watch a movie, and they can turn in early. I will keep them tomorrow, and you can go work with Brooks if you need to."

Everything about Ryan does it for me, without him even trying. Now, he works it. He bats his eyelashes and paints on his panty-melting smile.

I take a seat on the edge of the pool, my feet slipping into the water. Ryan, still in the pool, places a hand on either side of me. His thumbs caress my thighs. I lean in close to prevent the girls from hearing our discussion.

Ryan interprets my lean as a move; he closes the distance between us, his lips softly caressing mine. His kiss is slow, gentle, and sweet. It is PG with veiled meaning.

"Ryan," I giggle, his lips grazing mine, "the twins will see us."

He pulls back a couple of inches, still in my space.

"Stay," he implores. "Please."

"Ry," I groan.

"Yes, Mommy?" my daughter replies, now within ear shot.

Ryan attempts to bite back his laughter at my addressing him with the name my daughter now prefers.

"Girls, come here," I instruct.

Floating in their innertubes, they smile up at me.

"Daddy wants to know if we would like to spend the night here at his new house with him and his new furniture," I share.

"Please, please, please," they beg, hands pressed together in front of them.

I glance at Ryan before I answer to find him making puppy-dog eyes, hands pressed together like his five-year-old daughters. I laugh.

"It is a yes!" the girls cheer.

They know me too well. The fact that I did not immediately argue or say no meant I was giving in. *Heck, Ryan probably remembers this fact, too. It is three versus one; I never stood a chance. The odds are not stacked in my favor for all future decisions.*

"I will inform Josh we will need an early dinner," Ryan says, preparing to climb from the pool.

As much as I long to see the muscles of his arms, shoulders, and chest flex as he lifts himself onto the patio instead of using the stairs, I offer to talk to Josh instead. I need to pee anyway.

"Josh?" I call on my way toward the kitchen.

He magically appears.

"The girls and I will be staying. Would it be too much to ask that we eat dinner early?" I scrunch my face, hoping not to be too much of an inconvenience.

"I am grilling pizza for dinner," he smiles. "It will take 15 minutes tops. Shall we say five o'clock?"

I nod, smiling.

"I took the liberty of preparing two guest rooms downstairs. You will find pajamas and toiletries laid out on the bed for you." The sweet, middle-aged man smiles, awaiting my reactions.

I open and close my mouth several times.

"Ryan asked me to keep some items handy," he chuckles.

"He did, did he?" Sarcasm laces my voice.

Josh holds his palms between us. "He made it very clear you needed your own space downstairs. I set you up in the second master suite, and the girls will be in the room across the hall."

"I am sorry," I confess. "It caught me off guard that he planned for us to stay before he even asked us."

Josh winks at me. *He winks at me. Seriously? Am I that predictable? Or am I easy?*

"While you are here, can we go over a few things?" His sweet smile never falters.

I nod; I can hold off going to the bathroom for a bit.

"Do the three of you experience any food allergies?"

I shake my head.

"Allergies to soaps, shampoos, detergents, etc.?"

I shake my head.

"An aversion to any foods or textures of foods?"

Again, I shake my head. "The girls and I are adventurous when it comes to eating. We will try anything once," I share.

"How about Miss Brooks?" He looks down at his tablet to input my answers.

"Do not liquify or make smoothies out of solid foods, and she will be fine," I remark.

"You should invite her over for dinner tonight," Josh suggests. "I am sure she loves to spend time with the three of you. We do not want her to be lonely while you are here."

My brow furrows.

"That is if she does not share her evenings with someone special," Josh backpedals.

I shake my head. "That's a scary thought." I laugh, and he joins me.

"Between you and me, I see a spark between her and Maddux." Josh winks again, plugging the tablet into the outlet at his desk beside the refrigerator.

So, I am not imagining it; there is a spark between Brooks and Maddux.

"I will text Brooks and let you know," I say, race-walking to the nearest bathroom.

"There is a bathroom in the pool house," Josh calls over his shoulder.

Crud. I forgot about the pool house. Oh, well. I needed to talk to Josh about dinner anyway. I open up my texts while I pee.

> ME
> grilled pizza at Ryan's
> wanna join us?

> BROOKS
> what time?

> ME
> 5

> BROOKS
> on my way

An evil smile forms upon my face. I pull up the contact I thought I would never need to use.

Christy

> ME
> grilled pizza at Ryan's
> wanna join us?

> MADDUX
> yes!
> on my way

The little matchmaker in me does a happy dance. On my way past the kitchen, I inform Josh there will be two more for dinner, and he laughs, assuring me it will be no problem.

Ryan

My favorite people surround my patio table. Hot off the grill, Josh's homemade cheese, pepperoni, and supreme pizzas grace the center of the table, while Maddux, Brooks, Christy, and the twins join me.

In planning this house, I envisioned moments like this. Now, this is my reality, and I look forward to making it a permanent occurrence.

My girls grow more tired with each bite they enjoy. At this rate, I doubt they will make it through bath time, let alone a bedtime story.

I watch Brooks lean near Christy, whispering in her ear, and watch Christy's eyes grow wide as she shakes her head at her friend. Looking in my direction, her eyes dart away when they find me watching her. I glance at Brooks, and she winks at me.

Christy

Damn her. Brooks knows I prefer not to know about her visions. While she did not tell me any specifics, her hint will haunt me. "Say yes," she instructs as a hint to a question someone will ask me. Her prompting means my first instinct will be to decline. In her visions, she sees what lies beyond the question; she knows I should say yes. Now, I can only wait for this question to surface. I hate waiting for her hints to pan out.

Ryan

With our guests gone and the girls asleep, I can't pull my eyes from the woman opposite me at the kitchen island. I am fascinated at the way she watches the white wine swirl in her glass, the way she tucks stray hair behind her ear, the way she wets her lip with her tongue. Then her brown eyes are upon me.

"This feels like old times," I say.

Christy quirks a brow. "I did not drink wine in high school," she corrects.

"I mean us." I state what I am sure she knows. "It is easy and natural."

"Things are very different now." She rounds the corner of the counter, closing some of the three feet between us. "We are parents, and you are a tight end in the NFL." She presses her index finger into my chest to drive the point home.

My finger moves back and forth. "I meant between us."

Christy

She sets her nearly empty wine glass in the center of the island before positioning herself directly in front of me. No longer interested in my beer, I place my hands upon her hips, lifting her to sit on the island countertop in front of me. My eyes leisurely scan her from head to toe and back.

"You know exactly what I am talking about," my husky voice informs.

I watch a full-body shiver rack her. Her pulse in her neck quickens, and my nostrils flare, straining for the scent of her.

"I do not plan to fight my feelings for you," I admit. "I never stopped loving you. I tried to move on, but no one else could measure up. I could not bring myself to sleep with anyone after high school."

Her pupils dilate.

"Ryan," she whispers. "I must consider the girls…"

"So do I," I cut her off. "The best thing for our daughters is to be raised in a loving family with their mom and dad under one roof."

She opens her mouth, but I hush her, pressing my fingers to her lips.

"Sure, we can co-parent. We can shuffle them back and forth between our two houses. We can alternate weeks, carpool duty, and the like. We can toil over our individual calendars, focusing more on the logistics than the girls."

I remove my fingertips from her lips.

"Or we can all four live under one roof. You can move in here. Lord knows there is plenty of room. We can share a family space, a family calendar, and family time. Instead of you missing Harper and Ry while I spend time with them, you can be here, too."

"I love you," I confess. "I love you and always have." I pound my closed fist to my heart. "I kept you in here; I always will. And you love me."

I hold my index finger between us. "Do not try to deny it. I know you love me. I can see you love me. Heck, I can ask Brooks. I am sure she had visions of our happily ever after."

She lowers her eyes, but fingers to her chin, I raise her gaze.

"Move in with me."

16

SATURDAY, JUNE 17TH

Christy

Mic drop. This is the question Brooks prompted me to say yes to.

"Move in with me." Did Ryan really speak those words out loud? "Move in with me." He thinks it is that easy? That with the flick of a switch, I can make the decision, pack our bags, and move in?

He's right. I do love him. I never stopped loving him. He is correct that the logistics of visitation during the NFL season will be a nightmare, and I do not want that for my girls.

"Move in with me." He is stripping himself bare, he is putting it all on the table, and he is going all in on this bet. Sure, we could parent separately, but why do we need to? We love each other; we are not divorced. His house is large enough for all of us.

We love each other.

I look at him through my lashes to find him studying my face. I dart my tongue out, longing to taste him. *I need him.*

Ryan covers my mouth with his. His plump lips massage mine, and his teeth gently nip. I close my eyes, reveling in the sensation of his lips to mine.

"I..." He kisses the right corner of my mouth.

Christy

"Love..." His lips place a peck on the left side of my mouth. "You."

I pounce. My arms encircle his neck, and my legs wrap around his center. Ryan's strong arms anchor me to him.

"Your room," I instruct.

Following my instructions, Ryan carries me—still wrapped around him—to the primary suite. My lips tickle his neck and collarbone as we move.

"I love you, too," I confess a moment before I fall backwards onto his bed.

His mattress is nearly as big as the room the twins and I share at Brooks's apartment. Standing at the foot of the bed, Ryan's eyes move from my face to my chest, down my legs, then back up again. I watch his eyes turn liquid, and his tongue glides along his plump lower lip. I squirm beneath his gaze.

His right arm reaches behind his head, grasps his collar, and pulls the shirt from his back in one fluid motion. For years, his memory has haunted my thoughts. Now, before me, he is more god-like than before. His time playing Division I and NFL football sculpted his body into a chiseled, powerful beast.

Though I admired him as we played strip pool, in my inebriated state, I did not fully appreciate the mighty man before me.

I caught a glimpse of Ryan's tattoo Friday night, but my nerves prevented me from really seeing them. High on his right bicep sits his National Championship Georgia Bulldog tattoo. The red contrasts brightly against the grey and black. Above his right pectoral two red halves of a heart are split about two inches apart. His left bicep holds a Celtic knot pattern that repeats as it wraps around his bicep.

Ryan

We've barely begun, and I already know I will never find my fill of her. She will please me yet leave me always craving more.

For several long minutes, we struggle to control our breathing while I hold her hand in mine.

"I need you to know. There was never anyone after you left; I couldn't. I messed around in college, but even they left me longing only for you. After I cheated and hurt you that night, I never found satisfaction with another woman. It has always been you." I kiss her forehead.

Silence bathes the room while she processes my confession. Muted moonlight filters through the slats of the blinds.

Christy

"Tell me about your tattoos," I request, my fingers tracing the pattern, repeating on his left bicep.

"It's a Celtic knot," he explains. "Dad's family is Irish and Scottish. It symbolizes eternity."

"And this one," I prompt tapping the broken heart on his chest.

He shakes his head.

"Is this because of me?" I prod, and Ryan nods. "Broken heart?" my voice breaks.

"The pain of parting is nothing to the joy of meeting again," Ryan murmurs.

My breath hitches, and tears burn my eyes.

"Dickens?" I whisper.

"I had to read *Nicholas Nickleby* in college," he divulges. "I can't believe you knew it."

"It's almost identical to a Nicholas Sparks quote I latched onto," I confess.

"Still a veracious reader?" he asks.

"I have less free time, but I do read at night," I inform.

"What's the quote?" he prods.

"Fell in love with her when we were together, then fell deeper in love with her in the years we were apart."

Ryan chuckles as I finish the quote. "Dear John."

I sit up, placing my palm on his bare chest. "No way," I protest.

"What?" he scoffs. "Mom wanted to start a book club, so Maddux, Mom and I read the book."

Mouth agape I am unsure how to respond. I am equal parts impressed that he shared that moment with his mom and the quote meant enough for him to remember it.

Remembering his tattoo started this line of conversation, I trace my fingertips over the heart.

"I broke your heart," I rasp.

Ryan shakes his head, placing his hand over mine on his chest.

"My heart was not broken. Hearts don't break," he explains. "It hurts because the two parts that make it whole were separated." He taps the left part of the tattoo. "You." He taps the right part. "Me." He raises my hand to his lips. "Not broken, simply separated." He kisses my fingertips.

"I can't stay much longer; we should not risk it," I warn and let out a huff. "I wish I could stay in your arms all night."

Lifting up on one elbow, I kiss him.

"I love you," I declare, kissing him once more. "Tomorrow, we should discuss what a relationship between us might look like in front of our daughters and when the three of us should move in."

I slip from his bed, quickly dressing. I wave, smiling sweetly on my way out the door. *He will sleep like a baby tonight, knowing he won me back.*

17

SUNDAY, JUNE 18TH

Ryan

I drink my protein smoothie, seated at the kitchen island while I wait for my girls to wake and climb the stairs. I tilt my head. *Was that a thud?*

Josh laughs at me. "They have been up for about an hour," he informs, reading my mind. "I am sure they will be up here soon."

I nod. I do not like them in the basement. I want the twins in the bedroom on the same level as mine, and I want Christy in my bed at night. *Baby steps*, I remind myself.

Instead of the proverbial pitter-patter of little feet, I hear the thumps of a herd of elephants as the girls climb the stairs.

"Daddy!" they yell, running toward me.

"Good morning," I greet. "Where's Mommy?"

"Right here," Christy answers, emerging from the stairway. "Good morning."

Josh greets Christy and the girls while keeping his attention on pancakes on the griddle. Christy scans the sliced fruit and yogurt on the island with the plates, napkins, and utensils. I bite back my

Christy

smile; it kills her to let Josh do his job. When our lives grow hectic in late summer and fall, she will appreciate his help.

"What is on the agenda for today?" Josh asks, placing four saucer-sized pancakes on the counter.

I set down my now empty smoothie jug.

"Were you able to make all of the arrangements at the club?" I ask.

With a smile, Josh nods, pouring batter on the griddle for four more pancakes. I watch Christy expertly prepare two plates with pancakes, sliced strawberries, a spoonful of peanut butter, a dab of yogurt, and a small puddle of syrup. When she slides them to the twins, they thank her and Mr. Josh before taking a fork in hand.

I face 11 defenders on the field without fear, but caring for my little girls scares me. Burning fear rises up my throat. I am not sure what they need and when they need it. Christy fixes their plates as easily as she fixes her own, yet I have not the first clue what to do.

"You will learn," she promises at my bewildered expression. "They are old enough to tell you what they want and how they want it. Trust me; you can handle this."

Christy fixes a bowl of yogurt topped with slices of fruit then sprinkles granola on top. She slides onto the stool beside me, taking her spoon in hand. I notice she didn't opt for a pancake; I wonder if she is avoiding carbs. She does not need to worry about her weight. If anything, she is a bit thin.

"Daddy, do you have to work today?" Ry asks, big blue eyes looking up at me from her seat.

I smile; I will never grow tired of hearing them call me Daddy. "I will need to work out later, but I plan to spend the entire day with you," I answer.

"Yay!" they cheer.

"Eat up," Josh encourages, motioning to their plates. "He has lots of fun things planned for today."

"You do?" Christy murmurs, leaning into my side.

I smile down at the beautiful woman next to me. *I am the luckiest guy alive. I can't wait to spend the rest of my life with the three of them.*

Turning back to Harper and Ry, I share my plans for the day. "Uncle Maddux plans to join us if that is okay?"

The girls nod, their blue eyes excited by everything I say.

"Mr. Josh and I bought new golf clubs in the garage for you," I brag. "And another golf cart will be here next week," I tell Christy.

I turn back to my girls. "Uncle Maddux and I want to take you to the driving range and putting green to teach you how to golf. Does that sound fun?"

Again, they nod.

"Eat breakfast, then we can talk about some more fun things," I urge.

Christy places her right hand on my forearm. "You bought golf clubs? And why another golf cart?"

Spinning on my barstool to face her, I meet her dark brown eyes. "It is a family membership. Part of the reason I built the house here was to live at the country club and use the facilities, especially in the off-season. I'd love it if you would join us today, but I understand if you do not."

I search her face, dying to know her thoughts. I probably should have discussed all of this with her before I bought the golf clubs. I am so excited to spend time with my family that I do not stop to think.

"Why don't the two of you finish your breakfast on the deck?" Josh suggests.

I watch his eyes flick toward the twins and back.

"I will visit with the girls while they eat. Then they can help me fix snacks for the day," Josh offers, shooing us adults from the room.

I carry Christy's breakfast bowl as she follows me through the French doors. We sit at the end of the table, overlooking the pool below. A light breeze blows Christy's stray hairs that fall from her ponytail.

"You bought golf clubs?" she rasps.

Christy

Ryan smirks. "Last night, your parting words were 'I love you. Tomorrow, we will discuss what a relationship between us will look like in front of the girls and when we will move in,'" he states.

I scoff, caught off guard. He almost recited my words verbatim. I let out an audible breath as I place my spoon back in my bowl. I want to argue that I said "we should discuss" and "when we should move in," but essentially, they mean the same thing.

"Yes, that is what I said last night," I agree. "But you bought the clubs before…"

He interrupts me. "Whether you live here or not, the three of you are on my membership. That is why I bought the clubs. Golf is an activity I can do with my family. It is something we can enjoy together."

"You spoke like we already live together," I protest. "And Josh did not act surprised. Did you tell him I agreed to move in?"

Ryan's grin is all the answer I need.

"Ryan, tell me you did not."

"I did not *exactly*," he laughs.

I am woman enough to admit that, although I am upset, Ryan laughing turns me on.

"When I told him I bumped into you at the club, I shared about our past." He tucks hair behind my ear, his fingertips grazing my cheekbone. "When I told him about the girls, I told him I wished the three of you lived here with me. I may have shared a comment a time or two in between that my goal and ultimate desire was for the four of us to be a family."

Ryan pulls my chair closer to his. Our knees touch, and he places his palms on my lower thighs. The heat of his touch crawls up my bare skin.

"I love you. I can't hide it from anyone, especially Maddux and Josh," he murmurs, eyes burning through mine to my soul. "You love me. Is there any reason we should fight it?"

He moves his fingertips to my neck. His thumbs caressing my lips silences any answers I want to share.

"We do need to discuss the best way to speak to the girls. If you told them Daddy was busy with work, they will expect us to be together now that I am not busy. They will expect us to live together like the mommies and daddies of their friends."

His words make this sound simple. "Daddy was away at work, and now he is back." I did tell them he was busy with work, that he loved them, and that he wished he were with us. *He is right.* With the half-truth I told the twins, we were a family separated for some time. It stands to reason that we act as a family acts, and we live like a family lives.

Tears fill my eyes—happy tears mixed with tears of fear.

"In my wildest dreams..." Now, my tears threaten to clog my throat.

"So, you dreamt of me?" Ryan smirks.

I swat his shoulder.

"Like me, you spent the last six years fantasizing..." Leaning in, his lips graze my cheek. "Longing..."

He kisses the corner of my mouth. "And now, here we are..."

He kisses the other corner of my lips. "...in love...with children. We are a family."

His forehead to mine, our eyes locked, I find my voice. "So, what do we do?"

"We live as a family, and we love," he answers.

When I nod, his lips take mine. His kiss is soft and sweet. A banging sound interrupts us. On the other side of the closed French doors, our daughters clap and cheer. Smiling, Ryan opens his arms wide, inviting them to join us.

Harper swings the door open, and the girls run toward us. He scoops them onto his lap, swiveling to face me. With Harper on one knee and Ry on the other, their three identical smiles shine at me.

"I am going to let you golf with Daddy and Uncle Maddux while I talk to Miss Brooks," I inform them. "I will pack some clothes and toys so we can..."

Christy

My intelligent, outspoken Harper interrupts, "Move in with Daddy!"

My eyes dart to Ryan's for assistance.

"Would you like to live here with me?" he asks, smiling widely.

"Yes!" they yell.

"What about Miss Brooks? Where will she live?" Ry asks, more sensitive to others than her twin.

"Miss Brooks can come visit Mommy and you any time she wants to," Ryan answers.

"She will still live in her apartment." I add the one fact Ryan neglected to mention.

"We do not have a bedroom here," Harper blurts.

"Josh…" Ryan begins to answer.

"Mr. Josh," I correct him.

"Mr. Josh," Ryan smirks in my direction, "loves to shop. We will tell him what we want, and he will set a bedroom up for you in no time."

Again, I shake my head at the life Ryan now leads. His money affords him the luxury of snapping his fingers and things are done.

"Can we see our room?" Harper asks, hopping down from her father's lap.

"Why don't you go talk to Josh—Mr. Josh—and let him know what color you want your room to be?" Ryan suggests. "Mommy and I will be right behind you."

In a flash, the girls disappear inside.

"I want their room to be on the same level as ours." His eyes ping-pong between mine. "I mean, eventually, we will share my bedroom, and I would feel better if they were up here."

I press my hand to his cheek. His unshaven jawline prickles my palm. I feel my pulse quicken as I fantasize about his whiskers. I close my eyes tightly, brushing off that train of thought.

"I think your paternal instincts have kicked in," I remark. "I agree. Their room should be on the same level as ours until they reach their teens."

His blue eyes flicker with excitement briefly before a scowl crawls upon his features.

"What is it?" I ask, afraid I said something that upset him.

"Teenage boys," he snarls, his jaw tight.

I laugh. I laugh so hard I snort. I place the back of my hand over my mouth to stifle my humor.

"It is not funny," he growls. "I know exactly how a teenage boy thinks."

I take his hand in mine. "Let's not get ahead of ourselves. Let's focus on this week for now."

18

SUNDAY, JUNE 18TH

Christy

"Got a second?" I ask, walking into the back room of the tattoo parlor.

Looking up at me from her office chair, Brooks bites her lips, a smile peeking through.

"What's up, buttercup?" she asks, popping her "P."

"I know it is fast…"

My best friend interrupts me. "We knew the day would come when you would leave my nest." She shrugs, making light of this big life-changing event.

"You knew," I accuse. "This was one of the visions."

She nods, a wide smile upon her face.

"So, do you know where he and the girls are right now?" I further question.

"Nope."

"Maddux and Ryan took the twins and their new golf clubs to the driving range at the club," I inform her. "I am picking up a few toys and clothes. Then I am supposed to join them."

This news lifts her from her seat. She paces to the window, hands on her hips.

"Are you going to the club?" she asks.

"Ryan's keen on us using his family membership," I explain.

"How do you feel about returning there after they..."

"Fired me?" I finish. "I am over it."

I stand beside her, looking out the window to the alley behind the parlor.

"That being said, it will be awkward," I admit. "I expect members to whisper about me when they see us."

"So, you plan to be a member?" she asks.

"Let's take it one step at a time," I chuckle. "Today, I will watch the girls at the driving range. Want to come over tomorrow and help me set up the twins' bedroom?"

After I pull my car into the garage, I stand staring at a brand new set of women's golf clubs with a note tucked between them. *No way. He could not have.* I fiddle with the blade of one iron, stunned that they are the same brand of clubs I had in high school. *With all the brands available, what is the probability that he would randomly choose the same one?*

My mind drifts back over six years. Our parents belonged to the same club. Though we went to the same high school and I had classes with him, the first time he spoke to me was at the country club. My best friend and I were walking to my car. He and a friend had driven their golf cart over to check us out. They invited us to a pool party that night, and the rest is history.

I pick up the white paper from between the clubs, finding it is not a note but rather a drawing. The girls drew me a picture of the five of us golfing. In crayon—so I assume Josh bought craft supplies for the twins—across the bottom, the girls wrote "Cum gof with us." I can't help but laugh at the spelling of "come," and I wonder how Ryan reacted when he read it.

I am laughing when a golf cart pulls up the long driveway.

"Howdy, neighbor," Maddux's neighbor, Paige, greets as she parks her cart.

I am caught off guard for a moment. Then I realize that residents of Breakstone drive their carts on the road to the cart path to get to the club. Since she lives by Maddux, she probably saw me on her way by.

Wait. Ryan is the last house on this street, and there is not a turn around. He must drive by her house to access the cart path, not the other way around. I raise a brow and approach her red golf cart.

"I am headed to the club for my tee time with the ladies, and I thought I would drive by to see if your car was in the driveway to invite you to join us," she informs.

Arms crossed, my brow furrows.

Paige chuckles at my confusion. "Ryan asked Josh to reach out to me for input on purchasing your golf clubs," she explains, pointing at them in the center of the garage. "Josh and I purchased golf attire for you, too. The guys did not tell you?"

I shake my head, overwhelmed by it all.

"Let's go golf," Paige suggests peppily.

"Maddux and Ryan took the twins to the driving range," I inform. "I am supposed to text them to come get me."

"Pish." She swats the air. "I am headed that way; I will give you a ride."

"I need to change." I state the obvious.

"I can wait," she proclaims. "Chop, chop." She shoos me inside.

If I were Ryan, where would I put golf clothes? I did not see them in the room the girls and I slept in last night. I freeze mid-step. *He is just cocky enough...* I stride toward Ryan's bedroom. His closet is on the left, so I venture into the large walk-in closet on the right. It is no longer empty.

Crud!

I wonder what he would have done if I'd refused to move in with the girls? Would he have told me he bought golf clubs, a second golf cart, and clothes? Or would he have hidden them? Am I really this predictable?

Remembering Paige waits for me, I grab the first shirt and shorts I see, quickly putting them on. I must hand it to Paige and Josh--they fit. I even like the red polo and black shorts. I grab one of the two pairs of golf shoes from the nearby rack before returning to the garage.

"Perfect," Paige declares. "I loaded your clubs. Hop on."

There is no time to fret about the awkwardness of my first appearance at the club since they let me go. Paige maneuvers the cart towards the cart path, talking about the ladies she golfs with the entire way.

"You will have to join us soon," she urges. "We play for fun. Gibson is a phenomenal golfer, but the rest of us tend to drink to forget we're golfing. Promise me you will join us soon."

Wow. I am winded from listening to her.

"I have not golfed in six years." I make my excuse. "I should stick to the driving range for a while."

"Nonsense," she argues. "You have my number. Reach out to me for next Tuesday. If you do not, I will call Ryan."

Would she? Would she really call Ryan to force me to golf with her group of friends?

"We are here," she announces. "Before you go, let's take a selfie."

In a flash, she holds her phone in front of us, leaning into my side. I barely smile before she takes the photo. She removes her Birkenstocks. Barefoot, she hops from the seat, unfastening my golf bag like I do not know how to do it myself.

"Have fun," she calls, climbing back into the driver's seat. "Do not forget to take pictures of the girls with Ryan." With a wave, she's back on the cart path, headed to the clubhouse.

With my eyes closed, I draw in a huge breath. It is a beautiful, sunny summer day with a slight breeze. I heave the strap over my shoulder, carrying my clubs toward my family.

The irons in my bag clank together when I set my clubs in the rack of the open slot next to Ryan. The sound causes him to pull his eyes from Harper, glancing over his shoulder. He does a double take.

Christy

"Surprise." I fake my enthusiasm. "Paige dropped me off."

Ryan looks around the range and parked carts for Paige.

Not spotting her, he turns to face me. "You found the clothes." He motions toward my attire.

"Funny thing. They were in *your* closet." I lace my voice with sarcasm.

He smiles sheepishly. "I knew you would want to play with the girls, so I made sure you were ready."

I stand in the space behind the twins. "How are they doing?" I ask.

"They are naturals," Maddux announces, smiling at my arrival.

"Mommy!" the girls squeal, running to me with clubs in hand.

"Shhh!" I admonish.

"Remember what we talked about," Ryan directs. "We use inside voices on the golf course."

The girls nod.

"We do not want to mess up the other golfers," Ry explains to me.

"That is right," I agree. "Show me what Uncle Maddux and Daddy taught you. Ry, you show me first," I instruct.

I watch as both girls place their ball on a wooden tee. Ry turns her golf ball so the logo faces her; Harper does not worry about hers. Ry places her three-wood behind the ball and spreads her feet apart. I watch her little chest rise and fall as she steadies her breath before swinging. She connects solidly. With a loud ting, her ball takes flight, landing about 100 yards away. She smiles proudly, and I award her with a golf clap.

"My turn," Harper announces, her driver already positioned behind her ball.

I hold my breath as she draws her long club back then swings it forward, striking the ball, sending the tee flying with it. Her drive lands past the red 100-yard flag in front of us. Harper hugs her dad before looking at me for my approval.

"Wow! I think you hit better than Mommy," I tell my girls, only half teasing.

"You'd better practice, Mommy," Harper states.

"I will practice if the two of you keep practicing," I encourage.

I do not want them watching me swing the club for the first time in many years. I do not want Maddux and Ryan to see how out of practice I am. I will take a big hit to my pride if I can't strike the ball farther than my little girls.

"Hit some," I prompt the girls. "I will watch while I stretch."

I grab my nine-iron, placing my hands on each end. Raising it above my head, I stretch my arms and back. I watch the twins move to their irons, listen to Maddux and Ryan, then swing two times. They are little pros, and it is only their first time with clubs in their hands. I will need to up my game in order to play with them.

In my area, I take three practice swings, my body protesting to the motion. I am using different muscles from swimming and might be sore after today. With the face of my nine-iron, I roll a ball from my tipped over bucket to the grass in front of me.

I feel eyes on my back, but I do not dare to look. I am sure Ryan and the girls will watch me. I set my feet, shifting my weight back and forth. *Awkward.* It feels awkward, but I am not sure if that is due to my not playing or the way I'm standing.

I spread my feet two more inches. *That feels better.* Bending my legs slightly, I swing. To my surprise, the ball arches high and lands in the circle around the red flag. *Not bad.*

"Not bad," Maddux states from behind me.

I did not see him move there; last I knew, he was helping Harper.

"Bro, did you say, 'Not bad'?" Ryan chides. "That was great! Nine-iron, right?"

I nod.

"One hundred yards with a nine-iron for the first time in six years is spectacular!" he cheers.

"Biased much?" Maddux teases.

I point my club in Maddux's direction. He raises his arms, returning to the girls. While the girls hit shot after shot. I hit a few balls with each of my irons in order. Not wanting to overdo it on my first day at the range, I hit the final five balls of my bucket with my driver and call it good.

"Two more hits each," Maddux coaches the twins.

Christy

I note an empty bucket by each of their areas, and another bucket more than two-thirds empty next to it. I would not be able to move tonight if I hit more than a bucket of balls today.

Harper throws the strap of her bag over her shoulder, and Ry allows Uncle Maddux to carry her clubs to the cart for her. I secure my bag on Maddux's cart, allowing the girls to return home with Ryan.

"I am proud of you," Maddux states, pressing the gas pedal.

"Me? Why?" I ask.

"It was not easy for you to join us today, but you did it." He does not look my way as he follows Ryan's cart up the path. "It means a lot to Ryan to do these things with the girls, and he told me he's worried about you."

I stare at his profile.

"He wants you to enjoy all that the club has to offer and not let the loophole they quoted in letting you go deter you," he shares with a glance in my direction. "So, I am proud of you for joining us on the driving range today. By the looks of it, the twins get their golfing skills from you."

"Ryan golfs," I state.

"Not very well," Maddux chuckles.

"He's out of practice. That's all," I argue.

Maddux smirks.

Perhaps I am too defensive. *I am.* I am defending Ryan, and Maddux reads into that.

"What did Ryan tell you today?" I ask.

"About what?" Maddux inquires.

"About the girls and me," I answer. "Did he tell you we are moving in with him?"

Saying the words out loud makes it seem even more real.

"Do you want to move in with Ryan?" Maddux refuses to answer my question.

"The twins living with Ryan is how it should be," I state.

"That is not what I asked."

"It is fast," I admit.

"For who? For the girls? For you?" he counters.

"Don't *you* think it is fast?"

"Christy, it does not matter what I think. It does not matter what my parents think. It does not matter what members at the club think. All that matters is the twins, Ryan, and you," he says, parking his cart in Ryan's driveway.

I nod.

He lowers his voice. "Do you want to move in with Ryan?" A tender smile forms on his face.

"I do," I murmur.

He wraps his arm behind my shoulders, squeezing me. "Good. Because Ryan loves you."

His words warm my heart. Ryan and the girls waiting for me in the garage feels natural. I am not sure how it is possible, but this feels easy and meant to be.

"And…" he drawls, low for only me to hear. "I knew you were moving in with Ryan on Friday night."

I begin to ask how, when he explains, "Brooks told me when you "camped out" Thursday night with Ryan that you officially moved in with him and would not be returning to her apartment. She said you just didn't know it yet," he chuckles. "She really does see the future."

19

MONDAY, JUNE 19TH

Christy

Monday morning, the doorbell rings while we enjoy breakfast. I tell Josh I will answer it.

"Surprise!" Jackie cheers when I open the front door.

I'm shocked to see Ryan's mom and Maddux on the doorstep.

"What's up?" I ask.

"I coaxed Maddux into taking a day off. We've come to take my granddaughters shopping," Jackie announces.

I raise an eyebrow.

"They need to fill their toy room," she defends.

I look at Maddux.

"You spoil them enough already. They are happy children with what they already own," I state.

"Christy, dear, it is my duty as Gigi to spoil them rotten and leave it to you to teach them to appreciate…"

"Stop right there," I order. "I have a rule; if—and it is a very big if—I agree to let them go shopping, both of you…" I pause, pointing from Jackie to Maddux and back, "…must follow my rule."

The two look at each other.

Jackie rolls her eyes before asking, "What is your rule?"

I place my hands on my hips. "For every fun toy you buy, you must choose two educational toys or books," I explain. "Ry and Harper know this rule. Sometimes, they try to work around it, but as adults, you can't let them trick you."

I point at each of them again. Maddux smiles wide.

"I agree."

His smile differs from Ryan's in that it is not crooked on the left side.

"If it means you will let me take my granddaughters shopping, then I agree," Jackie relents.

I cross my arms over my chest. "I need you to promise, Jackie."

"I promise. Educational toys," she huffs.

I nod, motioning for them to make their way to the girls in their room.

Maddux leans in close. "I promise to keep her reined in."

"Thank you," I grin, patting his shoulder.

I walk to the refrigerator.

Josh laughs. "You know she will never follow through on that promise."

With the door open and cold air on my face, I admit, "I know, but at least she might feel guilty enough to buy a few educational toys."

He taps his temple. "You are already learning how to handle Jackie."

I laugh, closing the door, a can of Diet Pepsi in my hand. "No one handles Jackie.

20

TUESDAY, JUNE 20TH

Christy

I stand in front of the full-length mirror in a gray and black striped golf shirt and gray shorts with a matching hat and shoes. Of the three shirts, this is by far my fav; gray is my favorite color.

Josh offered to buy more clothes for me, but I told him I would ask Brooks or Paige to take me shopping. Living on the course, I will need an entire summer wardrobe to wear to the driving range and golf, to the courts, and to dine. I am no stranger to country club life; I grew up in a much smaller, less prestigious club. I know what clothes I need to fit in. Besides, Josh shopping for my clothes is just plain weird.

I snap a photo of my reflection before exiting the closet.

> ME
>
> (selfie photo)
>
> wish me luck!

> golfing with ladies soon

>> BROOKS
>> u look cute!
>> have fun!
>> share gossip with me later

> ME
> (thumbs up emoji)

This would be so much easier if Brooks was a member and golfing with me today. Together, we could meet these ladies. Together, we could play golf and laugh, and I would worry less about fitting in.

When I emerge from the hallway, the girls color at the kitchen island while carrying on a conversation with Josh. He nods his chin in my direction, his hands covered in flour.

"I am heading to the course. Wish me luck," I say, waving as I approach the door to the garage.

"Good luck," the three call to my back.

>> PAIGE
>> headed your way

> ME
> (thumbs up emoji)

I guess there is no backing out of this now. I sigh deeply before opening the garage door. I hear the hum of Paige's electric cart in the driveway as I begin to remove my golf bag from our golf cart.

"Ready to tee it up?" Paige calls as I refasten the strap holding my bag.

"As ready as I will ever be," I respond. "I think I will drive my own cart today, if you don't mind."

"Of course," she responds. "Can I ride to the club with you then hop on Gibson's cart while we play?"

"Of course," I smile, happy to have my cart to myself today.

She makes quick work of securing her bag on the back of my cart then joins me on the seat. I pull out and press the remote to shut the garage door behind us. She pats my knee with her right hand.

"Do not fret," she soothes. "We play for fun, and you will love everyone in the group."

She shoots me a quick smile that does little to calm my discomfort. It is not the golfing that concerns me. It is the fact that the club fired me a mere week ago, and now I return as a member instead of an employee. I know the women in our group today from their visits to the swimming pool over the years. I never dreamt one day I would be golfing with them as an equal. I tell myself my nerves will subside when we leave the clubhouse for the first tee box.

As I park our cart along the edge of the path, Sandy announces we are playing the Pyke course this afternoon.

"Good. You made it," Sandy greets. "I hope you are ready for all of us. We get pretty rowdy."

I glance at Paige at the rear of my cart, unsure what she neglected to tell me. She simply shakes her head. Paige moves her clubs to Gibson's cart parked nearby.

"The others will meet us on the first tee," Sandy informs, climbing into her cart.

21

TUESDAY, JUNE 20TH

Christy

We drive along the cart path to the tee box where other carts wait for us. Along with Sandy, our fivesome includes Gibson and Morgan. Of the ladies in this tight-knit group, Gibson is the one I spent the most time talking to at the pool. Paige informed me Morgan is the oldest at 34. Paige is 30, Gibson is 27, and Sandy is in her mid-20s.

Also at the first tee, the group behind us holds more of their tight knit group. Brett, Gwynn, Robin, Ruth, and Sam will follow us during our round. According to Paige, they will join us for drinks afterward.

The Pyke's first hole doglegs slightly to the left and is 325 yards. I lift my driver from the center of my golf bag and grab a ball from its pocket.

"Want to go first or last?" Paige asks near my shoulder.

"Last if no one minds," I answer.

"Sounds good," she assures, signaling for the ladies to go ahead.

Sandy struts to the women's tee box, her tight blue shorts barely covering her butt cheeks. I cringe and look away when she bends at

Christy

the waist, placing her tee into the soft ground. Paige catches my averted eyes and waggles her eyebrows. I am not the only one uncomfortable with Sandy's golf ensemble.

I watch Sandy approach, swing, and hit her ball to the right side, in the rough near the tree line. She mumbles something under her breath, returning to her golf cart, club in hand.

Next, Morgan's drive flies about 145 yards and lands in the middle of the fairway. My eyes bug out at the realization that my new Birkenstock-wearing friend, to my shock, golfs barefoot. She drives her tee shot to the left edge of the fairway, roughly 200 yards. The other ladies do not seem surprised by her lack of shoes, so I assume this is common. Gibson's drive soars gracefully down the center, even with Paige's.

I am up. I mindfully steady my breaths, planting my wooden tee into the earth between the women's tee markers. I rest the head of my driver on the freshly trimmed green grass behind my ball. Happy with the height of my golf ball, I fiddle with my grip as I lift the club head off the ground. I inhale then swing as I exhale. My hips shift through my swing, and I hold my finished pose as I admire my drive. I am pleased at my position in the center of the fairway, only feet from Gibson's ball.

Like ripping off a bandage, I relax now that my first hit is a success and immerse myself in the conversation around me. The women banter easily between hits and while driving their red golf carts along the path and onto the fairway.

Our four carts converge behind Sandy's ball. Seemingly unfazed that her drive fell short of the others, she walks up to her ball, an iron in her hand.

Paige was right; these women are a riot. Time flies by as we golf —if you can call it golfing. I struggle to catch my breath; I'm laughing so hard my side aches. My eyes scan the grass and weeds within feet of the green.

"What color ball is it?" Gibson asks.

"Ummmm..." Sandy ponders, hands on her hips. "Pink."

Good. Now I know what color golf ball I am looking for.

"My ball is pink," Morgan chortles, crossing her legs to keep from peeing her pants.

"Really?" Sandy slurs, tilting her head. "Was it yellow?"

I freeze.

Sandy rubs her fingers over her mouth in thought.

"For the love of all things golf," Paige grumbles. "Can we drop a ball already? She does not even know what color ball she is hitting. Did anyone see her last shot?"

The four of us exchange glances.

"Sandy?" I call, approaching her. "Did you hit your ball from the sand?"

I watch Sandy's eyes grow wide and her jaw drop. I close my eyes.

"Come with me," I urge, my hand on her arm.

I help her onto my cart, turning it around and driving 50 yards from the green to the bunker where her second shot landed. I hop from the cart. At the edge of the sand trap, I place my hands on my hips, standing in disbelief.

"Grab my wedge and come hit your ball," I instruct my new, inebriated friend.

"Heads up, ladies," I yell towards the green. "We found Sandy's ball."

Raucous laughter explodes. Apparently, in hitting our final approach shots to the ninth green, four of us neglected to make sure Sandy hit her own ball. My hand on her forearm, I do not let her hit the ball until the others step farther from the front of the green. This takes some time as the women are still laughing.

I release Sandy's arm, stepping backward several steps to grab the rake. She teeters a bit, losing her balance as the sand shifts under her feet.

"I am okay," she assures me with a quick glance.

Christy

I watch as she draws my club back then sends copious amounts of sand and her white ball into the air. Taking pity on the rest of us, the golf gods guide her ball within four feet of the green.

When we are back at the green, I hand Sandy her putter from my cart and grab my own.

"In my defense, Gibson and the new girl—" Sandy's loud voice slurs as she points to first me and then in the general vicinity of Gibson, "—made me do too many birdie shots today."

"For the record, I am Gibson, your neighbor, and the new girl's name is Christy," Gibson somehow corrects amid her laughter.

I think my appendix might burst if I laugh any more. Sandy, unlike me, took all four birdie shots and kept drinking beer during the round. The other women downed the two birdie shots earned by Gibson and the two earned by me while I covertly poured water into my shot glass for three of them. I am a lightweight when it comes to drinking. I knew better than to attempt to golf while doing shots. Heck, I probably could not stand up after four shots in under two hours.

As the group behind us watch, Sandy chips onto the green, and we all putt.

"I have never drawn so many snowmen on my scorecard," Morgan declares as we place our putters in our bags.

One by one the other carts pull away.

"Follow me to the club house!" Sandy announces.

I am not sure she realizes the other carts have already departed. I decide I will follow her to make sure she does not wreck on her way. We golfed the front nine on the Pyke course today. The closest course to the club house; I am thankful it is a short drive. I type a text to Ryan as I drive.

ME

shot 2 under

headed to clubhouse

> will text when head home

> RYAN
> great job!
> no rush
> (photo of girls in swimming pool)

Judging by the photo, he is home from his work out and entertaining the twins in the backyard.

Gibson insists I join the ladies back at her house and I follow her cart as we drive from the club house toward the traditional drinks and food at her place.

"It is about time," Gibson's husband, Aaron, teases, a wide smile upon his face and his hands upon his hips.

"Behave," Gibson chides, swatting his shoulder as she walks by.

Aaron wraps his arm around my shoulders, steering me to follow his wife inside. "I am glad you joined us," he greets. "Ty is a phenomenal chef. I hope you are hungry."

Paige prepared me for the cocktails and food post-golf. I hedged, but Ryan insisted I hang with the ladies for at least an hour, promising to pick me up if I needed to escape.

"Food. I need food. I do not know how these women plan to drink more alcohol," I groan. "I am not a drinker, but they are…"

"Persistent? Overbearing? Incessant? Relentless? Interminable?" Aaron finishes for me.

"Fish," I claim. "They drink like fish."

Aaron chortles at my side. His hand falls from my shoulder, and I find a seat on a cushion between Morgan and Paige on the deck.

Christy

It amazes me that Ty and Aaron wait on these women hand and foot from Gibson's outdoor kitchen every Tuesday. Josh would absolutely love this set up. The full outdoor kitchen boasts a large grill, mini-fridge, small sink, a built in cooler, and plenty of cabinets.

"Drinks," Ty offers, placing a tray on the ottoman before us.

I marvel as the other four take the fancy cocktails in hand.

"Today, I made rosé lemonade for you," Ty boasts. When Sandy opens her mouth, Ty quickly continues. "I added the recipe to our Pinterest board. It contains fresh-squeezed lemonade, sugar, water, and rosé." He gives Sandy a wink.

"Yummy," Sandy sings.

"Ty, this is divine," Paige praises.

Not wanting to miss out, I decide I will take a tiny sip from the final martini glass on the black tray. They were not exaggerating. This is to die for. One sip not being enough, I pull out my cell phone.

ME

@ Gibson's

Aaron promised food

RYAN

having fun?

ME

I'm staying

need designated driver later

RYAN

(thumbs up emoji)

I lay my cell phone on the cushion beside me before sipping more of Ty's concoction. As promised, Aaron approaches with a tray.

"These are Ty's prosciutto-wrapped melons," he informs,

replacing the empty beverage tray with this professionally decorated wooden one.

Before me, a small tower of red, orange, and green decorates the small wooden skewers.

"Did you make these?" Gibson inquires, two skewers already in her hand.

"First, I dressed the cantaloupe logs in prosciutto then decorated them with mint leaves before adorning them with red and green grapes," Aaron brags, much to the delight of his wife.

My brow furrows as I wonder if this is some kind of foreplay for the two of them.

Ty places small napkins and saucers on each side of the tray, smiling at our moans of pleasure. We enjoy two skewers each and sip from cocktails.

"Next, Ty created strawberry and nectarine fruit bruschetta," Aaron shares, laying yet another tray before us.

Ty returns with a pitcher of rosé lemonade. It sparkles in the sunlight as large slices of lemon and strawberries float inside the glass container.

"Sandy, this recipe is also on the Pinterest board," he assures his neighbor. "We made a French baguette brushed with olive oil then lightly toasted it, covered it in a honey and goat cheese mixture, topped it with a fruit salsa of strawberries, nectarines, and French basil, then lightly bathed it in balsamic glaze."

"Ty, this is the bomb!" Sandy cheers, her mouth full.

I pinch one small bruschetta between my fingers, placing it onto my tiny plate. A color explosion of fruit sits atop white cheese and bread. I am not sure I will like goat cheese, but with all the alcohol I consumed this afternoon, I decide to give it a try. *Explosion indeed. Ty is a culinary master.*

"How is it?" he asks, observing my facial expressions as I try it.

"This may be the alcohol talking, but I think I just experienced my first mouth-gasm," I announce.

While Ty and Aaron laugh, the women to my left and right agree with my assessment. *Bliss. Devine.* I never thought food could give me such pleasure.

Needing to regain control, I refrain from enjoying more rosé lemonade, opting instead for water. Ty and Aaron disappear into the house, returning from time to time to refill our glasses. My head spins as I follow multiple conversations at once.

"Blind as a bat," Gibson declares loudly.

All conversation ceases, and everyone listens to her.

"It is not rocket science," Gibson claims. "I can't be the only one."

Morgan bursts into laughter.

"What happened?" Sandy asks for those of us late to the conversation.

"I can't read without my glasses or contacts," Gibson explains. "I do not wear my glasses in the shower. More than once, I've used soap to wash my hair and conditioner on my skin. The manufacturers type the words 'shampoo,' 'conditioner,' and 'body wash' smaller than the other words on the front of the bottles. Of course, the bottles are the same color, too."

"I've never done that. Have any of you?" Paige asks the group.

I glance around the deck as heads shake in unison.

"You want me to believe I am the only idiot that can't figure out my soap and shampoo?" Gibson scoffs.

"Nope. You are the only one using conditioner on your nipples," Sandy proclaims for all to hear.

I gasp, still unaccustomed to her bluntness. While working at the pool, I heard stories and gossip of her inappropriate behavior. Other members spoke of Sandy's loud voice, vulgar mouth, and trampy attire with disdain.

"You will learn to ignore her outbursts," Paige murmurs. "I can't say you will grow used to it, but you will see that there is no changing her."

"Sandy, what did you do now?" Aaron scorns, emerging from the house.

22

TUESDAY, JUNE 20TH

Ryan

I scour my digital calendar. As the season draws nearer, my time grows busier. My publicist and agent add appearances and sponsorships on an almost daily basis.

"I suggest the evening of Friday the thirtieth or Friday the seventh," Josh states.

"Both dates work for me," I share. "Can we throw it that fast?"

"Plan what that fast?" Christy's voice inquires as she enters the kitchen, brow furrowed.

"How was golf?" Josh asks, grinning.

She shakes him off. "Do not change the subject. What are we planning, Josh?"

Turning my gaze to him, I chuckle when Josh raises his hands, hoping to excuse himself from the conversation.

"Josh thinks I should hold a housewarming," I share. "He thinks I should invite a few guests from the club and my team."

Christy's face lights up before doubt enters her thoughts. I turn on my stool, pulling her between my legs. I remove her red cap and tuck stray hairs behind her ears.

Christy

"Josh and I talked about it. If we invite a few couples, it would be a great introduction for you to some of the other wives before the season starts," I explain.

"But I am not a wife," Christy protests, her voice low.

"I love you," I murmur, eyes glued to hers. "The term in the league is WAGs; I choose to use the word wife instead."

I watch her eyes cloud as she attempts to work out the acronym.

"Wives and Girlfriends. And you are not my girlfriend," I say before she can argue.

I ignore the pit in my belly at the thought I am sure crosses her mind. *She's much more than my live-in girlfriend—so much more. I need to work on making her understand that, too.*

"So, this housewarming..." Christy begins, looking at Josh. "How elaborate are we thinking?"

"Casual," I inform. "I'm only agreeing to this if we can keep it casual."

I do not miss Josh winking at Christy.

"I think the two of you should plan it, and I will show up," I offer.

"It is your house," Christy argues.

"It is our house," I counter.

"Then you should plan it together," Josh states, putting that part of our discussion to an end.

23

SUNDAY, JUNE 25TH

Ryan

The slight sound of the motorized shades lifting from the wall of windows rouses me from sleep as the warmth of the sunlight touches my skin. I extend my arms above my head, stretching from head to toe.

Umph.

"Daddy!" the twins exclaim, bouncing on the bed and my chest. "Daddy, wake up! We made you breakfast!"

I open my eyes, unsure what they are doing. *What time is it?* I chance a glance at my phone. *Six-thirty.* The girls never wake before me. *How are they up and claiming to have fixed me breakfast?*

"Daddy, look!" they say in unison as Christy enters the room, a tray in her hands.

I prop myself up on my elbows before scooting to sit against the headboard. The girls scramble to sit beside me as Christy places the tray on my lap. My bewildered eyes look into hers.

"Happy Father's Day," she says.

"Happy Father's Day, Daddy!" the girls yell.

"I made the toast," Harper announces. "Ry helped Mommy with the eggs, and I poured the juice."

"This...looks...delicious," I stammer. "Thank you."

"Look under your plate," Ry encourages.

I lift the plate, sliding two handmade cards from beneath. Ry drew me doing a touchdown dance in the end zone on the front of hers. Harper drew me teaching the two of them to golf on her cover. Opening the cards, I struggle to read the words they wrote. Phonetically, I can make out some but not all the words.

"Ry, read your card to Daddy," Christy suggests, coming to my rescue.

"Happy Fodder's Day, Daddy. I love you," Ry reads. "And I love fut baw."

Harper reads hers next. "Fodder's Day menz I love you, and I play fut baw wit you aw the tim."

It takes everything in me not to laugh at their words and the spelling. I have not been around many kids in grade school to know if this is how they write or not. Christy told me they were too smart for their age; I assume that includes writing words. The urge to call Mom to see if she kept any of my writing samples from kindergarten and first grade rises. I would love to compare them.

Oh, crap! It is Father's Day. I forgot to buy a card for Dad. Reading my expression, Christy pats my shin from the side of the bed.

"I bought a card for Uncle Maddux, Mr. Josh, and Grandpa. They're in the kitchen, and the girls plan to deliver them later today. I bought a card from the two of us for your dad, too."

She is truly one in a million. I feel like I am perpetually thinking I am one lucky guy to find her by my side once again.

24

TUESDAY, JUNE 27TH

Christy

Dinner complete, I prepare a bath for the girls while Ryan returns a call to his agent. I need to share my conversation with Gibson and then Ty after our round of golf today. I hope his call is not something that will consume his attention the rest of the evening.

I help the girls climb into the bathtub, quickly stepping back as their splashing begins. I stand at the door to the room, watching them pour water on each other, squirt each other, and the like. One would think these girls do not spend nearly every day in a swimming pool.

"Trying to stay dry?" Ryan's voice surprises me as he snakes his arms around my waist from behind.

I look over my shoulder into his warm blue eyes. Raising my chin, his lips meet mine. I lace my hands behind his neck, holding him to me.

"Stop it!" the twins giggle from across the room. "Stop kissing!"

I remove my hands from Ryan, placing them over the top of his on my belly. His cheek presses to the crown of my head as we watch our daughters laugh and play.

Christy

"How was your call?" I ask.

"Some local celebrities plan to attend the first week of camp," he explains. "He wanted to give me a heads up so I can read up on them and make conversation as there will be cameras everywhere."

I nod, glad it was not too distracting.

"I got offered a job today," I announce, anxious to hear his response.

"Oh really," he drawls. "The club saw the error of their ways and begged you to come back?"

I shake my head before turning in his arms to face him. I attempt to read his face, wanting to see how he feels about me working.

"You've golfed with Aaron and Ty a couple of times, right?" I ask, not waiting for a reply. "Ty purchased the vineyard that borders the Vale course. He's hiring for several positions. Gibson mentioned them to me while we golfed."

With no sign of protest in his facial expressions, I continue. "At Gibson's house, Ty told me about the event coordinator position. He's hiring for 20 hours a week to start, perhaps more during wedding season. He offered me the job on the spot. I told him I needed to talk to you first. If I accept the position, I would be able to work remotely—scheduling weddings, updating the website, and booking vendors—and on the days I need to be on site, I could bring the girls." I smile, catching my breath. "Unless there was an event that day."

Ryan

I hate the idea. I hate the idea of Christy working at all. I do not want her to work because she will not find the flexibility to be available anytime I am. I am greedy; I am selfish. Look at her eyes light up as she shares about this position. I can't ask her to wait at home 24/7 for me to be able to spend time with her and the girls.

She pats my chest.

"Soooo… What do you think? Can I tell him yes and give it a try for a month?" Christy looks up at me through hopeful brown eyes.

She looks like the 16-year-old girl I fell in love with in high school. She is so sweet, so giving, so loving…and so excited.

"It sounds perfect for you and our family," I answer. "Ty is lucky to have you on his team."

"Really?" she squeals, jumping up and down. "I can do it?"

"You do not need my permission," I inform her.

"Why is Mommy happy?" Ry asks.

"Mommy is going to start working a new job with our friend, Ty," I explain to the girls. "She is excited, and we should be excited."

The girls cheer with copious amounts of splashing. I watch water fly from the tub onto the tile wall and floor. *Why do I take pride that my girls can create such a mess? Is it because I am a guy?* I brush away the thoughts.

"Why don't you go call Ty?" I suggest. "I will watch the girls."

With a quick nod, Christy darts from the room, phone in hand.

25

FRIDAY, JUNE 30TH

Ryan

Josh and Christy outdid themselves. Our guests enjoy the burgers and brats Maddux and I grill, along with the appetizers, sides, munchies, and desserts provided by the caterer. Younger guests play yard games or swim under the watchful eye of a lifeguard, while adults visit on the patio, deck, and inside. Josh ensures the bartenders and waitstaff keep guests happy, and Brooks remains at Christy's side to make sure she has no reason to panic. *The event is a success.*

As I hang out near the grill with my teammates, Christy chats with Gibson, Paige, Aaron, and Ty. Her story has even the guys laughing loudly. I excuse myself, curious if they laugh at my expense.

"What's so funny?" I ask the group when I walk up behind my girl, hands coming to rest on her hips.

"Ryan," Ty greets.

"Great party, man." Aaron nods his chin in my direction. "Christy was entertaining us with the story of her first day golfing with the ladies."

"I have yet to meet Sandy; she sounds like a riot," I add.

"She keeps it interesting," Ty retorts.

"When are we going to hit the links again?" Aaron asks.

"I love you," I murmur, and I place a peck on Christy's cheek before moving closer to the guys. "I only have three weeks left before camp."

"We can squeeze in a round anytime you can find an opening," Ty offers.

"Maybe guys one time and couples the next?" Aaron suggests.

"I like the couples idea," I praise. "I will check my schedule tomorrow and send you some dates."

My thoughts drift to a more pressing matter. With dinner over, the party is winding down, and I am running out of time to make my speech. As if reading my mind, Josh approaches.

"You are officially off the clock," I inform, stepping towards him.

He looks over his shoulder at his partner, Paul, who is holding two drinks. "I may have already called it a night," he discloses.

"Thanks again for everything." I grab him by the shoulder. "You know I could not do it without you."

"He is amazing," Paul declares, returning a half-empty drink to Josh's hand.

"Are you ready?" Josh asks.

My nerves ratcheted up when the guests started arriving and again when the meal ended. I nod, a burning taste in my throat as my adrenaline spikes. I am still nodding.

It is Josh's turn to place his hand on my shoulder. "Simply say what comes naturally, and remember to thank your guests."

Still nodding, I watch Josh approach the bar, instructing them to turn off the music. I guess it is now or never.

"Everybody," I call, hands cupping my mouth. "Can I get everyone's attention please?"

As the crowd's murmurs cease, Josh pats me on the shoulder before joining his guest. I tuck my hands into my shorts pockets as I begin. "Christy and I would like to thank each of you for joining us tonight to celebrate the new house."

Christy

Christy moves to my side while the group claps. I toy with the box in my right pocket. *It is now or never.*

"And I thought, while I had our closest family and friends as a captive audience, I'd..." I drop to my knee, extending the ring box towards the only woman I have ever loved.

I open the black velvet box with my left hand as it sits in the palm of my right. The crowd gasps, quietly awaiting Christy's reaction. I watch her eyes tear up as she fans her face. Then she laughs.

Laughs?

"Is this a joke? There's no ring," she asks out loud, laughing nervously.

"It is a joke," Maddux loudly announces to my horror.

What. The. Hell? He's ruining my perfect moment. *Does he not see I am proposing?*

He whispers something into Christy's ear, and she nods before he addresses the crowd.

"The joke is on Ryan," my brother tells the group, his hands cupping Christy's shoulders from behind.

He looks over her, down at me, a devilish grin upon his face.

Together, Christy and Maddux turn from me toward our guests.

"You see, unbeknownst to Ryan, Christy also planned to propose tonight," Maddux explains, and the crowd laughs. "She reached out to me earlier this week for help in getting Ryan's ring size."

Christy

That's my cue. I turn towards Ryan, extending my own little black, velvet box, opened in his direction as I drop to one knee.

I watch his shock morph to laughter while I wait for Ryan's answer. Instead, I watch him shake his head no. *What the heck? Is my proposal not valid since he asked me first?*

"But the joke is also on Christy," Maddux declares, and the crowd erupts.

I peek into the ring box to find it as empty as Ryan's. In horror, I look at Maddux. He stands beside me, a devilish grin upon his face.

"Seems these two love birds forgot to ask the two most important people to help." Maddux points to the pool. "Ry and Harper, it is your turn," he announces.

I watch my daughters emerge from the swimming pool, shaking their heads as they approach their uncle. Neither look in the direction of Ryan or me. Maddux bends down, allowing the girls a private conference. As they talk, their little hands and arms move animatedly until they both point behind them to the swimming pool. Maddux drops to his knees at the edge of the pool, peering into the deep end.

"I have got this," Brooks growls, passing me toward them. "What is going on?" she asks, loud enough for the guests to hear.

"I...um..." Maddux stammers.

"The rings are down there," the twins announce in unison, pointing to the pool.

I gasp, and Ryan wraps his arms around me.

"They are insured," he whispers as a reminder to both of us.

Maddux, no longer smiling, stares wide-eyed in our direction. One second his apologetic gaze is on me; the next, he dives headfirst into the swimming pool. As a group, we watch in horror as he dives over and over, only surfacing for a quick breath.

"Maddduxxx!" Brooks yells loudly the next time he returns to the surface.

All eyes move to my friend, who stands at the edge of the pool, the twins hugging her legs and her hands upon her hips.

"You just had to be a prankster," she scolds loudly. "You just had to ruin not one but two perfect proposals." She points at him. "Shame on you, Uncle Maddux. I can't believe you would use your little nieces in your evil plan."

She pries the girls' arms from her legs, taking their hands and leading them to us.

Christy

Turning back to Maddux, she asks what we all want to know: "What were you thinking?"

Still treading water in the deep end of the pool, Maddux defends himself. "I thought it would be cute to let the girls hand the two rings to their parents. So, I placed a ring on a safety pin and attached it to each of the girls' swimsuits."

The girls lift the outer leg of their swimsuits, displaying the large safety pins sans our rings. Then, while Ry leans in to whisper in my ear, Harper whispers in her father's. I stare, disbelieving what I heard.

"Really?" Ryan asks, and I see Harper nod in my periphery.

"Maybe if a few more adults hop in the pool, we will find the rings on the bottom," Maddux offers, looking at the guests.

Before anyone volunteers, Brooks announces, "That will not be necessary." She bends at the pool's edge, waving for Maddux to approach her. "You see, the joke is on you, Maddux."

The twins jump up and down, cheering, "We got you! We got you!" as they point to him.

"The joke is on you, Uncle Maddux," Brooks barbs. "You really thought it prudent to give expensive and important rings to five-and-a-half-year-olds?" she tisks, shaking her head. "What were you thinking?"

"First..." Standing once again, she holds up one finger. "They are little girls." She waves two fingers towards him now. "Second, they are not even six."

Now, as Brooks speaks, my daughters hold up their own fingers for the group counting.

"Third, your two nieces can't keep a secret," Brooks informs him. "The first time they saw me after you spoke to them, they told me everything. And I mean everything. Like how you originally planned to tie the rings to the suits until Ry asked, 'What if they come untied?' and you then decided to pin them."

Brooks raises her hands and shoulders as if asking what a woman is to do.

"So, when I arrived, I asked the girls to let me hold the rings. I can't believe you did not even ask to see the rings once in the past four hours." She pauses for effect, scanning the crowd.

"When it looked like Josh and Ryan were preparing for the first proposal, I shared a new plan to play a trick on you, Uncle Maddux. And to make sure they kept my secret for 15 minutes, I told them they had to swim until you asked them to climb from the pool."

She stands above Maddux as he sits on the pool's edge. "And that is how you pull off a prank of this magnitude."

The crowd jeers and boos at Maddux.

"Soooo…" Ryan yells, once again demanding everyone's attention. "So, now can I have the ring? I want to propose properly to…"

"Uh-uh," I protest. "I am proposing to you."

While our family and friends laugh, we exchange rings before Ryan plasters an inappropriate-for-public kiss upon my lips.

26

MONDAY, JULY 3RD

Christy

Ty emerges from his office, a giant smile gracing his face.

"It's a done deal," he announces.

I furrow my brow.

"I just got off the phone with Ryan's business manager," he explains. "By the end of the week, Ryan and Maddux will officially be my business partners."

It is a relief to see his excitement at this development. I worried it might seem as if my husband was forcing himself on Ty because I worked here.

"I think I will start gathering items to set up the wedding space to take promotional photos," I tell Ty as he passes my spot at the end of the bar.

He pauses at my words, pursing his lips.

"What?" I ask.

"I wish there was a way to take the promotional photos at a real wedding," he states. Thinking out loud, he continues. "The atmosphere would be realistic; we would have more than our staff to dress up and pose."

"It would save us money instead of faking it all," I add.

"Yep. But we need the photos to get our first bookings," Ty says, shaking his head.

"Not necessarily."

"How is that?" Ty asks.

Did I say that out loud?

"We could hold my wedding here," I share.

"When does Ryan report to camp?" Ty grows more excited by the second.

This would be a huge boost for the vineyard—not only its first wedding at the venue but a local celebrity wedding.

"July twenty-seventh," I answer.

"Can you do everything in less than a month?" Ty asks skeptically.

"First, let me text Ryan to see if it is okay with him," I say.

"Maybe this is something to ask over a phone call?" our restaurant manager Kirby suggests, chuckling.

I did not think all this through, I think to myself while the phone rings at my ear. *What do I say? "Hey, honey, I volunteered us to hold our wedding at the winery before you go to camp. I hope that is okay?" Maybe he will not answer, and I can think about what to say.*

"This is a surprise," Ryan greets.

"Hi, honey… um… I kinda did something," I stall.

He laughs. "Okay."

"I did not think you would find an issue with it, so I sort of volunteered us to do something, but… Ty suggested I call and make sure it was okay before we move forward."

"Babe," Ryan prompts.

"Oh, sorry." I regroup. "Want to get married—"

"Yes!" he interrupts.

"I am not finished," I chide, giggling.

"Okaaayyy," he chortles.

"Want to get married before you head to camp?"

I am no longer nervous about his answer. His quick "yes" to getting married settled all my nerves.

"Count me in," he answers. "When?"

Christy

"Umm...like Saturday the eighth or Saturday the fifteenth?" I suggest.

"You pick the date. Anything on my calendar is moveable for our wedding," he explains.

"Then let's say the fifteenth," I tell him, giving me an extra week to plan it all. "We can talk more about it after work."

"Let's do it!" he cheers and disconnects.

"He's all in," I announce. "Let's do this!"

Nerves flutter like butterflies in my stomach. *Did I really suggest I get married in 12 days? Ryan's mom is going to kill me.*

I begin making a mental inventory of all I need to do. *I need to utilize the barn, the catering we provide, the scenery... We should get photographers and florists. The guest list could be the same as housewarming... But add all the lady golfers. And do we need the entire football team? No. I prefer to keep it intimate. Brooks! Oh, my gosh!* I open my texts.

ME

call me ASAP

need 5 min

Immediately, I hear an incoming call from my best friend.

"Hello," I greet, still deciding what to say.

"What's up?" she asks.

"I am getting married," I state.

"Um...I know," Brooks chuckles. "I was in on the proposal fun. Remember?"

"Ha ha," I snark. "I am getting married on the fifteenth. The fifteenth!"

This time, she has no comeback. *I guess that means she did not see our wedding in her visions.*

"Now I have your attention," I tease.

"You could say that." I hear the door to her office close. "Why the rush?"

"Ty and I were brainstorming at work today," I share. "He

mentioned it would be nice to hold a practice wedding to work out all of the kinks and to showcase the venue the winery now provides."

"So, you volunteered," she surmises. "Should we see if Ryan is okay with it?"

"Duh. I asked him first," I laugh.

"So, we are really doing this in…" She pauses, counting the days under her breath. "…in 12 days. We are planning the perfect wedding and pulling it off in 12 days."

"It does not need to be perfect," I start to say, but she interrupts me.

"It has to be perfect," she argues. "My best friend's one and only wedding has to be perfect."

Well, I like her fortitude.

"I get to be the maid of honor, don't I?"

"Of course!" I squeal. "So, you will help me throw it all together in less than 12 days?"

"As your best friend and maid of honor, it is my duty to do it. But we are not throwing anything together; we will instead be planning your perfect, fairytale wedding."

I roll my eyes, although she can't see me. "I do not want a fairytale," I scoff.

"You want a happily ever after, don't you? Of course, you do. That is the only reason to get married. You deserve your fairytale. And I will be damned if I am not going to give you a fairytale wedding."

I do not dare to interrupt her rant.

"I guess we have 12 days to plan a fairytale wedding," I laugh.

Ryan

Christy

"Guys, I need to call it a day," I tell my teammates from my seat on the bench press.

"Coach does not like quitters," my quarterback, Nolan, taunts, standing over me as a spotter.

"It is urgent." I throw my towel in the nearby bin and snag my water. "Consider yourselves all invited to my wedding on Saturday the fifteenth at Tryst Valley Vines Winery," I mic drop as I exit through the door.

My fingers fly on my phone screen as I make my way to the parking lot and my SUV.

> ME
> call me ASAP
> urgent, not 911
>
> MADDUX
> 2 min
>
> ME
> (thumbs up)

I place my cell phone in its holder and set my path for home. I am not yet to the interstate when my brother's call rings through the hands-free of my vehicle.

"What's up?" Maddux asks as I connect the call.

"Are you free on Saturday the fifteenth?" I ask as the weight of this event settles in.

"Umm..." He draws out while accessing his calendar. "Maayybee. Why?"

Crap! I did not consider what I would do if Maddux was busy that day. I wonder if Christy made sure Brooks was free before setting the date.

"Dude," Maddux's voice booms through the speakers. "I am kidding; I am free. So, what are you planning?"

I breathe a sigh of relief.

"Ryan?" Maddux's voice grows concerned.

"My wedding," I answer.

I wait as he processes my words.

"Will you be my best man?" I ask.

"Of course! I owe you the wedding gift to beat all wedding gifts."

"Why is that?"

"In less than a month, you gave Mom a daughter-in-law and two granddaughters," Maddux states, and I chuckle.

"You laugh, but she has been riding me hard for over five years now to settle down and give her grandchildren."

I continue to laugh while I drive.

"It is not easy to be the oldest child," he informs. "She started in on me during my senior year of college, and the pressure has grown in each of the five years since then."

"C'mon," I scoff.

"I am serious. You bought me at least two years until she starts in again," Maddux chuckles. "And if you put a baby in Christy on your honeymoon…"

"Stop!" I bark through my laughter. "I will need to pull over if you do not stop making me laugh."

"So, why the rush to the alter? You put another baby or two into Christy already?" he jokes.

"Keep talking about my wife like that and I will find myself another best man," I tease back.

"I will behave," he chuckles.

"No, you won't."

"No, I won't," he agrees.

"Christy and Ty want to showcase the wedding venue, and instead of setting up a faux wedding for photographs, they thought it would be better to host a real wedding," I explain.

"So, Christy suggested yours, and you went along with it…" he thinks out loud, laughing.

"If I had my way, we would have eloped already," I confess.

"If you had your way, she would have been a child bride," he chortles.

"I would have waited until she turned 18," I argue.

Christy

"News flash, you did not wait until she was 18 to—"

"Touché," I interrupt before he can finish his statement.

"I got the call moments before I texted you. I am headed home to start helping Christy plan," I inform.

"I thought she planned to work until four today while Josh entertained the twins."

He's right.

"I need to let you go. I need to call and see where she is."

"I am happy for you. Congrats, brother," Maddux offers before disconnecting our call.

My car parked in the garage, an idea pops into my mind. I scroll through the names until I find Brooks.

ME
free tonight?

BROOKS
yes

if doesn't involve Maddux

ME
need a sitter

BROOKS
always

your place or mine?

ME
want to celebrate setting date

BROOKS
my place

I will keep girls

drop them off in morning

> **ME**
> you're the best!

> **BROOKS**
> I won't let you forget that

> **ME**
> (thumbs up emoji)

My mind scrambles; we can go out to eat, light candles, enjoy a bubble bath, then a massage before turning in for the night.

"Why are you grinning?" Christy asks.

"I have a surprise for you."

"Is it like me surprising you with a wedding date?" she counters.

"No." I kiss her forehead, taking her laptop bag from her. "I arranged for the girls to stay with Brooks overnight."

This gets her attention. My hand at the small of her back, I guide her inside. We remove our shoes and empty our arms in the mud room.

"I will meet you in the bedroom in a minute." I swat her butt, shooing her away.

In the kitchen, I share my impromptu plans with Josh, and I ask him to secure us a good reservation for tonight. He agrees to try but mentions it might be romantic for the two of us to cook our own dinner together.

"I bought all the ingredients. I can print the recipes before I leave. The two of you can still dress up to make it special." He leans against the counter, waiting for my response.

"What would we be making?" I inquire before I decide.

"I have everything to make shrimp scampi, steak and potatoes, or…" He peeks into the refrigerator and pantry. "…chicken parmesan."

"You gotta help me," I plead. "Which should I choose?"

"Christy loves shrimp and steak," Josh shares. "The shrimp scampi would allow the two of you to cook longer together, so I suggest shrimp."

Christy

I nod, patting him on the back. "Print the recipe then take the rest of the day off."

"I love my job," he sings, waving over his shoulder as he wakes his iPad.

"See you tomorrow," I call on my way toward the bedroom.

"I need a shower," I mouth to Christy while she talks to my mom via video call in our room. "Join me."

She swats the empty air as if brushing me off. I do not close the bathroom door. Instead, I drop my clothes to the floor and step into the shower.

To my disappointment, Christy does not join me in the shower. Wrapping a towel around my waist, I hear her voice along with my mother's in our bedroom.

I wonder if she dropped the wedding date bomb and how Mom reacted?

At the threshold of my closet, I decide on a different path. I stand at the foot of our bed, while Christy tries her best to ignore me, focusing on her video call.

Not to be ignored, I turn my back to her and playfully peek over my shoulder. With my thumb, I dip the towel, exposing some of my butt, teasing her. Her words falter, signaling I am affecting her.

Next, I unwrap the towel from my waist. I tug it to the right and left, lowering it an inch at a time. It is not a striptease; I plan to save that for a time Mom is not video chatting with her.

"Jackie, I need to let you go," Christy informs through her giggle.

I block out the boner-killing sound of my mother's voice when I secure the towel around my waist and turn to face Christy.

"What do you think you are doing?" She laughs, dropping her phone on the bed beside her.

I grab her ankles, tugging her down the mattress. She lies motionless before me, aware of my intentions. Taking her hands in mine, I pull her to a standing position in front of me.

Christy's eyes scald my abdomen and my chest on their way up to mine.

Christy

Back in the kitchen, we find the house eerily silent. Ryan strides to the refrigerator, pulling out a fresh water bottle while I scan our surroundings. I find a note in Josh's handwriting on the kitchen island.

> **Brooks picked up the twins.**
> **I emailed instructions for dinner to Ryan.**
> **Have fun, you two.**
> **—Josh**

I quirk a brow at Ryan, causing him to chuckle.

"At first, I planned to take you out to dinner to celebrate setting our wedding date but then decided we could stay in and cook together," he explains with a shrug.

"Really?" I ask, excited at the notion.

"Would you like to make shrimp scampi with me?" he offers, his sexy grin and dimple bright.

I clap like the girls often do when excited. Ryan opens the kitchen iPad and the recipe in his email. He places it on the counter in front of us.

"Confession time," he smirks. "I've probably only cooked two meals in the last six years. You may need to coach me."

I fight my smile for a moment.

"Let's set out all the ingredients first," I suggest, pointing to the items in the recipe.

"I love you," Ryan murmurs at my shoulder.

"I love you, too," I giggle, turning into him.

"I'll get the shrimp, lemons, and butter," he states before placing a kiss on the tip of my nose. "We need to send photos to Mom. She'll never believe I am cooking."

My heart feels as if it might burst. The man I love planned a perfect date night for the two of us. I love shrimp, and I'd rather dine in than in the presence of his fans. He loves me; I have no doubt. Ryan is a perfect father for Ry and Harper. He loves with all his heart. And yet, he is still a little boy, seeking his mother's praise.

27

TUESDAY, JULY 4TH

Ryan

"I am going to work out here today," I inform Christy as I fetch water from the refrigerator. "What time will you pick up the girls?"

Hearing laughter, I turn towards her. I am still awestruck that this gorgeous woman is back in my life, let alone living with me.

"Believe it or not, they are here," Christy tells me, glancing over her shoulder towards the bedrooms. "They are drawing pictures of the tattoos they want."

I quirk my head, hearing nothing. Christy nods.

"They are only this quiet when they sleep," I chuckle. "Did you threaten them or something?"

"Nope," she smiles. "They wanted new art to hang on their door, and since they left their latest drawings on Brooks's fridge, they wanted to draw new ones."

She raises her index finger to her lips. I stifle my groan. It is hard enough to work out for hours with them here. If I think of her mouth, I will never make it to the gym. *Look up. Look up.* I tell myself. I attempt to focus on her eyes, but even those attempt to distract me from my mission.

Christy

"Shh..." she urges. "Let sleeping dogs lie. Go workout. I am sure they will be glued to the two of us the rest of the day."

She shoos me away with a flick of her kitchen towel. Descending the steps, I wonder what she is doing in the kitchen and where Josh is. I find part of my answer in the basement. I see him on his knees, filling the lower shelves of the bar fridge with juice boxes and tiny water bottles.

"Hey," I wave, walking past him.

"Working out here today?" Josh asks.

I nod, smiling.

"Christy plans to use the fitness center, too," he informs, causing me to pause mid-step. "I caught her on her way down here. She's watching bars for me in the oven while I finish this task."

I feel my cheeks grow with a smile; I like the thought of working out with her for a bit. When my thoughts drift to Christy in tiny workout attire, I worry working out at home might not be a good idea.

"Done!" Josh announces, dusting off his knees and waving.

I stride towards the gym, needing to start my work out before she enters the room. When it comes to my woman, I only have a limited amount of willpower. I report to camp soon, and football season draws closer; I need every workout I can get to prepare.

I am five minutes into my session on the elliptical when Christy arrives.

"Room for me in here?" she asks, peeking her head and shoulders into the room.

"Get in here," I answer, not breaking my stride.

"I am gonna lift a few weights," she declares, running her fingers across the top rack of hand weights.

I fight the urge to suggest she start with the five-pound weights instead of the tens. I tell myself, *If she wants my advice, she will ask for it.* I know she is no stranger to weights and cardio; I have had my hands—and mouth, for that matter—on every inch of her recently. I chide my straying thoughts.

"Talk to your brother lately?" she asks, toying with her grip on the weights.

"Not since calling to ask if he would be my best man yesterday," I answer, wondering why she is asking.

"He had his first tattoo session yesterday with Brooks," she shares. "She mentioned it to me when she brought the girls home this morning. He was the last appointment she had. The twins watched some of it, and that is why they are now drawing their own tattoos."

I shake my head once, seconds before the preset workout program increases speed and tension on the machine.

"I do not like the thought of them getting tattoos," I state, bile rising in my throat.

Christy chuckles, her gaze meeting mine in the wall of floor-to-ceiling mirrors.

"You went straight to hidden tattoos and guys seeing them, didn't you?"

I grit my teeth, my clenching jaw the only answer she receives.

"Back to my story," she giggles, raising the hand weights overhead before lowering them to her sides again. "There was something about him helping her on the computer with a spreadsheet then inviting her and the twins to join him for dinner and a movie."

I watch Christy complete her first rep of 10 as she talks. Her words barely register as I enjoy watching the long, lean muscles in her arms and shoulders flex.

"Ryan?" Christy's annoyed tone catches my attention.

I shake away my thoughts, concentrating hard on listening to her instead of losing myself in the visual.

"Does it?" she asks, weights now on her hips and facing me.

Searching my mind, I can't figure out what she is asking.

With a huff, Christy continues, "It sure sounds like a date to me, but I will never tell Brooks that."

I smile, pushing through a difficult part of the workout.

"She can deny it all she wants, but I see the way she looks at Maddux; she is into him," Christy claims. "Entertaining the twins was an excuse for the two of them to eat together. If Maddux really found Brooks as annoying as he acts, he never would invite her out to eat, with or without the twins."

Christy

"Wait. What? Maddux went out to eat with Brooks last night?" I ask, having now heard her.

She gives me a knowing look. It is the "you did not hear a word I said" look. I pause the elliptical, toweling myself off while it slows down. I make my way across the room toward my gorgeous woman. Although she tries to be mad, she melts into my arms.

"I heard you," I murmur at the top of her head. "It took time to register. It is hard to focus with you dressed like this while lifting weights."

My hands start on her hips and move to her backside, squeezing suggestively, pulling her tighter to me. Her palms on my chest, she presses to escape in protest.

"I am not trying to keep you from working out," she states, wiggling in my arms. "I will go."

"No, you will not," I growl, my mouth nipping her ear playfully.

"That was hot," I rasp through my ragged breaths.

"I interrupted your workout," she murmurs, her face against my neck.

"I welcome this interruption any time," I say as I lift her face to mine. "I love you. I missed you so damn much. I love you so hard."

"I love you so hard, too." She laughs, stepping away. "I need a shower."

"I will join you," I offer.

She presses her palm to my bare shoulder.

"We were lucky to get this time alone. I doubt we will be able to walk through the house and to our room without being noticed," she states then places a peck on the corner of my mouth.

"I will offer them screen time," I counter, my hands pulling her to me.

"That's your answer for everything," she chuckles. "I will go shower; you finish your workout. We can't have you flabby at the beginning of the season."

"What would you think about golfing with Maddux this afternoon?" I ask, following her from the fitness center. "You could invite Brooks to ride with us."

Christy

"Let's talk colors and themes." I lead the conversation. "We need those in order to choose flowers, table settings, and everything else."

"Weeellll," Brooks chuckles, "it is your wedding, so what colors do you want?"

Hmm... I am not sure. When I envisioned my wedding, I wore white, and Ryan dawned a black tux. I never really imagined the bridesmaids and decorations.

"It is a summer wedding, and it is in July," she thinks out loud.

"Gray is my favorite color," I remind her.

"You can't have a gray wedding," she scoffs. "But you could do a dusty blue and yellow theme."

As I move our cart to the next hole, I try to envision it. Always helpful, she opens the Pinterest app on her phone, and she shows me several pins. She pulls her phone back, scrolling through other posts while I prepare to tee off.

I watch Ryan finally outdrive Maddux on the par three. Now, it's my turn; I approach the women's tee box, plant my tee into the ground, and address my ball. My swing is smooth, and my ball soars to the green. It bounces on the front edge, rolling within 10 feet of the hole. I turn back toward the carts amid golf-clap applause. I curtsy, which elicits laughter from the peanut gallery. I return my iron to my bag and drive the cart to the green.

"Here are some gray and dusty blue color schemes," Brooks says, showing me her phone as I steer. "Or we could choose dove—a.k.a gray—dusty blue, and yellow."

I look at more pins.

"You know I love my gray. I mean dove." I laugh. "Let's choose dove, dusty blue, and yellow."

"Yay! We made a decision," Brooks cheers. "Shot time!"

Of course, Maddux likes the idea of shots. He promptly pours four shots in our disposable shot glasses on the seat of the guys' golf cart.

"This is absolutely the last shot I am doing today," I profess. "I need to be coherent for the girls tonight."

"We chose the color scheme for the wedding," Brooks informs the guys.

"I also need to be sober to make more wedding plans," I add, looking pointedly at my friend.

We clink our plastic glasses, downing the peppermint liquor that Maddux packed today.

"I feel like I sucked off a candy cane," Brooks sputters.

"That can't be the worst thing you've swallowed," Maddux retorts, then promptly heads toward the green.

Brooks opens her mouth, venom threatening to spill, but I halt her with my hand.

"Please don't," I plead. "It is only the third hole, and we have at least six more to go."

She nods, stomping back to our cart. I bite back my laugh as I join the men on the green.

"Next decision," Brooks prompts when I return to the cart. "Time of wedding and reception."

I purse my lips. "I want it to be early enough that the girls are not crabby but cool enough to be outside in July."

"Well, it is July; heat is a given," she says.

"If the wedding is at six, cocktails at seven, and dinner at eight…"

"The girls are ready for bed at eight," she says what I know. "We could make them take a nap. I know they gave those up long ago, but if they know they have your wedding, they might not fight us."

"It is a gamble," I agree. "What if the ceremony is at six and dinner is at seven? Then, if they grow tired, they are done with all of their duties. We could do appetizers and cocktails at five."

"How would that work before the wedding?"

Reading her mind, I answer, "Ryan and I are not worried about seeing each other before the wedding. We can mingle between taking some photos."

She raises an eyebrow.

"Lady luck is on our side; she already brought us back to one another," I explain.

"So, the cocktail hour and photos will start at five, ceremony at six, and dinner at seven," she restates as she types it into my notes app.

"Band or DJ?" Brooks queries.

"DJ," we say in unison and giggle.

"Open bar, right?" she asks, and I nod. "That leaves flowers. I think that needs to be decided with the florist. I do not know enough to help you there. The rest of the details are for you and your event staff."

"Thank you for helping." I place my hand on hers.

"Shut up," she chides. "I am your best friend. Besides, it is in the duties for the maid of honor."

"Still, I appreciate everything you do for me and the girls." I lick my lips while fighting tears.

"Let's talk about my wedding gift." Brooks changes the subject. "I'd like to give each of you a tattoo."

That catches me off guard. As soon as the words are spoken, the idea grows on me. I stop the cart, setting the brake.

"I love it!" I hug my friend.

"Girls…" Maddux feigns disgust. "Not on the golf course."

Brooks opens her mouth, leaning in Maddux's direction.

"Play nice," I scold. "You are upset we talked you into joining us. Don't take it out on Maddux."

My friend scowls at me from the passenger side of my golf cart.

"I wanted to use this time to do some wedding planning with you," I remind her. "We are killing two birds with one stone."

"Fine," she spits.

"One of these days, I am going to talk you into golfing with me," I taunt.

"Good luck," she scoffs.

28

TUESDAY, JULY 4TH

Christy

Lounging by the pool in the late afternoon sun, I listen to the twins play with Ryan and Maddux in the water.

"Oh, my god," Brooks chuckles. "Did you read this?"

I tilt my head.

"Read what?" I ask.

"Today's *Back 9 Talk* post," she answers.

"Why the heck are you following that crap?" Ryan snarls, joining us at the patio table by the pool.

"I figured I needed to. Someone needs to know if they talk anymore sshhii...crap about you," Brooks defends.

"Swear jar!" Harper yells from the shallow end of the pool.

Caught up in the conversation, I did not notice the twins had moved to our end of the pool.

"Busted," Maddux chuckles, taunting Brooks.

"Anyway," Brooks drawls, giving Maddux a glare. "It sounds like we missed the drama of today's pool party at the club."

She slides her phone to me.

Christy

Back 9 Talk

Shame on you… The Fourth of July children's pool party paused for over an hour when several children found "balloons" (a.k.a. condoms to us adults). Shame on you for ruining it for the children. Parents of prankster teenagers, rein them in at club activities and on the premises.

"Gross!" I cringe. "Why would someone do this to kids?"

To my horror, Ryan and Maddux chortle loudly.

"Epic," Ryan laughs.

"I wonder if they blew them up themselves or used helium?" Maddux howls.

"What's so funny?" Harper asks, climbing the pool steps.

"Nothing," Ryan and Maddux shout, causing Brooks and I to giggle.

I do not look forward to the twins growing up, but these two already fear the dating years.

"I would opt for helium," Brooks states.

"What?" I ask, unable to follow her in our conversation.

"I would never put my mouth on a…" She looks sideways at the twins, who are now wrapped in towels on the nearby loungers. She shutters. "My lips do not touch prophylactics."

Oh. Now, I get it. The three of them were contemplating whether the pranksters used their mouths or helium to blow up the condom balloons. *Again, why would anyone do this? Yuck.* Ryan and Maddux chuckle like teenage boys, scrolling through the three photos included with the post.

"Grow up," Brooks chides, plucking her phone back from them.

"Can you imagine?" I shake my head in dismay.

"If my daughters found or touched those today…" Ryan growls. "Let's just say I would want someone's job."

"Let's not go there." I hope to put an end to this discussion.

Ryan pulls out his phone.

"What are you doing?" I inquire.

"Hmm... Nothing," he mutters.

"Found it!" Maddux announces, extending his phone to his brother.

"Followed," Ryan states.

Seriously? These two grown men now follow the gossip blog?

"Cheerleading is not a sport," Maddux states.

"Say what?" I scoff, as I return from putting the girls to bed for the night.

"You did not just claim cheerleading is not a sport," Brooks chides, glaring at him.

She mumbles something under her breath. I am sure they are obscenities.

"If anything, golf is not a sport," she counters.

"Now, you are smoking crack," Maddux retorts.

"Did you just say 'smoking crack'?" Ryan asks his brother.

"She's crazy to suggest golf is not a sport," Maddux defends.

"Crazy, huh?" Brooks jibes. "Golf is a long walk where you occasionally hit a ball. Is walking a sport?"

Maddux acts personally offended by her comments.

"And you think cheerleading is a sport?"

"Do you consider gymnastics a sport?" Brooks counters.

Ryan and I look back and forth between the two of them as they bicker.

"Yes," Maddux answers.

"Well," Brooks pauses, throwing her hands wide, "cheerleaders jump and tumble as they yell."

Maddux looks to his brother for help. Ryan shakes his head at him.

"Here," Ryan says, taking out his phone and thumbing to an app. "Watch this and see what you think."

Christy

I wonder what YouTube video Ryan found quickly enough to show his brother. Maddux watches the video, and Brooks looks over his shoulder. Her wide, green eyes dart from the screen to me then back.

"That's Christy!" she proclaims.

My brow furrows.

"You have a video of Christy cheering on your cell phone!" Brooks announces in disbelief.

Maddux points to the phone screen, looking over at his brother. "You kept this video on your phone for six years?"

Ryan's sun-kissed cheeks pinken.

Maddux taps and scrolls on Ryan's phone. "Every time you bought a new cell phone, you moved these photos and videos with you."

Ryan grabs his phone back, tucking it into his shorts pocket.

"Dude," Maddux lowers his voice, stepping closer to Ryan. "I know you loved her and missed her, but you never told me you kept these photos and videos."

A heavy lump lodges in my throat. It is one thing to store items on the cloud; it is another to download them over and over to new cell phones. I was not simply a memory to him. He made an effort to keep me in his life, too.

When my thoughts return to the present, I realize Brooks and Maddux no longer argue. Instead, they carry on a quiet conversation.

29
WEDNESDAY, JULY 5TH

Christy

Kansas City Cardinals
  <u>Preseason</u>
  8/28 Home   Houston Oilmen
  9/3 At   Dallas Wranglers
  <u>Regular Season</u>
  9/10 At   Arizona Blue Jays
  9/14 Home   Los Angeles Bolts
  9/24 At   Indianapolis Mustangs
  10/1 At   Tampa Pirates
  10/9 Home   Las Vegas Renegades
  10/15 Home Buffalo Bison
  10/22 At   San Francisco Miners
  10/29 Bye Week
  11/5 Home   Tennessee Giants
  11/12 Home Jacksonville Cats
  11/19 At   Los Angeles Bolts
  11/26 Home Los Angeles Knights

Christy

12/30 At	Cincinnati Tigers
12/10 At	Denver Grizzlies
12/17 At	Houston Oilmen
12/24 Home	Seattle Seagulls
12/31 Home	Denver Grizzlies
1/8 At	Vegas Renegades

I stare at the Cardinals schedule on my iPad screen. In past years, I excitedly printed this out and posted it on the refrigerator. This year, the schedule scares me. Ryan expects the twins and me to attend all home games in Maddux's suite at Cardinals Nest Stadium.

Glancing at the twins' school calendar, the Sunday, Monday, and Thursday night games will start at their bath time with halftime after their bedtime. The late nights don't bother me as much as getting them to school the next morning. Cranky girls preparing for school is not on my top 10 list of fun things to do. Add to that his desire for me to travel to away games. If he had his way, the twins would travel, too.

Frustrated, I print the football schedule, the school calendar, and a free printable calendar I find on Pinterest. Josh hears the humming of the printer as he passes by Ryan's office door.

"Is there anything I can help you with?" he asks, handing me the printouts.

I huff dramatically. "There is not enough room on this calendar. I am not sure how to make this all work."

I spread the papers on the table in front of me. Josh snags his iPad from the counter and joins me.

"Didn't Ryan show you my calendar?" he asks, tapping on the screen.

"Uh-uh," I respond, scanning the calendar he shows me.

"I have Ryan's practice schedule, game schedule, and the girls' school days all in here."

He scrolls from August to September and beyond.

"Have an app that allows me to be in two places at the same time?" I scoff.

"Nope. No magic pixie dust either," he chuckles. "I am available to help with the girls any time you want. I will help you survive the season." He taps on the screen. "I shared the calendar with you. When Mel, Ryan, you, or I add something, the event will show up on everyone's calendar." He stacks up my printouts. "I can print copies if you prefer."

I shake my head.

He places his hand on my forearm and advises, "Talk to Ryan. While he knows the rigors of his schedule during the season, he might need your help looking at the calendar through the eyes of a parent."

"How did you get so wise?" I ask.

"It is my job to keep this place running smoothly," he answers, returning to his daily tasks.

Although the calendar still haunts me, I can't talk to Ryan about it until tonight. I decide to swim laps to clear my head.

30

THURSDAY, JULY 6TH

Ryan

Maddux and I bend at the waist, catching our breath in his driveway. Running five miles on the neighborhood trails proved tougher than the treadmill. On my golf cart, I did not realize the course was so hilly. Slowly, the stitch in my side fades.

"What did you decide?" Maddux pants.

"About?" I encourage more information from him.

"The honeymoon," he states, standing upright once again.

"It is not easy to find something available last minute," I inform. "I want a honeymoon with Christy, but it will be the last week with the twins before camp and the season. I'd like to plan something shorter with Christy so I can still spend a few days with Ry and Harper before camp."

"So, plan a trip and take the girls," my brother suggests. "Make it a family honeymoon."

"Yeah, but…"

"But nothing," he argues. "Christy barely enjoyed herself the night the girls stayed with our parents. Can you imagine what she would be like after five nights away?"

Maddux walks to my side, patting me on the shoulder as he finishes, "Plan a family trip. Christy will love it."

A family trip. For our honeymoon? With Christy focused solely on the wedding prep and promotional photos for the vineyard, she has not even mentioned the honeymoon. Maddux is right; she hates nights away from the twins. My hours with the girls are numbered as the long NFL season looms nearer.

"Where do five-year-olds like to go?" I think out loud.

"Do not let Harper hear you call her a five-year-old." He chuckles.

"She is militant about being a five-and-a-half-year old and almost six." I laugh.

"Kids love flying, hotels, eating out," Maddux offers. "Zoos, and amusement parks." His voice raises an octave on the last suggestion.

I take his hint, and I feel like an idiot for not thinking of it myself.

"Gotta go," I announce, walking from Maddux's drive.

My head swirls with possibilities and creates a list. I will research the west coast and east coast attractions after my shower.

31

FRIDAY, JULY 7TH

Ryan

My jump rope stills, and my heart pounds as loud as *Hurricane* by I Prevail, which plays from the speakers. Finished with my workout, I return the rope to its peg and my dumbbells to the rack along the wall. I take a seat on the bench, toweling off my face, neck, and arms.

Snagging my phone, I turn down the music, noticing I have several social media alerts. I tap one, and Instagram opens on my screen. I am seeing the feed of the *Back 9 Talk*. I turn my phone sideways and upside down, trying to decipher the photo I am looking at. Perplexed, I move to the post below it.

Back 9 Talk
Excrement… Foul feces… Nasty #2… Fragrant fecal… Dirty doo-doo… Smelly s**t… Pungent poop… Big BM… Dark dung… Massive manure… Wicked waste… Stinky stool… Do you pick up your pet's piles of poo?
The club is cracking down on members that walk their dogs on the trails, cart paths, or other areas of the course and do not bag their

bowel movements. This is your warning; they plan to run DNA testing to determine the breeds of the frequent offenders. Use the walking trails with bags and receptacles or stay in your own yard. S**t happens, but not on our golf course.

I laugh out loud at the absurdity of it. This gossip writer must be hard up if this is all she can find to post.

My water bottle empty, I toss my towel in the hamper and carry my phone and bottle from our fitness center. Though I try, I can't hear the sounds of the girls; *I wonder what they are doing?* As I emerge from the hall, I see them splashing outside in the swimming pool. Walking to the floor-to-ceiling windows, I watch the twins splash about while their mom sits with Brooks under the umbrella.

A man on a mission, I take the stairs two at a time. I do not bother showering. Instead, I change into my swim trunks and head back downstairs. The hot July air hits me in the face the moment I slide open the patio door.

"Daddy!" the twins greet.

"Can I get in?" I ask, rounding the shallow end of the pool. "Ladies, you look like you are having fun," I tease, pointing to the slushy red concoction in the pitcher before them.

"Mr. Josh made us strawberry daiquiris," Christy grins.

"It is hard work, watching the girls swim in the sweltering heat," Brooks explains.

My eyes return to Christy.

"I think we should get a dog," I declare.

"Seriously?" she sputters. "As if our lives aren't crazy enough with the girls, you want to bring a puppy into it?"

"What kind of dog are you thinking about?" Brooks questions.

I shrug, tapping on my cell phone screen then raising it to my ear.

"Who are you calling?" Christy asks.

"Hey, Maddux," I greet, shooting a wink at the women. "I am thinking about getting a dog."

Christy

Brooks's face pinches at Maddux's name, and Christy acts put off that I called him. In my ear, my brother tells me he will be right over.

"We are in the pool," I inform him before disconnecting the call.

"Why did you call him?" Brooks spits.

I love fueling the flames of dislike she and my brother share any time I get the chance.

"It looked like the two of you did not like my suggestion that we get a puppy, so I called for reinforcements," I confess, standing at the edge of the pool. "Cannon ball!" I yell, jumping into the air as I wrap my arms around my knees.

I sink to the bottom of the shallow end of the pool, ensuring I splash everyone. Surfacing, I hear the cheers of my daughters and the stifled curses of the ladies on the pool deck. A proud smile upon my face, I keep my back to Christy and Brooks as my daughters swim to me.

"Throw me, Daddy," Harper encourages.

I take turns lifting the girls, my hands at their waists, throwing them towards the diving board end of the pool. They squeal as they flail their arms in the air before plunging into the deep end and cheer when they resurface.

"What's all this noise?" Maddux yells over the railing of the deck above us.

"Uncle Maddux!" the twins greet.

Christy

"Yay... Maddux is here," Brooks says sarcastically to my right.

"Be nice," I warn, filling her glass again.

"I like spending time with my best friend and wish that, sometimes, it was just us," she grumbles. "It is like Ryan can't stand to be outnumbered."

"Now, about this dog…" Maddux raises his voice loud enough for us to hear. "I think it is a terrific idea." He looks at me. "Pets teach responsibility and love. A dog or two would be good for all of you."

"Oh, no. We are not getting two puppies," I respond firmly.

"Good. Then we agree on one," Ryan states, a sly grin upon his face.

I open my lips to argue but fight down the urge. Once the shock of him blurting he wants a dog wears off, I decide it is something we could discuss. He tricks me into claiming out loud one dog is better than two. Yet again, he charms me into submission.

"Now, what size and breed?" Maddux prompts, furthering the discussion.

"It is none of your business," Brooks bites in his direction.

I love my friend's loyalty, but her constant need to get a rise out of Ryan's brother is not always convenient.

"My brother called me to discuss getting a dog. That makes it my business," he states.

"Let's table the puppy conversation until the girls go to bed," I suggest. "Until then, the four of us can think on it."

"Okay. Let's discuss this dog idea," I prompt, washing my face at the bathroom sink.

"About that…" Ryan smirks. "I know exactly which breed we should get."

I quirk my head, beckoning him to continue. While he speaks, I finish my bedtime moisturizing routine.

"Boxers are loyal, protective, and great with kids."

He now stands behind me with his hands on my shoulders as we make eye contact in the mirror.

"They do not require lots of grooming, they love to play, and they look fierce," he shares. "I will feel better about leaving you and the twins while I am on the road this season if there is a very protective guard dog with you."

I thought the idea popped into his head for the first time today, but clearly, he has done research.

"I like the idea of a dog that does not shed a ton or require constant grooming," I confess. "And yes, in a year, the dog would make a great guard dog, but you know this season, it will be a little puppy, right?"

Ryan kisses my temple.

"He will still be fierce as a puppy." His crooked smile and the solo dimple in his cheek melts my heart. "And I already picked the name."

I bite my lips to prevent laughter.

"What?" he challenges.

"Today, you mentioned getting a puppy for the girls. Now, I learn you already picked the breed and named it. Is this a dog for the girls or for you?" I tease.

"It is for all four of us," Ryan answers. "Want me to find a breeder?"

"By that, do you mean you'll ask Josh to find a breeder?"

He rolls his eyes at me.

"What are we naming it?" I relent.

32

SATURDAY, JULY 8TH

Ryan

I fiddle nervously with my cell phone in my pocket. Josh will text any time now, and I need to be ready for it.

"I thought you said you were wrapping it up," I remind Christy.

She promised we were ready to leave.

She huffs and explains, "I am waiting on a text from Ty. He usually texts me back immediately."

I know why he is not texting, but I can't tell her that. I need to ensure she is ready to leave in a moment. I tug my cell phone from my shorts pocket.

ME
is Ty there?

JOSH
yes

Christy

> ME
>
> Christy waiting on text from him
>
> says can't leave here til he texts

> JOSH
>
> on it

"Babe," I whine, "I want to go."

Man, I sound like one of the girls. I am laying it on pretty thick.

"Uh!" Christy groans. "Got a text from Ty but not an answer to my question."

"So?"

"Instead of answering my question, he is giving me grief for working on a Saturday afternoon," she grumbles. "I want to plan a perfect event for the promotional photos."

"Screw our wedding as long as the promo photos are good," I pretend to be offended by her comment.

"Stop it," she scoffs. "You know what I mean." She organizes some file folders in the basket on the corner of the desk. "Let's go."

"Finally!"

"You are such a kid," she scolds. "Now I know where the girls get it from."

"You promised under two hours," I remind her as we walk to our golf cart. "I promised the girls we would do something fun this afternoon."

"I know. What should we do?" she asks, climbing into the driver's seat of our cart.

"I guess you are driving," I state sarcastically.

As if she did not hear me, she suggests, "We could go to the zoo or the craft store."

"I told them to make a list while I rode to work with you," I lie. "We need to choose something from their list."

"You really need to start giving them limits and guidance. We can't give in to everything they want to do," she shares her parental knowledge with me.

My phone vibrates in my pocket.

JOSH
we r ready

ME
on way

As we reach the Breakstone course, I must begin implementing our plan.

"Hey, pull over for a second," I direct.

Caught off guard, Christy searches the area before pulling off the right side of the cart path.

"What's wrong?"

I exit the cart, pulling the blindfold from my golf bag.

"The girls and I created a surprise for you," I inform. "I need you to move to the passenger side and wear this."

She raises an eyebrow at me. I watch her eyes, able to read her thoughts as she contemplates arguing with me. Deciding better of it, she slides across the seat. With the eye mask securely in place, I drive towards our house.

"So, this is the reason you were antsy, wanting me to quit working," she surmises.

"Yep."

"This had better be good," she mumbles.

Good. We are about to surprise the hell out of her. She may even cry, it is that good.

"We are pulling into the driveway now," I inform. "Keep the mask tight, and I will help guide you out of the cart."

In the garage, I take her hand, leading her into the house.

"When we count to three, you may remove the mask," I tell her.

I hold up one finger to the twins, and they count in unison, "One... Two... Three!"

Christy

Removing the mask, Christy blinks rapidly as she adjusts to the bright light, and our guests yell, "Surprise!"

Christy

I am not sure what I am seeing. I stand facing the twins, Ryan, his family, and our friends. While they clap and cheer, I scan the room for clues for this surprise party. *It is not my birthday...* When I spin around, I find wedding shower decorations in the dining area and kitchen.

Josh offers me a glass of wine.

"What is this?" I chuckle nervously.

"It is your wedding shower, silly," he laughs.

"Mommy! Mommy!" the twins cheer. "We made you a party." They smile proudly. "You get to open presents."

Ruff! Ruff!

You've got to be kidding me. Yesterday he mentions a dog for the first time, and today we own a dog.

I spin to find a tan boxer puppy with giant paws and an adorable black face standing by the girls, barking up at me.

Happy wedding gift to me. Yippie.

"Who is this?" I ask the twins as I squat to pet the pup.

"We named him Waino," Harper says.

"This is Wainwright," Ry says at the same time.

At first, I cringed at Ryan's idea to use my maiden name as our new pet's name. My girls think it is the perfect name.

"Nice." I direct my comment in Ryan's direction.

He shrugs unapologetically.

"He is bigger than I expected," I state, standing again.

"He's four months old and already trained," Josh informs, winking at me.

Already potty trained. That is awesome.

"He will keep my girls safe while I am away," he murmurs near my ear.

My thoughts back on our guests and the party, I find Brooks.

"I will not open those gifts in front of everyone, will I?" I whisper in her ear. "The girls are here, and I do not want to open any honeymoon-type gifts in front of them."

"We made it clear that the girls would be here, so do not worry," Brooks informs. "The girls plan to take turns opening gifts for you. I will make a funny comment before the first gift to remind them to warn us if the girls should not open it."

That makes me feel a bit better. All eyes will still be on me as each gift is opened. I remind myself these are Ryan's family and our friends. Well, some are Ryan's friends that will become mine, too.

"Gift time," Josh announces. "Let's refill everyone's drinks and find a seat."

Ryan, Maddux, and Josh refresh the drinks while Brooks sets up a chair for me and the twins near the gift table.

"Ryan," I murmur, walking up behind him in the kitchen, "will you help me open the gifts? Everyone's eyes will be on me. I could use your support."

"Of course," he answers, kissing my forehead.

Ruff. Ruff. Waino barks beside us. I look from the dog to Ryan, shaking my head. He smiles proudly.

The next day, I focus on wedding plans. Leaning back in my chair, I stare absentmindedly at the laptop and tablet screens on the table in front of me. I open my cell phone, scrolling to the Notes app for my checklist. As I read the list, I highlight items not completed.

Colors? Check.
Minister? Check.
Food? Check.

Band? Check

Flowers? Check.

Hmm... My brain is fried. I need...help.

Waino nudges my knee with his snout. Absently, I reach down to scratch between his ears. My free thumb swipes to the internet browser on my cell phone, and I slowly scroll through the trellises.

"Which do you like?" I ask Waino, holding my phone up for him to see. "This one or this one?"

Waino licks my wrist.

"You are no help," I huff.

Ryan

Christy peeks her head into my office, causing Josh to pause mid-sentence.

"What's up?" I ask.

"Never mind. It can wait," she offers, preparing to disappear.

"Stay," I direct.

"We are finished," Josh informs her on his way out.

"It can wait," she apologizes.

I shake my head and reiterate, "We were done. Come on in."

I make to rise, but she finally enters the room, assuming the seat Josh vacated moments before.

"What can I help you with?" I ask, my hands folded on the desk in front of me, pretending to be a businessman.

"I am working on wedding planning, and..." She pauses as she pulls a file up on her cell phone. "Which arbor should we get married under?"

I take her proffered cell phone, looking at some large structure decorated in pink flowers and bows. I can't hide my snarl.

Christy laughs at me. "Look at the structure under the decorations. These are not our colors or flowers."

"Honey, I told you to do whatever you want."

I rise from my office chair, making my way to her side of the desk, phone in hand.

"The only detail I care about is you and me finally standing in front of a minister, reciting our vows."

She takes her phone from me with a slight huff. Leaning against the desk, my legs extend to the sides of her chair. I fold my arms across my chest.

"Pretend you are helping a bride plan her wedding instead of planning ours. What would you suggest for her big structure thingy?" I smile, hoping she is not angry that I do not remember what she called this thing. "Ask Brooks, Paige, or the ladies in your golf group for advice."

I unfold my arms. Leaning forward, I place my hands on the arms of her chair.

"I love you, and I want to marry you. I am not good with all this other stuff. Sorry."

"You are right," she relents.

"What did you say?" I pull out my cell phone, tapping a few buttons then holding the microphone towards her as if to record her statement.

"Bahaha," Christy scoffs. "I will ask the ladies about the wedding planning, but I do need one decision from you."

She looks pointedly at me, and I nod.

"A minute ago, you mentioned reciting our vows," she reminds me. "What would you think about writing our own vows?"

That sounds... Well, it sounds like a difficult task. Am I able to put my feelings for Christy into words for our family and friends to hear? I have no problem telling her. I guess I usually show her instead of using words.

"Ryan?" she calls, requesting my attention. "What do you think?"

She is asking me, so that probably means she wants this.

"I would be up for it," I lie.

I lose myself in the smile slipping onto Christy's face. *I got this answer right; this is important to her. I am not sure I can pull this one off for her. I'd better ask Maddux for help.*

33

MONDAY, JULY 10TH

Ryan

The bell above the door tinkles as I enter. I am pleased to find Brooks at the counter.

"Ryan," she greets, surprised.

"Brooks, I am in desperate need of your help," I reply.

Her face pinches. "What's wrong?"

"Oh, sorry," I assure her. "Nothing is wrong. I have…" I dig into my shorts pocket for my excuse for coming here today. "I came for a tattoo if you have an opening."

I feel like a giant jerk. I should respect her enough to make an appointment.

"I know you are busy, so I could…"

"My two o'clock canceled," she informs me. "So, you are in luck. Let's see the drawing."

Brooks extends her hand toward me.

Before I slip my design her way, I confess, "And I need some advice while I am here."

It is the real reason for my showing up unannounced at her parlor. She takes the folded paper in hand.

I explain, "The twins designed it, and I want to surprise them by really getting the tattoo."

She nods, "They love drawing tattoos."

I smile proudly, and I watch as Brooks places the girls' drawing on her scanner.

"Where are we placing this one?" she asks.

"I want it visible to me and others," I tell her.

"We could do your bicep." She studies the design again. "I could shrink it small enough for your neck or your wrist."

"Yes!" I turn over my arm, displaying my inner wrist. "If you can make it fit, I want it here."

Brooks smiles. "Give me a sec."

She fiddles with her laptop, while I look at the designs framed on her walls. Next thing I know, she prints a template.

"Follow me," she directs, already walking down the hall.

She applies black gloves over her blue ones and prompts me to sit.

"I am surprised the twins didn't insist on coming with you today."

"They don't know I am doing this," I admit.

Brooks's smile grows wider. "They are going to freak out."

"I know," I agree.

"You must film it for me," she declares. "Please promise me you will ask Christy to film it when you show them."

"Or you could be there when I show them?" I suggest.

She looks up and to the left for a moment before she answers. "I have no other appointments, but I can't unexpectedly close the shop."

"You are the owner," I remind her.

"I get relieved at four. I could text to see if he can come in at 3:30." She thinks out loud. "Position this where you want it."

She lays the tattoo template on the table by my wrist before grabbing her phone to text. Turning back, she adjusts my tattoo placement a bit. Soon, the two stick girls holding a big heart will permanently mark my skin.

"Ready?" she asks.

Christy

"Bring it," I taunt.

She wastes no time in starting her needle and inking my flesh.

"While I work, you should tell me the real reason you dropped in today," she prompts, glancing up at me briefly.

If she didn't wear two pairs of gloves, she could read my mind with her powers.

"I wouldn't mind if you removed your gloves. You could answer all my questions and then some." I chuckle, only half teasing.

"If I could pick and choose what I see, I would be more apt to oblige," she says, still focused on her work. "There is no promise I would find what you hoped, and trust me; there are some things between Christy and you that I should never see."

She dabs a bit of ink from my wrist.

"What's got you...um... What do you want to talk about?"

I sigh deeply. "A million things," I mumble.

"Like what?"

"Like..." I decide to let it all out. "Do I make Christy happy? Are the three of them better with me in their lives? Should the girls attend public or private school? Should we get a nanny? Is Christy taking another job a good fit for our family? Are we a family? I mean, we live under one roof, but are we becoming a family? Should I push for the three of them to attend my away games?"

"Is that all?" Brooks interrupts, laughing and sitting back on her rolling stool, crossing her arms over her chest.

I look down at my wrist to find my tattoo finished. Although the irritated skin is red, it is perfect. I smile at Brooks, nervous to hear her words of wisdom.

She covers my tattoo as she speaks. "You are a new father. Most of your concerns are normal for any parent. You will doubt yourself and worry until the day you die. Christy has more practice at it, but she still toils over every decision. Ryan, the girls love you. Christy loves you. And..." Brooks pauses, pursing her lips in thought. "Christy will kick my butt if you tell her what I am about to tell you."

When she waits for my approval, I nod.

"That day that Maddux and you first walked into my tattoo parlor and I shook your hand, I saw things."

My stomach does a flip-flop.

"Christy asked me long ago not to give her any hints when I see visions, so I didn't. Well, I did hint by saying, 'Happily ever after.'" She shrugs. "After touching your hand, I went home and touched both girls to see their futures. I wanted confirmation. I saw a blindside in my best friend's future, and I needed to see from another source. I saw you."

"You've got to tell me," I plead. "I won't tell Christy. I need something, anything to help me."

"Ryan, you are all four right where you are meant to be. I saw the four of you happy and healthy for many years to come. It killed me not to tell Christy that night that she would bump into you and that the four of you would make a beautiful family."

Brooks starts cleaning up the area.

"I had to let you scare the crap out of her. I had to let Ry break her arm, and I had to let the two of you talk it out."

"But you saw other stuff further in the future?" I pry.

Brooks grins. "Ryan, I try to avoid having visions and am not practiced at sharing them with people I am close to."

"Ah… I am growing on you," I tease.

"Actually, the visions make it easy to let you in. I mean, since you will be sticking around and are good for my bestie." She rises, crossing her arms over her abdomen, and continues, "All I will tell you is that I see your family many years from now, happy and healthy. I even saw your daughters and sons watching you play for the Cardinals well into the future."

Her eyes grow wide, and her hand flies to her mouth, suddenly aware she divulged more than she planned to.

"Sonnnsss?" I feel tears well in my eyes, my chest warms, and my mouth grows dry.

"Ryan," Brooks points at me. "You can't ever, and I mean ever, tell Christy. She is going to kill me for talking to you. I knew I shouldn't start telling you anything. Once my mouth starts, it is hard for me to filter myself. Ryan… Are you hearing me?"

Christy

I nod, unable to articulate more than that.

"She can never even get a *hint* that I told you about that—any of that." She is still pointing at me.

I raise my right hand. "I promise."

"And you need to wipe that smile off your face. Your grin will get us both in trouble," she demands.

"I will hide it by the time I get home," I vow.

I bend down, placing a peck on her cheek.

"Don't touch me," she mumbles.

"Wanna ride with me? I will surprise the fam with ice cream when we bring you home."

She shoos me out of the room, waving her hand.

"Give me five minutes," she states.

34

MONDAY, JULY 10TH

Ryan

In the lobby, I find Brooks's employee logging in on the iPad.

"Hey," I greet as he looks my way.

"Yo," he returns, coffee in hand as he heads for the hall. "Shoot!"

I hear his curse at the same time the liquid splashes on the concrete floor, the cup and lid rolling towards me.

"I will get the mop," he mutters, disappearing down the hall.

I return my attention to the sketches and photos on the wall. Motion out the corner of my eye causes me to turn. I watch in horror as Brooks, with her attention on her cell phone, slips on the spilt liquid. Her feet fly up as her body falls down. I attempt to break her fall, to protect her head, but I can't get across the room in time. I watch as the back of her head bounces on the polished concrete floor. Panic floods my veins.

"Shoot!" her employee yells, emerging from the back room.

"Get towels," I order, pointing for him to turn around.

"Lie still," I instruct Brooks.

I scan her scalp, gently moving my fingertips to the back of her head. Her coal black hair is damp from the caramel-colored coffee

Christy

she lies in on the floor. My fingers pause at the same time she hisses. Pulling my hand away, my fingers are red. I place my palm over the cut despite her groans.

Brooks attempts to get up; I keep her on the floor with my free arm.

"Easy. You could have a neck or spine injury," I warn.

"I'm fine," she spits. "I can wiggle my toes and my fingers. Stop touching me!"

The guy returns with two white hand towels. *Great. Her blood will look worse on the white cloth.* I immediately replace my hand with a towel; she takes advantage of my movement to ignore my concern and sit up.

"I'm fine," she states.

I shake my head.

"You're bleeding," I argue. "You need stitches."

"No, I don't," she bites.

I place the palm of my hand over her wound, showing her the blood-soaked towel.

"Head wounds bleed a lot..." she spouts. Then, her eyes roll backwards, and she passes out.

I groan, lifting her into my arms while trying to apply pressure with a fresh towel.

"Lock up," I bark. "You are driving my Escalade out front. I'll hold her in the backseat. Do you know how to get to the ER?"

"Yeah," he says, his keys in hand, holding the door for me to carry Brooks through.

He turns the sign to "Closed" and locks the door before opening the SUV door for me to climb in with my patient.

"Keys are in my pocket, so you should be able to drive with me in the car."

He presses the button, and my vehicle comes to life.

"I didn't catch your name," I state, realizing a total stranger now drives my SUV.

"Miguel," he answers. "I am a huge fan."

"Thanks."

With the hand not holding the towel, I wiggle out my cell phone.

"I am going to call Christy to meet us," I inform him as the hands free connects the call.

I groan as it goes to voicemail. "I am on my way to Liberty Hospital ER. Brooks fell and busted the back of her head open. She needs stitches. Please meet us there when you get this."

The less than 10-minute drive seems like an eternity.

"Drop us at the door. You can drive back to the parlor, and I will get my vehicle when Christy and I bring Brooks home later."

I pull the key fob from my pocket, tossing it into the empty passenger seat as he pulls under the awning at the ER entrance.

I carry a still unconscious Brooks through the automatic doors, scanning the reception area in search of help. I find four people in line at the desk and nearly every chair in the waiting room occupied.

"She has a bleeding head injury and lost consciousness," I state firmly above the voices at the admission desk.

The man points to the doors as he buzzes them to open. I am thankful they are taking the situation seriously. I worried I might need to throw my weight around to get her into a room.

"Lay her here," a male nurse instructs.

"She slipped on a coffee spill and fell backward, hitting her head. I held a compress to the gash. She was alert but quickly lost consciousness." I rattle off details.

"I need you to remove your hand so I can…"

I pull the saturated towel out with my hand, tossing it in the biohazard waste can.

"She's coming to," the nurse announces.

"Can you hold this to her scalp for me? I need another set of hands."

I bend at Brooks's bedside, holding the gauze to the back of her head. Almost instantly, Brooks loses consciousness again. Soon, more nurses join us, scrambling to take my task of holding the compress, taking her vitals, and barking out orders.

At that moment, it dawns on me that Brooks needs protection from touch. While all the healthcare workers wear gloves, I don't, and I've…

"Um…This may sound weird to you. Well, it is weird. Brooks has

Christy

an aversion to touch. Can we put a long-sleeved gown over her clothes, and may I use one, too?" I ramble.

I catch the female nurses off guard with this request. However, a male nurse smiles. "I will be right back, Mr. Harper."

"May I use some gloves, too?" I request while he is away.

"Of course." One nurse signals for me to help myself to the gloves mounted on the wall by the door.

I grab a pair of large for me and small for Brooks. I struggle but eventually succeed in slipping the blue gloves on both her hands before donning my own.

When they roll Brooks onto her side to suture her head wound, I slip her arms into the blue surgical gown then position one over my clothes. I can no longer ignore the incessant buzzing of my phone vibrating in my pocket. On its screen, I find my publicist's name. Unlocking it, I find multiple missed calls and several texts.

"I need to take this," I inform the medical staff. "If I step out…"

"I will walk you out and ensure they will let you back in," a nurse states. "We will take your friend to imaging soon."

I hedge at this knowledge.

"You won't be able to go with her."

Understanding I will be sitting in this room alone, I leave. On the sidewalk in front of the ER, I dial Mel.

"Tell me everything," she demands in greeting. "Social media lit up with photos of you carrying a woman into a hospital."

I scrub my free hand over my face then scan the area. Sure enough, people are looking in my direction with cameras poised. I take in my appearance. The physician's surgical gown and gloves I wear will guarantee more pics will soon be posted online.

"Tell me everything. Rumors are already flying around about you with another woman, a mystery woman, a possible wreck, and on and on. I need to get a statement out there and get ahead of it."

"Okay," I huff. "I went to Christy's best friend's tattoo shop. I got a new tattoo on my wrist. So, the bandage there in the photos is from a tattoo. Brooks fell, cut open the back of her head, and needed stitches. She was unconscious, so I had to carry her, bleeding, into the Liberty Hospital ER. I am still waiting with her; Christy is on her way to meet me. That is all."

A long silence falls between us.

"I will put out a statement on social media, explaining the situation with enough detail to end the rumors and keep the press from calling me."

"Sorry," I sigh.

"Ryan, it is my job. You need to focus on your friend. I will take care of everything on my end," she promises.

I spot Christy speed walking through the parking lot towards me.

"Christy is here," I say into my phone.

"Go."

I disconnect my call as Christy places her hand on my forearm.

"Why..." Her voice breaks, and tears flood her eyes.

I remember how I look.

"Brooks is fine," I quickly assure her. "I put all this on so I wouldn't accidentally touch her. I worried, with her head injury, having visions might..."

She cuts me off with a kiss on the corner of my mouth. "I love you. Thank you for caring so much for her."

I long to linger here, kissing my girl, but we need to focus on Brooks right now.

"C'mon," I urge, leading her inside.

When I wave at the desk, they buzz us into the patient area.

"Who was on the phone?" Christy asks.

"Mel," I answer, guiding her into Brooks's exam room. "Photos of me carrying Brooks are all over the internet."

She nods, looking around the empty room.

"They took her to imaging," I explain.

I allow Christy to sit in the chair while I lean against the wall nearby.

"So, why are you wearing that?" Christy asks.

I take my need to repeat myself to mean she is shaken by Brooks's accident.

"I am doing this to avoid touching Brooks," I explain slowly. "I even asked them to dress her in a gown and gloves. I told them she has an aversion to direct touches."

"That is sweet of you," Christy leans her head against my hip.

When Brooks returns, we learn she suffers from a concussion and sprained ankle. They release her into our care with instructions and concussion protocols. I am blessed to have never had a concussion, but I am very aware of the protocols from those suffered by my many teammates. Christy sits in the backseat of her car with Brooks, and I drive.

"What the hell?" Brooks grumbles when we round the corner near her apartment.

"You will need to park on the other side of the square," Christy directs. "I can't believe it is this full."

Walking to the tattoo shop, we spot an off-duty police officer directing traffic on the sidewalk. A line forms at the door to the parlor and extends down the block.

Not liking the crowd, I instruct, "Christy, hurry to the door. I will carry Brooks upstairs, then I will see what is going on down here."

In my periphery, I see cell phones aimed in our direction as I walk past Christy, ascending the stairs. I place Brooks safely on her sofa.

"No more touching! Can I have my cell phone?" she demands immediately.

"No screen time," Christy reminds her.

"Then I need you to call Madam Alomar," Brooks growls. "Do it now. Tell her to come here. It's urgent."

"Did you say 'Madame Alomar'?" I ask, worried this is a side effect of her concussion.

"Out! Now!" Brooks barks, pointing me to the door.

Not wanting to upset her further, I head toward the door.

"Call me if you need me," I tell Christy. "I will be downstairs."

I kiss Christy before leaving.

"Ryan! Ryan!" The fans in line call for my attention.

I smile and wave before opening the door of the tattoo parlor. I am shocked to find Josh, Paul, Ry, and Harper answering phones while manning the computer and iPad at the counter.

"What's going on here?" I ask.

"We're helping," Harper answers, placing the phone back in the cradle.

I arch a brow toward Josh.

"The girls worried when Christy left, and they convinced me to drive them here. I figured you would return with Brooks. The phones started ringing off the wall, and the crowd started showing up." Josh catches his breath while he points toward the line outside. "Miguel called in other employees, and we offered to help with the phones."

"Why so many people?" I wonder out loud.

"Your social media post," Paul answers. "It mentioned Christy's friend Brooks fell at her tattoo parlor. I think they figured it out from there."

The clock on the wall tells me it is after seven. Hands on my hips, I take in the long line outside and the non-stop ringing of the phone.

"Let's let the phone go to the answering machine," I instruct the helpers. "I will talk to Miguel and take care of the line waiting outside."

When I emerge from the back room, Christy joins us at the counter.

"I offered to spend the night, but Madame Alomar insisted she would take care of Brooks," she shares, her hair a frazzled mess.

I can't help but run my hands over it, coaxing it all back into place.

"Let's go," I suggest, ushering her toward the door. "Josh and Paul, please join us back at the house for dinner. You've earned it for helping here."

"Can we ride with Mr. Josh?" Harper asks.

Josh agrees, and we make our way toward the door. I flip the sign to "Closed" before I walk outside.

"Ryan!" the crowd calls.

"Hey," I wave, my public persona in place. "Thank you for stopping by. Unfortunately, the artists are slammed for the remainder of the night. I hope you will book an appointment online." I point to the website posted on the window as I speak. "Or call for an appointment. Brooks and her clan do great work." I hold up my bandaged wrist. "I got fresh ink here today. We appreciate your interest and hope you will visit Ink, Inc. again soon."

I smile and wave for a moment as several people snap photos with their phones. I shake the police officer's hand, thanking him for assisting with the crowd this evening, then follow Christy toward her car. I make a mental note to ask Mel to help me find another way to thank Officer Jones for his time this evening. He puts his life on the line each day he works, and he stepped up to help during his free time. The least we could do is gift him tickets or something.

Insisting Christy leave her car and ride with me, in the privacy of the SUV, I ask, "Who is Madam Alomar?"

Christy chuckles. "She owns a tarot card reading shop in Gladstone and has the gift of sight. She is someone Brooks can reach out to with questions."

She places her hand on my arm while I drive.

"You helped Brooks, and she is grateful for it. When you touched her after she fell, she had powerful visions. Brooks remembers your hand connecting with the back of her head, visions started, and they never stopped. For the first time, Brooks has visions without touching you. Madame Alomar claims that, when you touched her blood, a bond was made. She claims she can teach Brooks to block out the visions."

More visions. Powerful visions. Is it greedy of me to hope Brooks will share the details when she feels better? I won't ask, but I hope she offers up the information.

35

TUESDAY, JULY 11TH

Christy

"I got you something today," Ryan states, grabbing water from the refrigerator.

I look up at him from the table where I'm coloring with the girls.

"Think Ty will let you take Friday off?" he asks, taking the empty seat near me.

"I make my own schedule for the most part," I chuckle. "Our wedding is planned and there is not an event that day, so I am sure it will be no problem. Why?"

"I booked you a private suite at the Elms Spa Friday morning," he informs proudly.

"Why?" I scoff.

"I thought you would like a bit of pampering before the wedding," he defends. "Ask Brooks to join you."

"I do not need pampering," I argue. "I am not the type of woman that goes to get her nails done."

"But you need to from time to time." Maddux butts into our conversation. "You are a public figure now."

"No, I am not," I protest. "I am nobody."

Christy

Maddux chuckles. "You wish." He tugs out his cell phone, quickly tapping on the screen. "This is the *Cardinals Chicks Facebook Group*. Scroll through the posts."

Reluctantly, I take the phone. The first post is an order form for an awesome t-shirt with a Cardinals design on it. The second is the photo of Ryan's SUV with the four of us the night we ate at Sonic that went viral weeks ago. I skim the comments, finding many supportive comments about our family and about how cute the girls and I are. In other posts, I find a photo of me shopping at Target and the local Hy-Vee grocery store.

"I had no idea…"

"The ladies in my office constantly talk about photos of you," Maddux informs. "They even point out the ones I am in with Ryan or you. They want to know where you shop, what you wear, and everything about the girls."

My chest grows tight, and tears flood my eyes. There are random shots of the girls and me in public with and without Ryan. I did not even notice cell phone cameras pointed in our direction. *What if…*

Ryan takes the phone from my hand, scrolling through the long page of photos.

"It seems all the photos were taken in public," he states. "I do not see any that look to be following you."

Maddux agrees. "I see nothing stalkerish. Just the usual fan stuff."

Ryan pulls out his cell phone. I watch as he types a text to his publicist.

RYAN

remind me 2 talk 2 u about Christy on social media

"Just as a precaution," Ryan murmurs. "I need my team to ensure the safety of the twins and you."

I remind myself I love to watch Ryan play football, and this goes hand in hand with his success in the NFL. Though it is new to me, Ryan has grown used to this public aspect. He will suggest that I speak to one of the other…

"We will ask the other wives how they handle social media, photographs by fans in public, and photos of the kids." Ryan suggests exactly what I thought he would.

"I am not on social media, and I do not want the first conversation I share with them to be about public attention," I state.

"You met the important women at the housewarming and our wedding shower," Ryan reminds me. "Those are the only ones we should talk to."

"If I may put my two cents in," Josh says from across the kitchen. "I am in three of the most active groups, and I only see love for Christy and the twins. For many of us in KC, your family is like royalty. The fans are excited to see you in public and realize you shop or eat at the same places they do." He winks at me then turns his back to continue with dinner prep.

I need to talk this one out with Brooks. I open my texts.

ME
need 2 chat

BROOKS
Fri I know

it will b fun

just the 2 of us

ME
no

about KC royalty

BROOKS
urgent or Fri?

Christy

ME
Friday remind me

BROOKS
K

"You okay?" Ryan asks, concerned.

I nod. "Told Brooks we need to discuss it on Friday."

"I know the spa is not something you normally splurge on, but you used to go get your nails done with your mom. I thought you might like it. You spend all your energy on the twins and now me; you need to take time for yourself more often." He kisses my cheek.

"I want a kiss!" Harper announces.

"Me, too!" Ry joins in.

Both girls move to Ryan's side, awaiting his affection.

I love that they did not experience a stand-offish, getting-to-know-you period with him. I often worried that lying to them, saying that Daddy was very busy with work, would harm them emotionally.

Ryan's team, as he calls it, works fast. The next day, I welcome Mel for a meeting at our house. I place the iced tea pitcher in the center of the table near the lemons and glasses of ice Josh already placed there. I take my seat before pouring tea for Mel and me, then I smile at my daughters.

"So…" Mel begins, tapping her iPad to life. "Harper and Ryan, let's talk about social media."

"Ry," Harper corrects tersely. "Not Ryan. Call her Ry."

"I am sorry," Mel back pedals. "Do you girls know what social media is?"

"Mommy already talked to us about it," Harper informs. "It is like Snapchat."

"Correct. TikTok, Facebook, Instagram, Snapchat, Twitter, Tumblr, Pinterest, and BeReal are all examples of social media. Do you and your friends use these?"

My girls shake their heads. "Mommy doesn't let us. Sometimes, Daddy and Mr. Josh show us something on their phones."

"Ryan and I limit the screen time the girls are allowed each day for their iPad. We set parental controls and did not download any of those apps to their device. I know Ryan told you I have not been on social media until now," I share.

"Girls, you understand that your dad is in the public eye, so we need you to be careful how you behave," Mel attempts to explain.

"We discussed that Daddy is famous, and that means people like to take pictures with him and ask for his autograph." I put Mel's comments into words the girls understand.

"Because your dad is famous," Mel looks at me, clearly not liking the term, "it is important that, when you are with friends or shopping in public, any pics taken are positive for your image and your dad's."

I bite my tongue. She really does not understand how to speak to children. I did not plan to assume the role of translator during her visit.

"Mel wants what Mommy and Daddy want," I explain. "We want you to make sure you are being polite and making good decisions. The people that watch Daddy on TV take our photos when we are with Daddy. Sometimes, they take photos of the three of us." I swirl my fingers between my girls and me. "We may not know they are taking the photos. That is why we always need to make good choices. Okay?"

Harper nods her head.

"We were in Target with Mommy," Ry shares. "And a boy yelled at his mommy and daddy. He laid on the floor, crying really loud."

"Exactly," Mel smiles, happy the girls understand. "People might film that boy. If his daddy was famous like yours, they might post it

Christy

to social media. We wouldn't want something like that of you out there for everyone to see."

My girls nod solemnly. I reach out my hand to rest on each of theirs on the table in front of them.

"We are not upset with you," I declare. "You did nothing wrong, and we did not find any photos of the two of you that should not be on social media."

"I wanted to speak with you now to prevent this from happening," Mel states.

"Mommy and Daddy want to keep you safe and happy. We want to protect you from bad things. This is why we are talking today. Mel and I wanted to make sure you know about social media, phone cameras, and people that will think you are famous like Daddy."

Mel begins to object, but I stop her.

"We are not famous. You are two five-year-olds, just like your friends. I am a mommy, just like other mommies. But because Daddy plays football on TV, some people will think we are famous and want our photos."

I look to my daughters for understanding; instead, I find defiance.

"We are five-and-a-half," Harper argues. "Say that, not five."

I nod, fighting a smirk at her insistence.

"It is important that you understand," Mel reiterates. "I would like to show you some photos and videos from social media that display what we hope you will avoid."

I lean into Mel's line of sight, my eyes wide, expression stern.

"I assure you they are appropriate for little eyes," Mel promises.

I watch as the girls stare at the iPad screen as Mel flips through the examples.

"We want to make sure you know that people use cell phone cameras everywhere at all times," I explain. "If you remember there are always cameras, then none of this will happen to you."

"Okay," Harper promises, and Ry nods. "Can we go play now?"

Mel looks at me, concerned. I nod to my daughters, and they make a beeline for their room.

"Ryan and I will continue to remind them," I pledge. "At their age, we must talk to them in quick conversations. They have short attention spans. If we push too hard, it becomes a lecture, and they lose interest."

Mel nods. "Ryan claims they are well-behaved children. If so, I don't expect to have any issues."

"I guess now it is my turn," I grumble, causing her to laugh.

Over my shoulder, I hear Josh chuckle, too. I tap my iPad screen, waking up the display.

"Where do I start?" I ask, dread dripping from my tone.

For the next hour and a half, Mel logs me into the social media accounts she created for me on TikTok, Facebook, Instagram, Snapchat, and Pinterest. She shows me the profiles she created and photos she used.

She helps me make a post on each platform. We record a video introduction post, use hashtags, and even follow other accounts. Then I learn how to like and comment on other posts. My mind reels with the similarities and differences between each app.

"Now onto another topic," Mel says, sitting back in the chair, placing her hands in her lap. "Let's discuss your wedding photos."

Wedding photos? Does she think she has a say in the photos we take?

My furrowed brow and pinched mouth signal my confusion.

"Two publications approached me for rights to the wedding photos," she announces.

"Really?" I scoff.

"Christy, I thought you understood the reason for today's meeting. Your family is in high demand. My inbox overflows with companies wishing to send you free products. They hope you will be an influencer for their products. Restaurants, clubs, stores, and clothing lines vie for you attention on social media. Your fan base intrigues them. This is why the two national publications seek to be the first to post photos from the wedding of Ryan and Christy Harper."

"Fanbase?" I laugh. "I doubt one follower interests them."

Mell pats my hand where it rests on the table. "Trust me by morning, you will have 1,000, and within a week over a 100,000."

I fight the urge to roll my eyes at her. She slides her tablet toward

Christy

me. Pointing at the screen she explains, "This shows the name of the publication and how much they are offering."

I can't breathe. The room suddenly feels 100 degrees, and the air evaporates. When I cough, Josh hurries to my side with water.

"Oh my!" he whistles.

"I don't want the money," I state, pushing the iPad toward Mel.

"This isn't about the money," Mel claims.

Is she serious?

"I am not Ryan's business manager, and I would never presume to advise you on finances," she argues. "Money you and your family receive could be used for Ryan's childhood leukemia or colon cancer foundation."

"This is your chance to do good," Josh suggests. "Philanthropic work benefits the entire community." His hands on my shoulders squeeze me in support. "Ryan and you should discuss this," he urges. "Decide if you want to sell the photos and if so how to use the money. Celebrities do it all the time with wedding and baby photos. Don't let others decide; the two of you know what is best for you." With that Josh returns to the kitchen.

Mel squints at his back before she speaks. "I did not mention this to Ryan as I figured he would refer me to you. This is a huge opportunity for you. I hope you will consider it."

I nod.

When she leaves, I breathe a deep sigh of relief, flopping into a stool at the kitchen island. Josh slides a glass of white wine in front of me. I chuckle; he read my mind. From the table, my iPad beeps, and my cell phone chirps. I glance at Josh over my wine glass.

"Welcome to the world of social media," Josh snickers.

"Can you help me silence those alerts?" I plead, taking another sip of wine before fetching my devices.

"Social media is a time suck," I complain when I return.

"Not necessarily," he argues. "If you are selective in the accounts you follow and post content that is important to you for the masses to see, it can be a valuable tool."

"Did you just quote Mel word for word?" I ridicule.

Though it was not verbatim, he restated her many comments of the over two-hour-long lecture.

"And you will help me create such content, like you promised," I moan pathetically.

"You will quickly find your way," Josh promises. "Tomorrow, I thought we might film you with the girls, making the peanut butter protein balls they enjoy. I bought all the ingredients. I'll film on the iPad and take photos, too. We will post the recipe for all your followers."

"I don't have any followers," I debate.

"Let's see about that," he argues, tapping my screen. "You now have five followers on Instagram, four on Twitter, five on TikTok…"

"Okay. Okay. So, I now have followers," I relent. "Can we see who they are?"

Josh helps me see that Ryan followed me on all platforms. My other followers were a couple of Ryan's teammates, Mel, and Josh. *The sneaky little turd.* We tweak my notifications to vibrate only, and I follow people back.

"I have thousands of followers. Do you want to take a selfie with me?" Josh jeers.

For many years, I hid in plain sight. I tried hard to blend in and not stand out. Bumping into Ryan at the club sent my life soaring in a new direction. I can no longer hide in my safe little world with the twins and Brooks. Maddux's comment about KC royalty haunts me daily. I no longer keep my head down; I must be alert.

I let my guard down when it is only Ryan, the girls, and Josh at home. When we host visitors or leave the safety of our house, cell phone cameras lie in wait. Any photo a friend takes, members at the club, and other shoppers at the store holds the potential to be posted to social media or sent to the press. At the same time, I am making new friends and starting new activities, I am also constantly aware of many eyes on me. I remind myself it is worth it; my new life with Ryan brings many wonderful opportunities.

36

SATURDAY, JULY 15TH

Christy

"Knock, knock," Maddux calls from a tiny crack in the doorframe.

"Come in," I invite, signaling we are decent.

"Special delivery," he announces.

"Uncle Maddux is being funny," Harper giggles, walking past him to join Brooks and me.

"I am dropping off two girls," Maddux states. "But I need to hurry back."

"What's wrong?" I panic.

He raises his palms between us. "Nothing is wrong. I promised I would hurry. That is all."

"Ryan is okay? Is he nervous?" I ask, my hands clasped in my lap at the make-shift vanity.

"Nervous, yes," Maddux chuckles. "He's ready for the afterparty and honeymoon."

"He will be ready for photos in 20 minutes," Brooks states instead of asking after looking at the time on her nearby cell phone.

"I will take care of my best man duties. You worry about yours."

He looks around the attic space. "Ry and Harper, Miss Brooks is now in charge of you." With that announcement, he closes the door behind him.

"Mommy looks pretty," Ry says, standing beside me in the mirror.

"I am finishing one more curl, then the two of you can help her slip on her wedding dress," Brooks informs the girls. "Why don't you go potty now?"

Excited for our big day, the twins do not argue. Although usually they hate being told when to use the bathroom, claiming they are not babies, they quickly comply today.

Ryan

Finally! Today is the day. Today, I tie the woman I love to me for the rest of my life. Today, I get to declare in front of our family and friends how much Christy means to me as well as show how much I love her.

"Ready?" Maddux asks from the doorway.

His smile grows as do his dimples. He strikes a pose, leaning against the door frame in his cream and dusty blue Cuban shirt and khaki slacks. I am glad Christy opted for a casual summer wedding instead of tuxes. Today's high is 90; a tux would be miserable.

"You're ready," he answers for me. "You have been ready since the day she popped back into your life."

"I am ready," I agree. "But I am more ready for the ceremony to be over. I am ready for our happily ever after."

"You are just nervous about your vows," my brother surmises, and I nod.

"Public speaking does not bother me, but not cracking jokes while doing so does," I admit.

"They are your vows. If you want to joke, you should," Maddux states.

Christy

"I can't use humor and make light of our love," I argue.

Maddux places his hands upon my shoulders, all traces of his smile gone. "Christy asked you to write your vows. She loves you and expects the real you to speak. The Ryan that she loves is honest and fun-loving. That is the guy she wants standing with her at the altar today."

Maddux is more than my big brother; he is my best friend. He always has been. While he has given me advice over the years, he has never been so wise. I pull a note card from my pants pocket, tearing it to shreds over a trash can.

"Let's do this," I announce, following Maddux from the room.

As I emerge from the employee breakroom at the back of the kitchen, I am greeted by the kitchen and waitstaff. Maddux and I ease our way through the busy workers into the dining space where I am caught off guard by the family members and guests that have arrived early.

"I forgot about the cocktail hour," I murmur near Maddux's ear.

My brother chuckles, patting my shoulder. "As your best man, I am supposed to help you socialize with guests when we are not posing for wedding photos," he informs me.

It is as if my brain turned to mush. I forgot about the cocktail hour and photos before our ceremony. Hell, I even forgot what time the ceremony was set to begin. My wedding day jitters are worse than the NFL locker room jitters before a playoff game. My fear must be written all over my face because Maddux pulls me to the side.

"Dude," he chuckles. "Breathe. You are turning green."

I close my mouth, drawing long breaths in and out through my nose. I keep my eyes trained on his.

"I forgot everything," I confess.

"Your vows?" He quirks a brow.

"No. Everything." I wave my hands around the space we stand in. "The pregame, kickoff time, everything."

Maddux chortles, and I nervously scan the area, afraid others will hear us.

"This is not a football game," he reminds me through his laughter. "You said pregame and kickoff. We are at your wedding."

He shakes his head, moving beside me as he lays his arm along my shoulders.

"I have got you," he promises. "I will take you where you need to be and tell you what to do. Right now, we are to greet your guests while we wait for the photographer to find us."

I nod, looking around the large room, unsure who to approach first. Fortunately for me, my parents join us.

"He looks a little green around the gills," Dad tells Maddux.

"Honey..." Mom takes my hand in hers. "I peeked in the attic. Christy looks lovely. She will be down any minute to start the photos."

"Chin up," Dad orders. "It is not the defensive line of the Grizzlies; she is to be your wife."

I can't let Christy see my nerves. I do not want her to confuse them for doubt of my love for her. *Talk.* I will distract myself by talking with family and guests.

"T-minus one hour," I jest. "I am ready to wear a ring and move on to the afterparty."

My father chuckles, and my mother shakes her head.

"What?" I defend. "I am being honest. I am sure Christy would say the same."

Behind my parents, I notice a couple with cameras around their necks, each with a camera and giant lens posed to their face. As I carry on conversation with my family, they snap photos from every angle.

"Right about now, I am wishing I paid closer attention to Christy when she shared the details about the wedding she planned," I admit.

"There are five photographers," Maddux explains. "Three will be taking candid shots while two will be posing the wedding party around the vineyard."

I hope my smile conveys how happy I am that my brother listened to Christy's details. He truly has my back today.

"It really is hard not to make eye contact with them as they snap pictures," Mom states, her eyes motioning in the direction of the photographers. "I hope Ty recognizes how big of a favor you are doing for him by letting them use photos from your wedding."

"Didn't Dad tell you?" Maddux answers for me. "Ryan and I invested in Ty's vineyard. So, Ryan and Christy's wedding is serving as a launching point for our business."

"You own a vineyard?" Mom both asks and exclaims. "I hope that means I get to taste copious amounts of wine."

"Sorry to interrupt, but the photographer is signaling they are ready for us," Maddux states, waving across the room.

"*Ciao*," Mom calls as we walk away.

I chuckle. "Her Italian lessons are paying off."

Maddux laughs with me, "Dare you to tell her it is '*Arrivederci*.'"

I shake my head, holding the door for my brother. I freeze in my tracks after rounding the side of the building. I am equal parts surprised and impressed as I take in the scene Christy created for our vow ceremony.

In the shade of a ginormous white, open-sided tent, white cloth-covered chairs line up at angles toward the center aisle. At center stage stands a large bamboo trellis, draped with a thin, dusty blue and gray fabric and yellow flowers. The beautiful display before the field of vines moves me.

"I need a favor," I tell my brother. "I want to buy the trellis for my yard."

Maddux bumps my shoulder with his. "My brother, the romantic," he teases.

"Just do it for me," I order. "No matter what it costs. I want that exact one, not one like it."

He nods, now understanding I am serious.

"Gentlemen," the photographer's assistant calls to us, "we are ready for the best man right here and the groom here."

For 10 minutes, I pose with Maddux and then my parents within the romantic scene Christy created before Maddux leads me back to the cocktail hour. I nibble on shrimp as I move amongst the crowd. My nerves evaporate as I speak with my teammates and neighbors. That is until Maddux tells me it is time for more photos.

"Are you ready to see your bride?" he murmurs.

Instantly, the hair on the back of my neck rises, and my heartbeat quickens. The one part of Christy's planning I do remember is our decision to take photos together before we exchanged vows. While we are both superstitious, we felt me not seeing my bride before the ceremony was unnecessary.

I am standing at the altar, like I would be if we had waited, when I see her for the first time. In a wispy, ivory sundress, she walks up the aisle towards me.

My heartbeat pounds in my ears, and every cell sparks to life at the sight of her. My fingers tingle with the need to caress her bare, sun-kissed shoulders the halter neckline displays, and I lick my lips, longing to taste her. Mentally, I tabulate the time remaining in the cocktail hour, ceremony, and reception to follow.

"Hello, Mr. Harper," she greets, assuming the position beside me for the photographer.

"Hello, soon-to-be Mrs. Harper," I return with a smile.

It is not lost on me that Brooks wipes the inside corner of her eyes, and my mother frantically searches for a tissue at the sight of us. I have attended three weddings in the past two years. I found them to be emotional myself. While my teammates exchanged vows, strong emotions stirred within me. It renewed my longing to reconnect with the woman standing beside me now.

Ryan

Christy

Time passes in a blur. Before I know it, it's my turn to share my vows.

"When you proposed writing our own vows, I knew it would be a monumental task to put into words all you mean to me. I do not like to fail, so here it goes. You are a hole in one…"

As the crowd interrupts my vows with raucous laughter, I am forced to pause. I spent over a week perfectly picking my words, and I chose to throw them away two hours ago. While I want to speak from my heart, I do not want to embarrass myself or Christy. *Why did I think I could try to improvise my vows?* I clear my throat before continuing.

"Bear with me," I beg our guests. "I am a simple man, and while I am up here in front of my closest friends and family, I ask that you not judge me as I spill my heart to this magnificent woman."

While *ahh*s sweep through the crowd, I take a deep breath to steady my nerves and collect my thoughts before I continue. I spin the engagement ring on her finger.

"Christy, you are an expertly grilled steak and a Super Bowl victory rolled into one." I ignore chuckles as I continue. "From the day you chose the seat beside me in my senior calculus class, I have been under your spell. Though we spent time apart, my heart always belonged to you, and it always will. I can't wait to spend the next 80 years in love with my sexy-as-hell wife."

I kiss the back of Christy's hand as a blush creeps upon her cheeks, and the tent erupts with catcalls and applause.

"You should write greeting cards when you retire," Maddux says over my shoulder.

37

SATURDAY, JULY 15TH

Christy

Our wedding reception passes in a blur.

"Ladies," Maddux greets, walking toward us.

"Do not look now, but the uptight suit is approaching," Brooks grumbles.

"Be nice; you're in public," Maddux chides. "I am here to remind you the twins need to leave in about an hour. So—"

Brooks interrupts, "We need to cut the cake, dance the first dance, and throw the bouquet." She begins scanning the area for Ryan.

"Ry, Harper, and Ryan are making their way to the cake as we speak," he informs, his smirk aimed at my friend.

I swear these two will ignite when they finally get together. That is if they do not kill each other first.

"May I escort the two of you?" Maddux offers his arms to us.

I slip my arm through his elbow; Brooks hesitates before begrudgingly following my lead. Arm in arm, the three of us make our way toward my daughters, who are waving from in front of the wedding cake. I note the photographers flanking them from every direction, snapping numerous photos.

Christy

"Who is ready to eat some cake?" Brooks asks the girls, causing excited squeals.

"Shall we?" Ryan asks, entwining his arm with mine.

We assume our spot behind the three-tiered cake, Ry between Brooks and me while Harper stands between Ryan and Maddux. The DJ cuts the music, and all eyes swing in our direction. With a raised voice, Maddux announces it is time to cut the cake.

"Do it, Daddy!" Harper cheers.

"Behave," I warn, not wanting icing smeared all over my face.

Ryan's crooked grin does nothing to ease my worries. I lose myself in the shape of his lips and the glimmer in his eyes. It is the same smile he will flash at me later tonight when we are alone in our hotel suite. It causes a flutter in my belly and excites every part of me.

Ryan clears his throat. I find he has a small piece of cake perched inches from my mouth. I arch an eyebrow, to which he flashes his dimple at me. I can't very well refuse him in front of our guests. I slowly lick my lips in preparation. His eyes track the movement and desire grows within them.

I open my mouth, watching his pupils dilate as he places the cake. I slowly close my lips around it and his fingertips. I take my sweet time retreating, allowing the sensations of my mouth upon his fingers to transport his thoughts elsewhere.

"Now who is not behaving?" he growls at my ear, causing goose-bumps to cover my flesh.

Focus. Focus. Focus. There are hours left here before we can escape. I carefully feed Ryan a piece of cake, ready to pose for a few photos and move on to the next item on our itinerary.

"My turn!" Harper announces. "Do me! Do me!"

Ryan and I exchange glances. He nods then cuts two small pieces of cake. He hands me a slice and takes one in his hand.

"Ready?"

I nod. At the same time, we squat. I feed Ry while he feeds Harper. The girls giggle as cameras flash from every angle.

"Time to toss the bouquet," Maddux instructs, taking his best man duties seriously. "Brooks, gather the single ladies, and I will make the announcement."

He walks to the DJ stand, taking the microphone in hand.

"May I have your attention please?" Maddux's voice sounds smooth and sultry over the sound system. "In a moment, Mrs. Harper will toss her bouquet, so all the single women should make their way to the left side of the dance floor. Now, it is time for the couple's first dance. This will not be the traditional first dance between Mr. and Mrs. Harper. The couple opted to share this dance as a family. Ry, Harper, Christy, and Ryan, please make your way to the center of the dance floor." He returns the mic to the DJ and slips into the crowd, gathering to watch us.

I bend between the girls. "You know that TikTok dance you like to practice?"

They nod.

"Think you can do it with Daddy and me right now?"

Again, they nod.

"But who is going to record?" Harper asks.

I point to the center of the crowd where Brooks stands with a cell phone aimed at the four of us. Both girls wave excitedly, and she waves back.

Ryan signals the DJ, and the four of us strike the first pose. When the music starts, we perform the dance routine as the guests laugh and cheer us on. The girls jump up and down excitedly when the song ends.

"We did it! We did it!" the twins cheer. "Miss Brooks, did you record us?"

Brooks nods, extending her phone for the girls to see the video. Josh instructs Brooks to share it with him so he can post it on my social media.

"Time to throw the bouquet," the DJ announces.

We hurry to complete the traditional tasks before our daughters make their exit.

Brooks takes the girls by their hands, walking them toward the other women. Maddux hands me my bouquet. Ryan spins me away from our guests and plants a chaste kiss on my lips before retreating to the edge of the dance floor.

I hold my left hand in the air, extending fingers as I count. "One...two...three!"

I place both hands on the stems and launch it over my head behind my back. I immediately spin as the flowers hit Brooks in the shoulder and fall into her reluctant hands. She quickly tosses it to the twins to her right and wipes her hands on her dress. She acts like I coated it in cooties before launching it towards her.

The DJ restarts the music, our guests return to their seats or take the dance floor. I join Brooks and the girls as Ryan and Maddux approach.

"Congrats on catching the bridal bouquet," Maddux says to Brooks. "I think that means you are the next to get married."

"Two words, one finger." Brooks spits venom back at him.

"Touchy," Maddux continues to prod.

"Truce," I demand, looking between them. "Harper and Ry, you have 15 minutes to dance before Gigi and Grandpa take you home."

In a flash, the two find a spot in front of the DJ to bust a move. Ryan and I disperse into the crowd to mingle with our guests. Brooks remains at my side and Maddux with Ryan.

After half an hour, Brooks taps me on the shoulder. "Sorry to interrupt, but you need to see this," she says under her breath, bending between Gibson and me as we sit for a bit. "Ryan's friends are shedding shirts. We. Are. The. Luckiest. Women. Alive."

We follow Brooks's gaze across the barn. I see the Cardinals quarterback, wide receiver, running back, and kicker dancing, sans shirts, for a group of laughing women.

"I am going in," Ryan announces from behind us.

I watch in stunned silence as he jogs toward his teammates while unbuttoning the front of his shirt. Like a stripper, he teases with his shirt before tossing it into the crowd of nearby tables where it lands on, of all people, his mother. He joins the others in moves that remind me of *Magic Mike*.

"No way..." Brooks interjects.

I turn to see where Brooks is looking. Following her line of sight,

I find Maddux on the far-left side of the barn, removing his shirt. I look back to my friend, finding her unable to pull her eyes from him. *Mm-hmm. I warned Ryan there were sparks between those two.*

Returning my eyes to my husband, I watch as the men attempt to perform as a group. I pray someone captures this on video.

38

MONDAY, JULY 17TH

Ryan

The twins safely secured in the backseat and Christy comfy in the passenger seat, I drive our rented SUV back toward the hotel. My phone, connected to the handsfree Bluetooth in the vehicle, signals a text. Christy taps the screen to see it is a text from Maddux. Not wanting it over the speakers, I ask Christy to read it.

"He wants to know our hotel name and room number so he can send us something," she tells me, astonishment in her tone.

Glancing to my right, I see she is responding to the text. When she sets the cell phone back in the cup holder, she informs me that she gave Maddux all the information.

"What could he be sending us?" she asks.

"Who knows?" I respond. "It is probably something for the girls. He spoils them rotten."

"I bet that is it," she agrees.

Christy

While the girls enjoy 30 minutes of screen time, Ryan takes his second shower of the day and I check my messages. I see three work-related emails that can wait until I return. I open an email from Mel to find our wedding photos posted online. Ryan and I removed all social media from our phones for our honeymoon. Our photos going public today will light up our social media accounts with alerts. Thankfully, Mel takes care of all that in our absence. Bored, I decide to see what Brooks is up to.

> ME
> what's up, buttercup?

Minutes pass with no response.

> ME
> day 3 @ Disney World done
> resting @ hotel before dinner

While I hope for a response, I stare blankly at the movie the girls are watching on the television. A knock at the door startles me. I don't believe my eyes when I look through the peephole. I blink rapidly and look again. *What is going on?* Dumbfounded, I open the door.

"Hello," Maddux greets, entering our room.

"What are...you doing here?" I stammer.

Christy

As I close the door, Ryan emerges, freshly showered with wet curls drooping adorably around his face.

"Maddux?" Confusion creases Ryan's face.

"I'm here to spend time with my nieces in the most magical place in the world. I plan to entertain them each evening to give you two some honeymoon alone time," Maddux explains.

Temporarily stunned by my brother-in-law's grand gesture, I pick my jaw up off the floor. I can't believe he took time off from work to fly to Florida for us. I mean, he is Ryan's brother and uncle to my daughters, but I never expected this of him.

"I secured a room two floors up," Maddux states, sliding a key card into Ryan's hand. "I plan to hang out with the girls this evening. I will sleep in this adjoining room to keep an eye on them while the two of you spend the night upstairs." He points at the ceiling.

I can't speak. I look at Ryan in wide-eyed disbelief. He shakes his brother's hand as he pats him on the back.

"You are the best brother in the world," Ryan chuckles.

"You will owe me one," Maddux laughs. "Now, off with you. Gather your clothes and toiletries and relocate to the room upstairs. Go."

We quickly grab our clothes from the closet, our suitcase, and items from the bathroom.

Excitement flutters in my belly at the thought of Ryan and I having alone time on our honeymoon. The only night we spent alone was at the hotel on our wedding night. I lick my lips.

Ryan extends his hand to the doorknob, pausing inches away as a knock sounds for the second time in 20 minutes.

"Expecting someone?" Ryan asks me.

I shake my head.

Without looking through the peephole, he swings the hotel door wide open.

"Brooks?" We say in unison.

"Surprise!" Brooks exclaims.

"What are you doing here?" I ask, my voice rising an octave.

"I came to be your nanny for the rest of your honeymoon," she announces proudly.

Ryan and I exchange glances before looking in Maddux's direction.

"Beat ya to it, sweetheart," Maddux taunts Brooks.

My head whips back to my friend, now inside the room.

Ryan chortles, grabbing his stomach. "I can't believe the two of you had the same idea and arrived on the same day only minutes apart." He points between Brooks and Maddux. "I bet it kills you that you think alike."

Tears clog my throat. *Brooks and Maddux are the greatest friend and brother-in-law I could ever hope for.*

"Let's get out of here while we still can," Ryan murmurs, his hand holding a duffle and nudging against my lower back.

My thoughts war for a moment, but I choose to go with my husband rather than remain here to figure out the sleeping arrangements for Brooks and Maddux.

39

WEDNESDAY, JULY 26TH

Ryan

Why do I feel like a dead man walking? I love football. I love my job. It is not football that I am dreading; it is the time I will be away from my three girls over the next seven months.

"Daddy, one more," Ry whines from my right side.

I opted to read their bedtime story in our bed tonight. In the center of the bed, I lie with Ry on my right and Harper on my left. Both rest their heads sleepily near my shoulder.

"One more, but do not tell Mommy," I whisper, turning the page in the first Harry Potter book, starting one more chapter. "Close your eyes, and I will read."

I look down to each girl, ensuring their eyes are, indeed, closed before I begin to read out loud. I will miss this each night I am at camp. My nights at football camp in St. Joe will lack… Well, they will lack females.

I read this chapter slower than the last, drawing out the inevitable, and find the twins are asleep a few pages in. I lay the closed book upon my stomach, enjoying the cuddles.

"They can sleep with us tonight," Christy murmurs from the bedroom door.

I like the thought, but I envision other plans for our bed tonight. As much as I will miss my daughters, I will miss my wife, too.

"Nah. I plan to entertain my wife tonight," I whisper as I carefully sit up.

Christy raises a brow. "Entertain? Will you be dancing or jumping on the mattress?"

Giggles slip out from behind me. Turning, I spot my daughters laughing with their little hands over their mouths. They were not asleep; they were faking it.

"Busted," I scold, eliciting more laughter.

"Party is over," Christy announces. "Time to go to your bedroom."

The twins crawl from our bed, padding down the hall to their room. They share a conversation in their twin language all the way.

"No more books; they need sleep," Christy instructs.

"Plleeaassee?" I pretend to beg. "One more."

Christy bites her lips, shaking her head. "Nope."

I place a kiss on the tip of her nose.

"Gotcha," I answer.

The girls lie in bed with the lights on, waiting for us. Waino sits between their beds, on guard. When we walk into the room, he spins three times before plopping down on his dog bed beside the open door.

"I do not want you to go," Ry states, wiping a tear from her eye with her little hand.

"He has to go so he can play football this year," Harper tells her twin.

"I am gonna miss you." Ry's little voice quivers, and her lower lip trembles.

"Aww, sweetie," I soothe, lifting her head from the pillow and wrapping my arms around her. "I must go back to work. But I am going to miss you very much."

"Daddy has to sleep over with the team at camp, but we will go watch him practice on Saturday." Christy shares the information we conveyed multiple times in the past two weeks. "Daddy will call us when he can, and when he does, you can tell him all about your day."

"I will call you every day after practice, and every night before you fall asleep, you will call me," I promise, looking from Ry to Harper and back. "I can tell you a bedtime story over the phone."

"But I want you to read me my bedtime story," Ryan cries.

I look over my shoulder, hoping Christy will give me guidance. I am a sucker when the girls cry. In fact, right now, I am searching my brain for a way to see them each night after practice and before team curfew.

"Wellll," Christy drawls, "I packed a present for Daddy to take to camp in his suitcase. Maybe I should share that surprise with all three of you now."

"Yes!" Harper cheers as Ry nods and wipes her eyes.

Christy disappears for a minute, returning with a rectangle wrapped in brown paper and tied with twine.

"I slipped this into Daddy's suitcase when he was not looking," she explains. "Harper, climb onto Ry's bed so the two of you can open the present. It is for all three of you."

Christy's brown eyes sparkle with her smile. I slip my hand into hers, tugging her onto my lap. I wrap my arms around her belly, resting my chin upon her shoulder while I watch my girls.

"It's a book!" Harper squeals when a tiny corner is revealed.

"It's lots of books!" Ry proclaims.

"One, two, three, four, five." Harper counts the books out loud.

"I bought a copy of each book for us to read here as Daddy reads to you over the phone before bed," Christy explains.

"Daddy, what does this say?" Ry asks, pointing to a title.

"Let's see," I begin, scooping the books into Christy's lap.

One by one, I lift them for the girls to see.

"*Charlotte's Web, The Tale of Peter Rabbit, Peter Pan, The Wizard of Oz*, and *The Boxcar Children*," I read, and the girls clap. "Wow. We have a lot of stories to read," I say, looking at Christy.

"This book is thick," Harper states.

"These are chapter books," Christy shares. "Soon, the two of you will be reading these thick books at school."

The twins listen with wide eyes; their attention hangs on Christy's every word.

"Now, it is time for two little girls to go to sleep," she orders. "Tomorrow night, we will pick a book from the stack, and Daddy can read to us over the phone as he watches you fall asleep."

Reluctantly, Harper and Ry climb under their covers, resting their heads upon their pillows.

I tuck them in, placing a kiss upon their foreheads and both cheeks before instructing them to close their eyes. I pause at the door frame, burning the sight of them into my memory, as I turn off the overhead light. Leaving their door open a crack, I close my eyes, leaning against the wall of the hall.

"Hey," Christy soothes, taking my hand in hers. "They are tired. Everything seems worse when they are tired. They will miss you. Heck, I will miss you." She takes my face in her hands. "We love you, we will miss you, and we will visit when possible. Your time at camp will fly by. The girls are already counting down the days until the first preseason game."

Her brown eyes look up at me through her dark lashes. I press my lips against her brow, holding them there as the pain of leaving tomorrow whirls within me.

"Ry," she murmurs, and I pull away. "We will be right here. You are not losing us. This is not goodbye; this is see you soon."

She is right. I think part of the pain I feel is fear that I will lose her again—that I am losing them. I can't bear the thought of my life without them in it. Christy fills the vacant parts of my soul; I am a better man now that I've found her.

"We will use webcams and video calls," Christy continues. "You may be at camp, but each evening, you will still spend time with the girls."

"And with you," I whisper, rubbing my thumbs along her jaw, my hands upon her neck. I swipe my tongue over my lower lip as I slowly move toward hers. "I still need alone time with you."

Christy's eyes scan mine, unsure of my meaning.

Christy

"After the girls fall asleep, it will be sexy phone time," I state.

"Ry," Christy swats my ribs.

"I need you," I growl.

"Sexy phone time?" she scoffs. "I do not know..."

"We will prop our phones on the pillow. The rest will come naturally," I explain.

"Have you ever...?" Christy does not finish her question.

I find it cute that she stammers nervously about sex. She is not a prude; she is out of practice and struggles with parenting while allowing for the things she enjoys.

Christy's hands wrap around my waist. "Three days. The girls and I will be at camp on Saturday. After that, we can drive over for dinner some evenings. Camp will be over before you know it, and you will be back here most nights."

She tries to comfort me. The guys said it gets easier to leave with time. I wonder if it is harder for me because I became an instant father to five-and-a-half-year-olds a month ago. I feel pain in my chest.

"C'mon," Christy prompts, removing her arms from my abdomen.

Telling myself I will see the girls at breakfast tomorrow, I follow my wife down the hall. Her hand in mine, I tug her to me. I kiss her like there is no tomorrow. I kiss her like it is our last night together. I kiss her to forget the painful thought of not being with them every day.

※

Christy

"Hmm..." I sigh, my muscles blissfully exhausted.

"I am going to miss you," Ryan whispers, staring at the ceiling.

Rolling onto my side, I rest my head on his shoulder and lazily trace the plains and valleys of his chest muscles then abs.

"We plan to visit," I remind him.

"Yeah, but you will not be in my bed at night," he grumbles.

"It is only two weeks before you get twenty-four hours off to come home. You can make it through two weeks."

He releases a loud sigh. "I waited six years to find you; I do not relish the thought of any time away from the three of you."

"But you love football," I argue. "During the season, you will be home most nights with a little travel here and there." I twirl my finger in his hair. "The girls and I love watching you play for the Cardinals. We can master family life during the NFL season."

Ryan rolls towards me. He tucks my hair behind my ear, his thumb caressing my cheek. "Tell me how the girls watched…" His voice chokes as he speaks.

"Well," I smile, "living in Brooks's apartment, the four of us took turns choosing the menu for each game. Ry, Harper, and I are superstitious; we wear the same things for every game and sit in the same spot. Brooks is not really a football fan. She watched the games with us and often asked questions about the referees and scoring."

Ryan hangs on my every word. I pause to place a sweet kiss on his lips.

"I am afraid the girls share a tendency to yell at the officials during the game." I bite my lip. "They learned that from me."

"So, they yell and cheer?" he asks.

"Yes, they do," I answer. "They know a lot about football for their age. Although they did not know you were their father, they knew the Cardinals were my favorite team. They chose you as their favorite player all on their own."

I trace my fingertips along the scruff of his jaw.

"I wish I could watch a game with them," Ryan murmurs.

"There is always the bye week, and you can watch Monday or Thursday night games with them when the Cardinals play on Sunday," I suggest.

I witness a smile grow upon his face at my words.

"And Brooks and I can record them from time to time during your games," I offer.

"What do you think they will do when they get to come to the stadium for the first game?" he thinks out loud.

I shake my head, unsure how they will react, and I watch his eyes glaze as he imagines.

"I can't wait for them to visit me on the field during pregame warmups," he smiles, his thumbs brushing my jawline. "You will love watching the game in the birds' nest?" Ryan props himself up on one elbow.

My brow furrows.

"That is what we call Maddux's suite," he explains. "You will record their reactions, right?" he urges.

I nod.

Thursday, July 27th
Ryan

"Daddy, I made this for you," Ry announces proudly, holding a drawing in front of her.

"Tell me about it," I prompt, using the words Christy taught me when I am not sure what their art is.

"Here's me. Here's Mommy. Here's you. Here's Harper. Here's Miss Brooks, and this is Uncle Maddux." She points proudly at each of us in her drawing.

"Why is my hair blue?" I chuckle.

"That's a blue hat." She giggles.

"Can you do me a favor?" I ask, pulling her against me as I am seated on the sofa. "Please write your name on it and how old you are."

She nods firmly, disappearing to the art table in her playroom to complete my request. I bite my lips between my teeth as tears threaten. Glancing at my cell phone on the table in front of me, I find there is a little more than an hour until I need to leave my family. I rise from my seat and make my way down the hall toward the twins' bedroom.

"Hey, Daddy," Harper greets, smiling at me.

I lean my shoulder against the doorframe, extending my right arm to rest on the opposite side.

"We are drawing pictures for you to take to camp," Harper states.

"I will hang them up in my room," I promise.

"Did you pack tape?" Ry inquires, looking skeptical.

"I packed tape and magnets," Christy's voice answers from behind me.

She ducks under my arm, leaning into my side and snaking her palm up my chest. I soak up every touch and every interaction my girls give me. I marvel at how much my life changed in the course of a month. I am blessed to have the three of them in my life, in my home, and in my heart. Though I dread leaving them for camp, knowing they will be waiting here for me lights me up. *This will be my best season yet; I know it.*

"Where is Waino?" Ry asks, scanning the bedroom.

"Oh, no," Christy groans, quickly off to find the puppy.

Taking their pet ownership duties seriously, the twins join us as we search upstairs and down. I find him napping between an air conditioner vent and my open suitcase on our bedroom floor.

"Found him," I announce down the hallway.

While the four of us stand at the door, Waino turns his head in our direction.

"He wants to go in Daddy's suitcase." Harper giggles.

I want to pack my three girls in my suitcase, I think to myself.

"Girls, please take Waino out back to potty before I go," I suggest.

When they are out of earshot, I pull Christy tightly to my chest, resting my chin on top of her head.

"This is killing me," I rasp, my voice heavy with emotion. "It is taking everything in me to hold myself together."

She squeezes me in her arms.

"It is okay for them to know you are sad to leave," she soothes.

"Promise me we'll video call each other every night," I beg.

Christy

"Maybe each night before the twins fall asleep and again before we fall asleep."

Christy pulls her lips tightly between her teeth, her eyes serious. She stares at me for a long moment.

Tightness forms in my chest, and tears trail down my cheeks. My heart is full in ways I never knew possible.

40

TUESDAY, AUGUST 15TH

Christy

"Who is ready for Uncle Maddux's first birthday gift?" Maddux raises his voice for the girls to hear.

The sound of their feet running from their room is heard before they respond, "Me!"

It is hard not to laugh when Maddux joins in their cheering and clapping, jumping up and down. He asked to take the twins to Worlds of Fun and Oceans of Fun today while I work a bit this morning and golf with the ladies this afternoon.

"Where are we going?" Harper asks.

Maddux extends his arms over his head and mimes riding a roller coaster, opening his mouth like he is screaming.

"Worlds of Fun!" the twins scream, hopping up and down. "Mommy! We're going to Worlds of Fun!" they squeal.

"I know," I reply. "I packed your backpack with sunscreen, towels, and some money to buy stuff."

"That will not be necessary," Maddux argues. "It is my treat. I will buy everything today. Well, what are you waiting for? Go put your swimsuits on under your clothes, and let's go."

Christy

The girls dart down the hall, jabbering the entire way.

"Are you sure you are ready for this?" I ask, fetching the backpack from its hook in the mudroom.

"Amusement rides, water, and sugary treats. How can I go wrong?" he jests.

"It is hot. Please make sure they drink plenty of water and apply sunscreen every two hours," I instruct, passing the backpack to him.

"Will do," he chuckles. "I will text when we head back this way in the morning. Enjoy your day and night of freedom."

With Ryan at camp, this will be my first night alone. When the girls slept at their grandparents', Ryan, Maddux, and Brooks were here. This will be the first night I sleep alone in a house…ever. I went from my parents' house, to the unwed mother home, to Brooks's apartment with the twins. I have no idea what I will do with myself tonight.

I place my snack plate in the dishwasher, then stand at the kitchen island pondering what to do now. This house is too big and too quiet tonight. Golfing with the women this afternoon then enjoying drinks and appetizers with them at Gibson's helped to pass the afternoon and early evening hours. Once home, my hour-long phone call with Ryan only caused me to miss him more.

The clock on the microwave shows a bit after nine. Maybe a glass of wine and a long soak in the tub will put me in the mood to sleep.

Several chapters and an hour later, I close my Kindle app and step from the now luke-warm water of the tub. After I secure my robe around my waist, I move the half-empty bottle of Chardonnay and my iPad to the table beside our bed. Back in the bathroom, I sip from my wine glass as I transport it from the tub's edge to the vanity. I moisturize my face, slip into one of Ryan's old tees, and climb into bed, taking my tablet in hand. I lose myself in the pages, letting it transport away.

I read and read until I am disappointed at the book's end. It had a wonderfully happy ending, but I am not ready to fall asleep. I scan the other books, lining my to be read shelf as I contemplate starting another. It's after midnight; I finished off my wine bottle long ago.

Maybe it is the scent of Ryan's t-shirt, tormenting my mind and senses. I step into my closet in search of different sleepwear. Distracted, I open the wrong drawer. I slide my fingertips over my favorite red swimsuit.

I need a swim.

Lap after lap I kick, paddle, and glide. Lap after lap I attempt to clear my mind. As the number of laps grows, my muscles and lungs begin to protest. I push through, completing ten more laps before I emerge from the pool on shaky legs.

I've never been on my own; I've never been alone. Through all the tough times and struggles of being a teenage mother of twins, I never once regretted the choices I made or the life I lived. My daughters gave me the love and unity of a family, I always longed for. Living in my parents' home for sixteen years I was alone. I dreamt of a husband giving me a family. I fantasized about a house with a large yard and white picket fence, of children playing on a swing set while my husband grilled, and of surrounding myself with love to wash away the loneliness.

I fall upon the mattress, my body exhausted, sleep setting in, missing my family.

Ryan

In the past, camp was a fun introduction to my new teammates and bonding time with the guys. This year, it seems like a job; a job

Christy

that drones on. The days in meetings, workouts, and practices fly by. My evenings—well, nights—torture me.

I talk to my three girls after practice each day; then I eat dinner. Sometimes, I chat with the guys before I read the girls their bedtime story, but most nights, I study in my room. My calls with Christy at ten each night only make me miss them more. I lie awake, staring at the ceiling, telling myself other dads do this every year. *If they can do it, then I can do it.* I cross each day off the calendar, counting down the time until I return to my family and sleep in my own bed.

After dinner tonight, I set to the task of reading through the resumes Mel sent for a potential nanny. I study each photo; I stare at their faces, looking for any sign they might not be right for my girls.

When I read through their education, skills, and work history, I highlight positives in pink and possible red flags in yellow. Of course, none claim to hate children or worship the devil. I look at the length of their previous positions; if they are under a year, I highlight them in yellow. I scan each resume multiple times. Only the best is good enough for Ry and Harper.

My cell phone vibrates, signaling Christy's call. I answer, propping it against the base of my desk lamp.

"Hi, honey," I answer, loving the sight of her face filling my phone screen. "The girls stay asleep for you?"

"Yes," she drawls.

I ask this every night, and it is always the same answer. They play hard all day and are sound sleepers. Once their heads hit the pillows and their eyes close, it is snores-ville until morning.

"I looked through the resumes. How should we do this?" I ask, organizing my stack of papers in front of me.

"I picked my top three," Christy states.

"I found my favorites. Let's see if they match," I prompt.

I suddenly worry we might not agree on this. *Then what?*

"You start," she encourages me.

I take a deep breath, hoping that I match hers. If so, my fatherly instincts might be working.

"My top pick is Ken, and Collins is my second choice. Who names their daughter Collins?" I share.

Christy laughs. *Is she laughing at my question? Or did I make a horrible mistake in my choices?*

"My number one is Ken, and number two is Collins," she confesses.

I breathe a sigh of relief. *I did not screw this up. I made the same decision without her years of experience.*

"My only fear with Ken is..."

Christy shakes her head, cutting me off. "Don't go there. The agency screens these applicants. They talk with the previous families. If there were any red flags, he wouldn't be available for us to consider."

"But what about the girls changing into swimsuits?" I query, cursing the years ahead and the constant fear I will carry for my daughters.

"Ry..." Christy's voice is warm.

I love the rare occasions that I still get to be Ry for her.

"The twins are old enough to change their own clothes." She states what I know. "We leave them with Josh, and you have no worries."

She is right. I did not bat an eye at trusting Josh with them. I have known him for two years, but I trusted him from day one with personal details for me.

"Let me meet with Ken and Collins in person for an interview," Christy suggests.

"I wish I could be there," I grumble. "I could ask to take a morning off."

Christy shakes her head as she speaks. "Let me interview them once with Brooks, Josh, and the girls present. Then, if you want, I could arrange a video call for you with my choice. The two of us could have a conference call for the second interview."

I like that idea. I'd still prefer to be there for the first meeting, but I can work with this.

"Okay," I sigh.

"I will call them tomorrow and text you when I set them up," she says through a yawn.

Christy

"You are tired," I state. "You had a big day with work, swimming with the girls, and golf."

She nods, yawning again.

"I need to look over my play book again before I sleep," I lie, letting her off the hook. "I will let you get some sleep. I love you," I tell her.

"I love you, too," she returns, blowing me a kiss.

"Good night." I disconnect the call.

I am too keyed up to sleep. I contemplate going for a run but remember it is sprinkling outside. I could work out or…

I turn off the desk lamp, grab my phone, and move to the two small twin beds I pushed together in my dorm room. I pull up a photo of Christy on my phone before I lean it on the nightstand.

41

WEDNESDAY, AUGUST 23RD

Ryan

"So, how was the first day of first grade?" I ask.

"Are you calling from practice?" Christy's voice is higher than normal.

I stand at the water station on the sideline of our camp practice facility. I am sure she can hear the coaches yelling, whistles blowing, and the guys chatting as they wait for their next drill.

"Coach gave me a short break to check in on the girls' first day of school. How did it go?" I ask again.

"They seem to like it," Christy informs. "They brought home new artwork for the refrigerator, and they can't stop talking about friends they played with."

"I worried all day," I confess. "It is a big day for them; I wish I were there."

On my screen, I watch Christy approach the girls' bedroom. With the camera pointed forward, I see the girls playing with Legos on the floor before they spot me.

"Daddy is on the phone," Christy announces, and they cheer.

Christy

Christy changes the camera lens back to the front and passes the phone to Ry.

"I am going to grab a water. Girls, Daddy only has a minute. Quickly tell him all about your day at school," she says as the twins' faces fill my screen.

Of course, the girls speak at the same time but not in unison. I hear the words "friends," "recess," "finger painting," and "story time." They are smiling as they speak animatedly, so I assume they like school. They finish their stories at the same time, and the line goes silent. I open my mouth to ask a question but am interrupted.

"Daddy, what's a gold digger?" Harper blurts.

I feel like a bullet pierces my chest. My lungs burn, and my mouth goes dry. *What the heck? I mean, seriously?*

"Where did you hear those words?" I ask, still looking for an appropriate definition.

Harper tells me a boy at recess said he saw us on TV, and his dad says Christy is a gold digger. *That's it!* I had my reservations about public school before, but now, it is done. I will not allow my daughters to be taunted by boys like this. If he said this on day one, I am sure it will only get worse with him and others.

"First of all, Mommy is not a gold digger." I look firmly at my girls on the screen, hoping they understand the importance of my statement. "A gold digger is someone after another person's money. Mommy is not stealing my money. Mommy loves me, so she would never take my money and run away."

I banished the smiles from my daughters' faces. I hate that I dampened their excitement about school. Ever the emotional twin, Ry looks to be fighting tears.

"Sometimes people say things to hurt other people. Right?"

The girls nod.

"Calling your mommy a gold digger is this boy and his dad trying to hurt our family," I explain.

I attempt to keep my emotions from my words when all I want to do is ask the boy's name and pay a visit to his father with my fists.

"Why are we talking about this?" Christy asks, now in the background of the girls' room.

"Harper!" Coach yells. "Break's over."

Crap!

"I gotta go," I inform my family, but I am sure they heard my coach. "Christy, I will call you as soon as practice is over today. We need to talk about this."

"Bye, Daddy." The girls wave, smiling once again.

"I love you," I state before disconnecting and tossing my cell toward a nearby trainer.

Today's camp sucks. I drop a couple passes and mess up on running my routes. Coach actually pulls me aside to ask what is going on with my head. I apologize, telling him there was an incident with the twins' first day of school. He asks if it is urgent enough I should leave. When I tell him no, he reminds me I have a job to do, and I am at work right now. He urges me to let it go until after six. The last two hours of practice pass like a turtle walks.

I towel off and gulp the sports drink a fitness intern offers as I scan the area for the trainer I asked to hold my cell phone for the day. Everything I need to discuss with Christy haunted me for over two hours. I need my phone.

"Mr. Harper?" A young woman holding a tablet with a large camera hanging around her neck approaches me. "I have your phone for you," she informs nervously, extending her hand toward me.

The pass hanging from a lanyard assures me she works for the head office and is not a random person from the press.

"Call me Ryan." I smile, taking my phone. "Thanks for this." I lift it between us.

"Of course." She grins, not making eye contact, and walks in the direction of the defensive coaches.

Christy

I select Christy's name as I remind myself not to let my anger get the best of me.

"I do not like it," I argue. "It is senseless when we have other resources available for them."

"We went to public school, and we turned out fine," Christy counters.

I wish we were having this conversation in person, not on our phones. Even though I can see her, I long to be with her for this.

"Our girls will live a very different life than we did," I argue. "Homeschooling will allow them the flexibility to travel to away games, be free on days I am home, and stuff like that. They can sight see and learn on the trips, all while avoiding bullies or classmates trying to befriend them only to get to me. When we hired Ken as the nanny, we said we liked the fact he had an education degree; let's let him be their tutor. You are one of the smartest people I know; you will have no problem teaching them when he is not around," I state.

Christy's appalled reaction makes me smile while shaking my head at her.

"We can afford to pay him more as a dual nanny and tutor." I state what she already knows.

"Let's wait until I meet with the teacher before we pull them out of school," Christy suggests, her tone like my mother's.

Feeling helpless, I run my fingers through my hair, frustrated.

"I know you will not want to hear this," I hedge. "We should meet with my publicist before we talk to the school. We are new to this, but things are easily distorted in the media. I would not want someone from the school to post it all over social media." Christy opens her mouth, but I continue. "As a precaution. That is all. I will call Mel now, fill her in a bit, and ask her to contact you."

"Ry…"

I absolutely love hearing my former pet name.

"I love you," I state, putting an end to this part of the discussion.

"Fine. Call her. I will set up the time to meet with the teacher and let you know what we all come up with."

"I want to be with you to meet with the teacher. It is not quite…"

"Ryan, I have got this," Christy assures me. "I will keep you posted every step of the way. This is not something for you to miss work over. I hope there never is, but this is not an emergency."

After contacting Mel, I debate finding one of the guys to offer some dad advice or a workout. I opt for the weight room; I will take out my frustration on some free weights.

42

THURSDAY, AUGUST 24TH

Christy

The twins remain in their chairs at the main office with the administrative assistants while I follow the principal to her office with Brooks at my side. When I called her to vent, she insisted she would attend with me in Ryan's place.

"Thank you for meeting with us today," the principal begins, motioning for the two of us to sit in chairs at the table in her office.

It seems large for a school office. It contains an over-sized desk and shelves at one end, a round table with four chairs in the middle, and a sofa against the far wall.

"I am Ms. Anson," she introduces. "I invited the twins' teacher, Miss Smith, and our elementary counselor, Mr. Rodriguez, to join us."

I smile at the three members of the faculty as they pull up chairs at the table.

"I brought my friend, Brooks, with me today," I explain. "Ryan Harper," I pause, looking at the additional people at the table, "the girls' father, is at NFL camp this week. We thought it might be best if he did not attend to keep this from becoming a local celebrity issue with the press."

I keep secret the fact that it was his publicist's idea that he does not tie himself to volatile topics if he can keep from it. Beside me, Brooks clears her throat, placing her cell phone between us.

"We will be recording this meeting," I inform them.

This is met with raised brows, eyes looking towards the administrator, and the teacher shaking her head.

At their balk, I explain, "Our lawyer instructed us to do so, in case any of this leaks to the press. It will serve as physical proof of everything discussed today. We take these incidents seriously and feel the press and public would, too, if it were to be leaked."

"Incidents plural?" the counselor asks the teacher next to him in a whisper.

The principal clears her throat. "I believe it is important that we speak with each of the girls separately about the allegations before we discuss where to go from here."

I nod. First in is Harper.

The principal begins by making sure Harper knows all the adults in attendance. Next, she asks Harper what it means to tell a lie then to tell the truth. Once it is clear that my five-year-old plans to tell the truth, we move to the reason for our meeting.

The counselor prompts, "Harper, do you know why we are here today?"

Harper nods.

Mr. Rodriguez continues, "Please tell us what happened yesterday."

"At first recess, Jackson came over to the swings with Juan and Justin. He told me his dad said my mom is a gold digger. I told him to leave me and my sister alone."

"Do you know what the words 'gold digger' mean?" Mr. Rodriguez asks.

Harper nods. "I asked Daddy last night, and he said it is a bad word for someone that steals."

Mr. Rodriguez nods. "Did anything else happen?"

Harper looks my way; I smile at my little girl.

Christy

She continues, "He punched Ryan in the tummy. She fell off her swing, and he told us he knows where his dad keeps his guns. If we tattled to the teacher or our mom like we did last year, he would bring his gun to school and shoot us."

The adults in the room attempt to school their features as they share concerned glances.

"Did you tell your teacher…"

Harper interrupts Ms. Anson. "We did not tattle. We do not want him to shoot us."

When the door closes behind Harper, the principal inquires if any of us had heard the second part of that story before today. The educators all shake their heads before I respond.

"Initially, they did not tell me," I begin. "As I asked more and more questions, Harper finally told me everything. She was crying and scared about the gun."

I am more nervous when Ry sits at the table. Of the two, she is my tender one. Things bother her that do not seem to faze her sister.

Again, Ms. Anson makes sure my child knows the difference between the truth and a lie before the questioning begins.

In her own words, Ry recalls the same story that Harper shared and then some.

"Jackson still calls me a dike," Ry informs, and my stomach plummets as it does every time I hear this story.

He called my daughter a dike last year. This Jackson is the same Jackson that I had to email the teacher about in kindergarten. Ryan cried an entire evening before confessing that a boy at school kept calling her a dike.

"I told on him last year, and the teacher told him to stop, but he did not." Ry divulges information she kept from me until yesterday. "He punches everybody when the teacher is not looking. He takes our stuff."

"What stuff?"

"Crayons, pencils, and food at lunch," Ry answers. "We told the teachers last year, but he did not stop. It got worse."

After hearing once again, in detail, the ongoing bullying my daughters endured last year and again now, I am resolute in my decision to pull them from this district. I glance one more time at my girls through the large window as they play with the iPad in the outer office.

"At first, I balked at the thought of pulling my children from the district," I admit. "With each passing hour, however, my anger festers. A teacher was made aware of Jackson bullying my daughter by using a word that might be interpreted as hate speech to the LGBTQ community. I learned yesterday that, after the teacher spoke to him, the name calling continued, along with threats if the students tattled on him."

I scan all the eyes at the table. "Fast forward to first grade. Jackson continues to bully, name call, and is threatening gun violence to the students in his grade. In the district's handbook, it lists a zero tolerance for weapons, bullying, and hate speech. Even with the zero tolerance, this child is still attending classes. Our family takes threats of gun violence by a child seriously; we do not condone bullying in any setting, and feel the names this child chose to call our daughters are hurtful."

I slide my large brown envelope toward the principal.

"Here is my affidavit, signed and notarized, with the information I shared with you here today. This paper, along with the recording on our cell phone, will show that the school was made aware of all three offenses in case the district opts to do nothing, this child escalates, and something horrific happens in the future."

"We are not going to the press and prefer not to go to the school board. We are quietly withdrawing our girls from the district to cut all ties with this child and the situation. I beg you to follow the guidelines laid out in the handbook, as every parent in your district assumes you are, indeed, protecting their children."

No one speaks; all eyes look to the administrator for guidance.

"I will take your silence as an end to our meeting," Brooks states, rising from the seat beside me.

"Thank you for your time." I follow my friend from the room.

"That went better than I thought it might," I say for only Brooks to hear.

"We did all we can; the rest is up to them," she says.

Christy

"Who is ready for ice cream?" Brooks asks the girls.

They hop from their chairs, a smile upon their faces. Usually, they would be cheering and clapping at Brooks's announcement. This inquisition by the principal and counselor shook them. I will make it my mission tonight to cheer them back up and put this hideous situation behind us.

I love how close my best friend is to my girls. We co-parented for many years; I hope she will always feel this close to all of us.

43

MONDAY, AUGUST 28TH

Christy

"Mommy, I love my necklace," Harper proclaims, her hand upon her lanyard.

"It is not a necklace," Ry chides. "Mr. Ken, what's this called?"

"It is a lanyard," our tutoring nanny answers, guiding them.

We follow Mel through the underbelly of the stadium as we make our way to the field. Our lanyards allow us to stand on the sideline during the pregame warmups today. Ryan arranged for the twins to see him on the field since it is our first game at the stadium. He thought it would be a good idea for our nanny to attend, too, since today is his first day with us.

The hot, late-August air signals our arrival. As we climb the four stairs to the field, butterflies flutter in my belly. I am as excited as the girls are; I may even be more excited. Despite being a Cardinals fan my entire life, like the girls, this is my first time in The Cardinals Nest Stadium. I can't believe I get behind-the-scenes access. I feel like a little girl on Christmas morning.

The sun blazes above, and the heat seems to reflect off the grass at our feet. I spin, in awe of the red and gold stadium surrounding me. A few eager fans make their way to the front rows for a close look at the teams warming up while most continue tailgating in the parking lots surrounding the stadium.

"I see Daddy!" Harper yells and points toward the nearest endzone.

My eyes instantly lock on red number 87, who is running routes with the quarterbacks. My breath hitches, and my heart skips a beat. I recognize this feeling; it is the same effect he had on me in high school.

The saying, "There is something about a man in uniform," holds true. Ryan in a football uniform proves to be my kryptonite. I press my libido back into its box and distract myself by focusing on my daughters.

"He will not wave at me," Ry pouts, hands on her hips.

"Honey," I bend to her eye level as I speak, "Daddy is working. He can't make touchdowns if he is looking at you on the sideline."

I appeal to my daughter's competitive nature in my explanation. Ry nods, happy with my rationale.

Standing again, I catch Ryan dancing to the music blaring through the stadium. I stifle a giggle. *Oh. My. Gosh.* I feel as though my eyes will pop out of my head. Ryan turns around; his back now faces me. *His dance moves...* I chew on my lip as I watch him gyrate deliciously to the beat.

"Daddy's being silly," Harper laughs, breaking my lusty haze.

Damn those uniforms.

"Daddy's coming! Daddy's coming!" the twins cheer.

In his football uniform, Ryan looks ginormous, dangerous, powerful, and... Stop it! This is not the time or the place for my wanton thoughts.

"Hi, Daddy!" the girls shout, waving animatedly.

In one fluid motion, Ryan scoops them into his arms, standing in front of me.

"Time for good luck kisses," he announces, "from all three of my girls. Come here, Mommy."

The twins kiss Ryan's cheeks while he gives me a peck. The sounds of cameras click around us.

"I love you," he murmurs.

"We love you, too," the twins giggle.

"Ken, I am glad you joined us this evening." He greets the man standing behind us.

Ken smiles and nods nervously.

Ryan looks towards his teammates as they disappear under the stadium. He tilts his head in that direction.

"I gotta go." He smiles, before lowering the girls to the ground.

"Bye, Daddy!" they yell, waving at his back.

I find myself biting my lip again as I ogle my husband's tush in his tight, white uniform pants while he jogs away.

The birds' nest, as Maddux refers to it, is a large luxury suite stocked with catered food, snacks, and desserts. The two mini-fridges hold beverages with and without alcohol. While Maddux introduces me to his other guests, my girls stand at the windows overlooking the field. In addition to Jackie, Warren, and us, Maddux has two employees and two clients with him today. I keep a watchful eye on the girls as I listen to the adult conversations. When the topic moves to real estate, I excuse myself.

"Daddy looks so small," Harper giggles, pointing to him on the far sideline after the national anthem.

Maddux's suite sits on the 45-yard line behind the visitor's sideline. It gifts us with a view of Ryan on and off the field.

"Guess how many seats there are in this stadium," Ken prompts the girls.

Ry mulls it over while Harper shouts out guesses. After five guesses each, Ken informs them over 75,000 seats surround us. The girls quickly lose interest in learning and focus on the field again.

"Mommy, we're waving at Daddy," Harper shouts.

"Sweetheart, remember Daddy is working right now," I remind her in a hushed tone. "We need to use our indoor voices. Uncle Maddux has other guests with us."

Christy

I watch my daughters scan the suite behind us, nodding.

"What do you say? Let's open the windows so we can hear the crowd better," Maddux suggests as he moves the glass.

The girls bounce excitedly in their seats.

Soon, the special teams players line up for the kickoff, and the music begins. Without missing a beat, my daughters wave their towels over their heads, as is tradition for every kickoff in this stadium. I join in, easily caught up in the electricity of the crowd. As a sea of red towels wave, the Cardinals catch the ball, running it back to the Houston Oilmen 40-yard line.

I sit on the edge of my seat; I am always anxious for the first series. In past seasons, I often paced the room at home until I settled down.

On the next play, our quarterback quickly hands off to the running back for a gain of 15 yards. We crossed the 50; now, I relax a bit. On our 45-yard line, the center snaps the ball, and the quarterback drops back to pass.

"Daddy's open!" Harper yells and points.

I follow the tight spiral arching through the air into a pair of gold-gloved hands.

Ryan! It is Ryan! Ryan caught the pass. Standing now, I clap and cheer. Ryan dodges a defender, spins past another, and easily enters the endzone.

"Touchdown!" I scream.

Our suite erupts, as does the entire stadium. I continue jumping on my toes and clapping while Ryan's teammates pose like bowling pins, and he rolls the football at them. One by one, they fall, imitating a strike. They bump chests and pat each other's butts before leaving the field for the special teams players to line up for the extra point.

My eyes remain on my guy. He trots towards his coaches. Five yards from the sideline, he pauses, turning to face our suite. He kisses the tip of the fingers on his right hand, then his left hand, and his right hand again, throwing all kisses in our direction.

I've watched every one of Ryan's games. Never before has he blown a kiss into the crowd or pointed to his brother's suite.

"Mommy, Daddy pointed at me," Harper cheers.

"Mommy, did you see?" Ry asks.

I can't speak; I can't breathe. Tears fill my eyes as adrenaline from his touchdown speeds through my veins. Maddux approaches, gifting me a side hug.

"He wanted to surprise you," Maddux explains. "The two of us discussed a few options, and he asked me to keep it a secret. He wanted to surprise the three of you if he scored today."

I look up at him, stunned.

"Breathe," Maddux laughs.

I focus on my breathing. I am not sure what affected me the most: witnessing his touchdown or the gesture he made towards us in front of 75,000 people.

"I will take that as an indication that you liked it," Maddux chuckles.

"Uncle Maddux," Ry calls, and he bends down to her level. "Daddy scored a touchdown."

"I saw that," he chortles. "Did you see him blow you a kiss?"

Both girls nod, smiling widely.

"Maybe he will score another one," he says, standing.

"Two," Harper suggests, holding up two fingers.

"No, three," Ry adds before returning her attention to the field.

Maddux returns to my side.

"I thought he was an idiot," he says for only me to hear. "I cursed the memory of you that he held tightly onto."

He looks from the Cardinals defense on the field to me.

"He never gave up hope. He never stopped searching for you," Maddux informs.

For the second time since the start of the game, I fight tears. Maddux faces me, placing his hands on my shoulders. He turns me towards him, embracing me in a tight hug.

"I am thankful the two of you found each other again," he murmurs on top of my head. "You and the twins mean the world to him and me."

He squeezes tighter before releasing me to return to his guests.

44

THURSDAY, SEPTEMBER 14TH

Ryan

Fall games test an athlete's body. Even with this Thursday night game, the heat attempts to wear me out. Whistles blow; the Bolts called a timeout. I drink the water offered by the hydration staff as I listen to our offensive coach. Less than a minute remains in the game, and we trail by three. I signal for my special bottle. A staff member quickly runs it to me in the huddle near the sideline. I take a long drink of the pickle juice. *Damn. That stuff is not good warm.* I chug water to wash down the taste. Having never left a game due to cramps, I do not plan to do it tonight. It is time for the offense to step up; my team needs me.

The refs' whistles signal the end of the timeout; our offense returns to the center of the field. It is first down with the ball on the 48-yard line. Coach calls a passing play to a wide receiver. Nolan shouts the cadence. At the snap, I roll to the far right before cutting back to the center of the field in a short route. Nolan drops back to pass, looking to number 42. I watch my quarterback's head turn and eyes scan the field. Our receiver is not open; Nolan looks for an open man. I wave my right hand over my head, not breaking stride.

Nolan cocks the ball back and launches a pass in my direction. My eyes lock on the spinning ball as it hurls toward me. On my next step, I leap into the air. Both hands connect with the pigskin. I grip it with all my might as my feet connect with the turf. I tuck the ball to my chest with my left arm and run toward our endzone.

I point in the direction of an approaching cornerback. My teammate tries and fails to block him. I am pushed out of bounds at our 39-yard line. My 13 yards moves our team across the 50-yard line with enough for a first down.

Coach calls a running play. Nolan hands the ball to our rookie running back, and we gain another four yards. It is second down and six yards to go with fifty-two seconds left in the game. When the center snaps the ball, I run my short route up the middle; Nolan throws a long pass to another receiver, but it is incomplete.

After our running back gets us a first down, Nolan throws two incomplete passes. It is third and ten on the twenty-eight-and-a-half-yard line with eight seconds on the clock. This is it, the offense's last play of the game. We must score or leave enough time for our field-goal kicker to attempt to tie it for us.

Nolan shouts out our cadence, the center snaps the ball, and I sprint like there is no tomorrow. I don't look at my quarterback. I have faith in our lineman and in Nolan; I run my route, knowing the ball will greet me in the endzone. My job is to get there, break free of defenders, and make the catch.

I turn toward the middle of the endzone for four steps, then cut back to the far side of the field. I look up, finding the tight spiral aimed perfectly. I take two more steps, spring from my feet, and reach for heaven.

I glance at the defender's arms extended like mine, hoping to swat the ball. My vertical is higher than his. I close my right hand around the tip of the ball, squeezing so hard it stings. I bring my left hand to the side of the ball and pull it toward my abdomen as my back hits the ground.

Flat on my back, a defender on top of me, I hear the whistles but can't see the officials' signal. I do not need to see his arms. I caught the ball; it is a touchdown.

Christy

My offensive teammates pull the L.A. player off then help me up. We celebrate with chest bumps then an endzone shuffle dance before leaving the field. I send my three kisses toward my ladies in the suite as I step off the field.

Game one of the season places a tick mark in the win column. The victory feels sweeter with Christy, Ry, and Harper to help me celebrate.

45

SATURDAY, OCTOBER 28TH

Christy

I am buffed, polished, styled, and staring at my reflection in the three-way mirror in my closet. The tight, strapless red dress I purchased on this week's shopping trip with Brooks matches my heels perfectly. The shoes are surprisingly comfortable. Since I avoided heels for years, I figured they would kill my feet as I attempted to balance on their pegs.

The last time I dressed up like this was Ryan's senior prom. I had no idea the complete one-eighty my life would take in the two weeks that followed it. We were young, in love, and planning on a long-distance relationship while I finished high school and he attended college.

Pulling myself back to the present, I scan my reflection from head to toe, turning to one side then the other. Amazed that this is now my life, I exit my closet in search of my husband. It feels weird to say "my husband," even after three months.

I peek into his closet to no avail. *Hmm...* He dressed quickly. I exit our bathroom and bedroom. I hear male voices.

Emerging from the hallway, I find Josh working at the table while

Ryan leans against the kitchen counter and Maddux occupies a stool at the island. I pause at the entrance to the hallway, admiring Ryan's snug, royal blue button-down. He left the top two buttons open; already, I long to trace my fingers along his neck and sneak my palm from his collar to his shoulder over his strong pectoral muscles. The striking blue shirt causes his blue eyes to pop. He rolled the cuffs once, exposing a bit of his strong forearms. His dark gray slacks only hint at the powerful thighs beneath.

Josh clears his throat, looking at me. Maddux and Ryan turn their heads to Josh then follow his line of sight. Maddux smiles appreciatively. Ryan's eyes... Well, Ryan's eyes feel like Superman's X-ray vision, appraising my dress and flesh beneath. My skin heats, and my body zings to life.

Ryan prowls towards me as I remain frozen in place. I am a deer in the headlights, not sure how to react. His fingers scald my bare shoulders seconds before his mouth encases mine. His desperate kiss further fuels my flames. When he pulls away, panting, he rests his forehead against mine.

"You...that dress... You look stunning," he stammers between his heavy breaths. "I am not sure I will keep my hands off you tonight."

I take a step back, tapping my index finger to the tip of his nose. "Well, you'd better try, or your publicist will find lots of photos and posts to clean up tomorrow."

Ryan shakes his head, leaning his left hand on the corner of the wall. "You are going to be the death of me."

I look into my phone's camera as I apply lip gloss.

"But you will die a very happy man," Maddux chimes in.

Eyes still on me, Ryan replies, "A *very* happy man."

I swat his hard chest as I walk past him. I need water to cool down.

"Mom made me promise to send her a pic before we leave," Maddux informs. "I told her there would be photos taken at the club, but she wants one from here."

I pose next to Ryan, my side pressing to his. Maddux takes two photos before he prompts us to move closer together. We turn, facing each other, my soft curves tight to his hard muscles.

Stop! I can't fantasize about Ryan for the next four plus hours. We must behave in public tonight, or my thoughts will cause us nothing but trouble.

"Maddux, please send me the photos," Josh requests. "I will post one or two to Christy's social media."

Josh winks at me. His duties in running Ryan's household grew to helping me keep up with my posts.

Worrying about dressing up and going to a club for the first time, posting to social media did not come to mind. Lucky for me, Josh will post now, and Ryan's publicist will post throughout the evening.

"The car is here," Josh announces after reading an alert on his iPad. "You kids go have fun. I will want all the details in the morning."

Ryan's driver parks our SUV in front of Ink, Inc in downtown Liberty 15 minutes before we planned to pick up Brooks.

"I will text her to let her know she can come down as soon as she is ready," I tell the guys.

"Let me tell her," Maddux suggests from his third-row seat. "I need to use her restroom."

Ryan and I turn around to peer at Maddux.

"What?" he smirks. "She will let me use her restroom, won't she?"

I nod, sure my eyebrows arch near my hairline and mouth falls agape. Maddux opens his door and makes his way to Brooks's door.

"That seems odd, right?" I ask as I watch him open the door as if he is familiar with her stairway.

"He got a tattoo here," Ryan states.

That is true, but the entrance to the tattoo shop is separate from the door to her apartment above. I wonder if maybe the night he took the twins and Brooks out to eat, he also received an invite to her apartment. Hmm... Something is fishy.

Christy

"Has he said anything?" I ask.

"About what?" Ryan turns slightly in his seat to face me.

"About Brooks," I urge. "For two people that fight like cats and dogs, he seems pretty familiar with how to enter her apartment."

Ryan's confused face lets me know he has not paid any attention.

"Mark my words, their constant bickering is foreplay," I smirk.

"No way," he argues. "She is soooo far from Maddux's type. You must be imagining things."

"Whatever," I scoff.

"You really think they are?" he asks.

"They are what?" Brooks asks, opening the car door.

We were so caught up in our conversation, we did not notice Maddux and Brooks approaching.

"Let's go," Maddux encourages when all doors are closed.

Movement restricted in my seat; I turn as best I can to see Brooks.

Brooks wears a spaghetti-strap, little black dress with a tight bodice and flowing skirt. From the front it looks like something I might wear, falling to mid-thigh. However, the straps turn in to black angel wings in the back. They are small and beautiful lying flat to her tattooed back. Not wearing her signature fishnet tights, she opted for bare legs between her hemline and treaded platform combat boots that nearly reach her knees. Her vibrant leg tattoos contrast with her black attire.

"You look fabulous," I tell my friend.

"Fabulous? I said she looks damn sexy," Maddux shares.

Ryan's wide eyes find mine as I bite my lip to keep from smirking. *Yep. Something is fishy indeed.*

When the SUV pulls to the front of the club, the valet opens my passenger side door. I take a deep breath in preparation before climbing from the vehicle. I stand awkwardly, waiting on my husband to join me.

"Ready?" Ryan asks, lips near my ear, then kisses my temple.

"Ryan! Ryan!" fans call.

I force a smile upon my face and wrap my arm through his. To say I am nervous would be an understatement. It seems every outing becomes a big production. Ryan's celebrity status draws a lot of attention, and I prefer to blend in rather than stand out. Add to that the fact I have never ventured to a nightclub, and I am truly a fish out of water. I turned 21 this year, and I focused on the twins rather than going out with friends. I never partied much. I only know what to expect from what I've watched on TV and in movies.

"Relax," he coaxes, patting my forearm. He speaks through his charming smile. "Cameras out here then we get to relax and chill."

Right. Cell phone cameras will be everywhere. There will be no relaxing for me until we are safely back in the vehicle.

"Ryan! Ryan!" fans call from both sides of the ropes.

My husband halts, waving in one direction and then the other. Although he declines requests for selfies and autographs, his fans seem okay with it.

"Tonight, all my attention is on my wife." He grins, and the fans eat it up.

I need him to give me lessons on working with fans and the press. He is gifted in that department. I chuckle to myself. *He is gifted in many departments.*

"Thank you." Ryan waves to the crowd before escorting me past the line of people waiting to enter the club.

I imagined the club to be darker than it is. Strobe lights flicker around the upper and lower dance floors while spotlights highlight the bar areas.

Ryan's publicist greets us, ushering us to the right side of the room. A bouncer the size of Ryan's linemen in full pads opens the velvet rope, and we are led up a dimly lit staircase to the less-public second level.

The space overlooks the two main dance floors and three bars on the first floor. I am looking over the glass railing at the crowd below, when Brooks nudges my shoulder.

"You okay?" she asks as we take in our surroundings.

I nod.

"Nervous?"

"Yes," I answer. "This world is nothing like our apartment life with the twins."

Ryan's large palm presses into my lower back. "Ladies, our booth is ready." His deep voice and touch takes the edge off.

Maddux follows Ryan's publicist, and we follow him. Our booth is actually a large, round red sofa with a short round table in the center. The area is dim compared to the brighter lights downstairs. I assume this allows the VIPs more privacy from the general public.

Mel leads the owner over. Ryan rises to greet him and introduces him to me, Brooks, and Maddux. Having spent my entire life in the KC area, I know he is part owner of the professional baseball and soccer teams in town, in addition to his family owning vast amounts of real estate across the metro. The two make small talk for a minute while I fidget in my seat.

Returning, Ryan stretches out his arm on the sofa behind me. His hand on my shoulder, he pulls me closer to him. I begin to look up at him when our waitress approaches.

"Oh, my gosh!" Kirby squeals.

"Hey," I greet. "I didn't know you worked here. I mean, you told me you worked at a club downtown, but I never thought it might be this one." I am rambling.

"You know her?" Brooks asks over the music.

Kirby looks toward Brooks and Maddux at my side. "My name is Kirby, and I will be your bottle girl this evening."

"Kirby is a member at the club," I inform the group. "She frequents the pool."

Kirby's smile lights up her face. This is my first time seeing her in makeup, and she is gorgeous. She is beautiful without makeup, too. I bet she makes great tips.

"I brought bottles of water and glasses of ice for you now," she informs as she places them on the table in front of each of us. "Would you like a beverage menu?" She looks from Maddux to Ryan.

"1492," Ryan says, looking to Maddux for confirmation.

Maddux nods.

"And for the ladies, Ciroc Peach," he requests.

I hear him order, but I am lost in the lights shimmering in his blue eyes. I want to freeze this moment. My heart speeds up when his sexy smile spreads across his lips. I want to sneak out the back door and hurry home with him. When I break free of his tractor beam smile, Kirby no longer stands in front of us. I squeeze Ryan's thigh while I watch Maddux lean toward Brooks as they talk.

"Leave them alone," Ryan says near my ear.

Turning back to him, I ask, "Will you be drinking tonight?"

"I will have…"

"Two," we say in unison.

Does that mean that Maddux will drink the rest of the bottle? I can't imagine what he will be like after that much alcohol. *Ryan better not think Brooks and I will finish off an entire bottle of vodka.*

As if reading my mind, Ryan states, "We will not drink it all. If someone drops by our table, we will offer them a drink or leave it when we are ready to go."

I worry my lip.

"Pretend the four of us are in our basement," he suggests. "Talk and watch people dance; we are in our own little bubble up here." He chuckles. "Even our server is a friend."

He is right. I need to relax; I am here with friends. Before I know it, Kirby returns with two bottles and four glasses. She pours our first drinks, asks if she can get us anything else, then excuses herself to tend to the table next to ours.

Brooks raises her glass, asking, "Whose turn is it to toast?"

Maddux does not wait for an answer. "Here's to family, friends, bye weeks, and a record-setting football season."

We clink our glasses, and I watch the other three drink before I take a tentative sip. I enjoy the sweet peach scent and flavor. Seconds pass before the warmth of the vodka burn coats my throat.

"Like it?" Ryan asks, and I nod.

Christy

"I've had it a couple of times before," Brooks admits, listening in on our conversation.

Ryan smiles, proud of his choice. Sensing motion out of the corner of my eye, I watch Maddux speak near Brooks's ear, she nods, and he moves to sit on the opposite side of Ryan. I move a little closer to my friend, making it easier for us to chat for several minutes. She does her best to keep me calm in my new environment.

We talk until two women in tiny swaths of fabric walk past the two of us to approach the guys. Brooks nudges my ribs with her elbow. I pray my friend keeps her cool. She can be a spit fire and protects those dear to her.

"Ryan, can we get a photo with you?" the busty redhead asks.

"Ladies, like I told the fans out front, I am keeping all my attention on my wife and guests tonight," Ryan states.

"C'mon," Red urges, crossing her arms under her chest, further accentuating it. "We're here with..."

"You take the brunette; I get the redhead," Brooks growls in my ear, drawing my attention.

I watch Ryan rise to his feet, preparing to scoot past his brother.

"Your friend should join us, too," the brunette encourages, hopeful.

Of course, Maddux jumps at the opportunity. He positions himself between the women, his arms slinking around both their waists.

"Ryan in the middle with..." the redhead coos.

"I am his brother, Maddux."

The women seem to be enamored with both men. While one presses tightly to Ryan's side, the other does the same to Maddux. Several long seconds pass before the women realize they have no one to take a photo for them.

"Be a dear and take our photo," the redhead says, waving her cell phone toward us.

"I am gonna shove that phone..." Brooks grumbles as she rises.

I grab her arm, halting her progress, "Be nice. Cameras will be recording Ryan from everywhere."

Brooks rolls her eyes at me. I can see her lips moving the entire time she takes the pictures. I hope the women can't hear what she says.

"All done!" Brooks announces louder than she needs to.

To Ryan's credit, he quickly peels the woman from him and returns to me. Maddux struggles, but Brooks comes to his rescue.

"Honey, I need another drink," she pretends to whine, pulling on his hand.

Hoping for an invitation to join our group, the ladies stand before us, admiring the photo on their phone.

Kirby returns to our table, refilling glasses and replacing empty water bottles while chatting a bit. Before she leaves, she discreetly tilts her head toward the women. Ryan shakes his head. A moment after Kirby disappears, the bouncer ushers the women away from our table.

"I am not sure how they made their way into the VIP area, but I *had* to take a photo with them. You know that, right?" Ryan's sincere eyes search mine.

"I know, but they wanted more than a photo," I state.

"I did my best to keep her from humping my leg and grabbing me." He chuckles, causing me to swat his shoulder.

"Do not look now," I murmur near his ear, my fingers playing with his long waves. "Brooks seems to be staking her claim on your brother."

"Is it possible for dynamite and a flame not to explode?" Ryan teases.

"I fear we are about to find out," I retort.

I am equal parts excited and scared by their interactions. I believe the two of them would make a great couple if they could refrain from challenging each other on every topic.

46

FRIDAY, DECEMBER 22ND

Ryan

I am bone tired, nursing a bruised rib, and enduring a sprained middle finger on my right hand. With two games left in the regular season, it is time to dig deep, fight through the pain, and secure our spot in the playoffs. There are no days off; workouts and practices remain intense.

Work over for the day, I camp out on the chaise lounge in the family room. I place ice on my hand and heat on my ribs. Lifting my water jug with my free hand, I groan, finding it empty.

"Daddy, what's wrong?" Ry asks from the floor near my feet.

My girls color in the new Santa coloring books Mom dropped off yesterday with her most recent Christmas presents to place under our tree. Christy often shares her dismay at the sea of gifts flowing from beneath it.

"What do you need?" Josh calls from the kitchen.

"My water is empty," I tell my daughter.

"It is my turn!" Harper scolds her sister, taking the jug from my hand.

The twins take my recovery between games seriously. To prevent fighting over me, Christy started a rotation for the girls to assist. They long to be helpful for me, claiming it is how they help the Cardinals win.

Taking advantage of Harper's distraction, Ry tucks herself into my good side with two colors and her coloring book in hand. She uses the side of my chest as a hard surface to continue her art project.

"I love you, Daddy," she states, eyes remaining on her task.

"I love you, too, Ry," I murmur and kiss the crown of her head.

"Hey! No fair!" Harper complains, returning the water to me.

"There is room down there," Ry informs, pointing her green color at my feet.

Harper places her hands upon her hips, ready to argue with her twin.

"If you are careful, you can cuddle in here," I suggest, pointing to the heat pad on my ribs.

To her credit, she does slowly climb into the chair beside me, tenderly laying her head against my shoulder.

My soreness evaporates; this is the life. I look at the mirror images on my sides. I can't deny they are my daughters. They share my hair, eyes, and nose.

This is a crazy week; the team holds practice, meetings, and workouts every day because we play a game on Christmas Eve. I forgot the excitement a kid feels for the holidays. I am not sure who is more excited for presents: the girls, my mom, or me.

The girls love lifting the presents in an attempt to predict their contents. Mom can't stop buying them gifts, and I swear Christy may explode if she drops off any more.

Josh and Christy went crazy on the holiday decorations. A 14-foot Christmas tree stands in the family room, visible from the kitchen and dining areas. Gifts seem to be multiplying beneath its branches. The basement holds an eight-foot tree, decorated in a sports theme. The girls display a small tree in their bedroom, which Christy insists they use as a nightlight. My wife loves sleeping under Christmas tree lights, so we enjoy a four-foot tree on a table in our bedroom, too.

It seems every shelf and railing holds greenery with lights. On each kitchen cabinet door hangs a small holly wreath, and sprigs of mistletoe hang in every doorway. Even the exterior of the house, in front and back, shines brightly with lights.

Josh and my family shared many laughs as I spent four days attempting to synchronize the interior timers to turn on at the same time. Apparently, my OCD was showing. Harper and Ry created a larger swear jar to hold more money due to my verbal tirades until the lights and timers bent to my will.

Christmas spirit does help motivate me through the late-season stress. The girls keep me active each evening, giving me less time to brood over my work wounds. I am happy to be binging less TV and enjoying more time with family this season than in years past.

Maddux and I enjoy our shopping conversations as we each attempt to find the perfect gift for the twins and Christy. I planned a family vacation for us to Washington D.C. for a week this summer. I will earn brownie points from my wife because the trip is both fun and educational. Uncle Maddux joined in, stating the twins placed 'meet the President' on their birthday gift wish list. While he can't make that happen, he plans to take them on a tour of the White House while giving Christy and I a day to ourselves.

I bought them each a backpack and carry-on luggage to use on this trip and all our travels. I placed the trip itinerary inside the bag, wrapped it, and placed it inside the suitcase, then wrapped that. Of course, I purchased them several other gifts, one of which is sure to make Christy upset with me. In my defense, Waino needs a sibling, and she never said we could not get another pet.

As for me, I do not need any gifts; I received the greatest gift of all in June when I bumped into Christy. If Santa insists on bringing me a gift, I guess I want to play in the Super Bowl this February.

EPILOGUE

Ryan

"Three...two...one!"

Fireworks light the sky; the stadium erupts. I throw my hands in the air, screaming at the top of my lungs.

"We did it!" Nolan yells, bumping his chest to mine.

"Super Bowl!" a lineman cheers at our sides.

I pat my hand hard against Nolan's helmet. Our eyes are wild with this achievement. *We are going to the Super Bowl.* Our entire team celebrates, closing in around us. I jump up and down over and over, attempting to find Coach in the crowd. Misinterpreting my movements as celebration, the guys around me begin jumping as they cheer, making it more difficult.

I remove my helmet, grasping it tightly at my side. Nolan's quarterback coach shimmies his way between us. He barks instructions in Nolan's ear. I follow the two of them as they force their way through the crowd. I assume they head toward Coach or maybe the press. Either way, I am eager to escape the calamity at the center of the celebration.

A staff member places a ball cap atop my head and a t-shirt over

Christy

my shoulder. I don't need to look; they are our AFC Champions merchandise.

I lose sight of Nolan and spin, searching. Players, coaches, assistants, agents, and staff cover half the field. In the center, a temporary stage appears. Red and gold confetti rains down from all directions. For the moment, the fireworks cease. I am not quite sure what I look for. The adrenaline coursing through my veins causes my heart to race.

"Super Bowl, baby!" a young trainer screams, darting past me.

"Ryan! Ryan!" a member of the press calls.

I smile. *Let the interviews begin.* A microphone appears, followed by large cameras from the network. In my periphery, local members of the press extend cell phones, hoping to catch a quote.

I find it hard to focus on the interview questions and look into the cameras. My body wants to run, to tackle, to exert this immense energy. I finish one interview to turn directly into another. *I get that this huge moment makes great headlines, but I need...*

Christy!

My heart skips a beat at the sight of my wife carrying Ry and Maddux carrying Harper towards me. *Family. I need my family.* That is what I felt the need to search for. I wave them over.

"Oh, my god!" Christy squeals, hopping up and down with Ry.

The cameras fade away. I place my hand on the back of her neck, pulling her lips to mine. My need to run settles at her touch.

"Daddy, stop!" Ry yells, her little palm pressing against my cheek.

"Your turn," I announce, kissing both her cheeks as she giggles.

I turn toward my brother, who is holding Harper.

"I'll pass," Maddux says with a raised voice.

I ignore his quip. Instead, I kiss both Harper's cheeks and pull her into my arms. Not to be ignored, Ry holds her arms out to me.

Here I stand, a daughter in each arm, my wife and brother at my sides, a man headed to the Super Bowl. Cameras surround us, capturing every perfect moment. I follow my girls' lead, looking up as red and gold tissue paper still falls from the sky like snow.

"We won," I tell my daughters.

"Daddy won!" They cheer and clap.

The owners stand upon the stage, preparing for the trophy presentation. Nolan stands in a champions hat and t-shirt at their side. Soon, I will be called up on stage, and this moment with my family will end.

"I love you," I say, looking from Christy to Maddux. "It means a lot that my wife and brother were here to celebrate with me. I hope you will always be at my games. I love to play with my family in the stands. Thank you for letting my wife and daughters watch the games in your suite," I direct to Maddux. "In the future, I hope you will have room for my sons to watch, too."

Christy coughs loudly at my side. Maddux squeezes her shoulders, shaking his head at me. I rewind my words, replaying them in my mind.

"You are in trouble," Maddux chortles.

I follow his gaze to Brooks, who is approaching with my parents. Next, I follow Brooks's eyes to Christy. She stands slack-jawed, eyes on me.

"Crap! I wasn't supposed to let you know I know," I sputter.

Christy's face morphs from shock to anger to happiness.

"Really?" she asks, looking at Brooks before returning her tear-filled eyes to me.

She places her hands upon my cheeks.

"Really," I affirm.

One day, my family—including my sons—will watch me play on this field. I am a blessed man.

"Super Bowl bound, baby!"

The End

I hope you will look for future stories in ***The Lynks at Tryst Falls Series*** of stand-alone books releasing Soon.

Help readers find this story and give me a giant author hug--please consider leaving a review on Amazon, Goodreads, and BookBub—a few words mean so much.

Check out my Pinterest Boards for my inspirations for characters and settings. (Link on following pages.)
Brooklyn Bailey's Social Media links—scan QR code:

ALSO BY BROOKLYN BAILEY:

Lynks at Tryst Falls Series-
Gibson -- #1

Christy -- #2

Ali's Fight

Country Roads Series-
Memory Lane

Dusty Trail to Nowhere

Fork in the Road

Take Me Home

The 7 Cardinal Sins Series-
Bend Don't Break

Behind the Locked Door

Starting Over

Whatever It Takes

Chance Encounter

Trivia Page

1. Character names in this book are those of famous MLB Baseball players.
2. Tryst Falls is a natural waterfall located in Excelsior Springs, Missouri to the north and east of Kansas City. Its name came about as young couples often met and picnicked here. I dare say it has witnessed a tryst or two.
3. Kansas City is in Missouri-well, most parts that you think/hear of are. (KCI Airport, the Chiefs at Arrowhead, the Royals at Kauffman, Worlds of Fun, the Power & Light District, & zoo are all in Missouri) I've attended many concerts where the lead singer says something along the lines of "Kansas how are you tonight?" when the concert is held in Missouri.

ABOUT THE AUTHOR

Brooklyn Bailey's writing is another bucket-list item coming to fruition, just like meeting Stephen Tyler, Ozzie Smith, and skydiving. As she continues to write sweet romance and young adult books, she also writes steamy contemporary romance books under the name Haley Rhoades, as well as children's books under the name Gretchen Stephens. She plans to complete her remaining bucket-list items, including ghost-hunting, storm-chasing, and bungee jumping. She is a Netflix-binging, Converse-wearing, avidly-reading, traveling geek.

A team player, Brooklyn thrived as her spouse's career moved the family of four, fifteen times to four states. One move occurred eleven days after a C-section. Now with two adult sons, Brooklyn copes with her newly emptied nest by writing and spoiling Nala, her Pomsky. A fly on the wall might laugh as she talks aloud to her fur-baby all day long.

Brooklyn's under five-foot, fun-size stature houses a full-size attitude. Her uber-competitiveness in all things entertains, frustrates, and challenges family and friends. Not one to shy away from a dare, she faces the consequences of a lost bet no matter the humiliation. Her fierce loyalty extends from family, to friends, to sports teams.

Brooklyn's guilty pleasures are Lifetime and Hallmark movies. Her other loves include all things peanut butter, *Star Wars*, mathematics, and travel. Past day jobs vary tremendously from a radio station DJ, to an elementary special-education para-professional, to a YMCA sports director, to a retail store accounting department, and finally a high school mathematics teacher.

Brooklyn resides with her husband and fur-baby in the Des

Moines area. This Missouri-born girl enjoys the diversity the Midwest offers.

Reach out on Facebook, Twitter, Instagram, or her website...she would love to connect with her readers.

- amazon.com/~/e/B0B57RYXZ2
- goodreads.com/BrooklynBailey
- bookbub.com/authors/brooklyn-bailey
- tiktok.com/@haleyrhoadesauthor
- instagram.com/brooklynbaileyauthor
- facebook.com/BrooklynBaileyAuthor
- twitter.com/brooklynb_books
- youtube.com/@haleyrhoadesbrooklynbaileyauth
- pinterest.com/haleyrhoadesaut

Made in the USA
Monee, IL
10 November 2024